（汉、英）

三维往事

THREE DIMENSIONAL PAST

古靖云/著

深圳报业集团出版社

出 版 人：胡洪侠

责任编辑：王 鹏

技术编辑：何杏蔚 杨铖彦

装帧设计：奔流文化

插 画：小山云设计工场

图书在版编目（CIP）数据

三维往事：汉、英 / 古靖云著. —深圳：深圳报业集团出版社，2023.11

ISBN 978-7-80774-074-2

Ⅰ . ①三… Ⅱ . ①古… Ⅲ . ①幻想小说—小说集—中国—当代—汉、英

Ⅳ . ① I247.7

中国国家版本馆 CIP 数据核字（2023）第 173877 号

三维往事
SANWEI WANGSHI

古靖云 著

深圳报业集团出版社出版发行

（518034 深圳市福田区商报路 2 号）

深圳市和谐印刷有限公司印制 新华书店经销

2023 年 11 月第 1 版 2023 年 11 月第 1 次印刷

开本：787mm×1092mm 1/16

字数：142 千字 印张：20.5

ISBN 978-7-80774-074-2 定价：68.00 元

序言

◎丁时照

（一）

十几岁同学写的东西，让几十岁的人追着看。

这个十几岁的同学就是古靖云。他写的这本科幻小说，没有当下的生活，只有想象出的存在。书里的世界观、人生观、价值观，超出了他的父辈的人生经验，是别样的演绎。

在为这本书的序言动笔的时候，古靖云还未满12岁。叫同学正当年，叫同志得几年。都说小说源于生活，他的资历很浅，生活经历简单。但是，他正处于无拘无束的年龄，思维如风，天马行空，让他的这本书自成体系，逻辑自洽。我的感觉，书里生活的成色最多30%，其他的，都是想象的功劳。

因为全新，所以陌生。换个方式说，《三维往事》讲述的是闻所未闻的故事。

（二）

当然是关于星际战争。不同的是，书里不经意间触碰到了最新的科研成果，是当今科学家关于宇宙的最新判断。

膜理论的出现意味着一种全新解释宇宙大爆炸的说法，该说法表明我们生活的整个宇宙是一层可以随意弯曲和拉伸的膜，也称为三维空间。在不远的地方也有一层膜，可以说是另一个宇宙，也是三维空间，当中的空隙，是四维空间。在某种未知力，有可能是暗能量的作用下，两层膜以极慢的速度接近，推想的距离为10万亿光年；当膜接触后，相互碰撞，宇宙中的万物开始毁灭，然后冷却，开始新的循环，这就是新的宇宙大爆炸理论。当碰撞后，两层膜又弹回原来的位置，重新在未知力的作用下，缓慢接近，如此往复，宇宙开始新循环，永不停止。

古靖云的"三维往事"就是此宇宙的故事。此宇宙里有爱恨情仇，有攻守防备。"虫洞理论"在本书是一个高频词，作者在本书中，将其设定为一个通过四维空间来快速穿越三维的工具，之所以能穿越时间是因为它可以通向时间流速异常的区域。目的地是新世界、新宇宙、新的开始，然而，新的并不都是好的，或许，隐藏着更大的风险。

（三）

所有的小说都是构建，这样的构建不多见。

在"三维"里，太阳系八大行星都可以清空，太阳和月亮都可以再造，月亮还被再造三次。有星际移民、星际逃生，还有星球买卖。有个人钱不多，就买了一颗恒星：黄矮星，没想到，这颗星竟然是太阳。

还有星际武器。譬如反物质炸弹。也有很原始却是真实世界的映射的"武器"。譬如，有个星球想攻占地球，这个星球上的人就制造了一块用于撞击地球的直径大约50公里的岩石。虽然是星际的新石器时代，却是真的流星撞击地球的暗喻。

也有审美。一个星球爆炸后的碎片形成了地球的行星环，像一串项链挂在浅蓝的天空。月球消失了，但是它化身成了地球的光环，这个光环就像斜挂着的一条美丽而壮观的银丝带。

想象奇特。当地球被行星发动机推回到太阳温暖的怀抱之中时，地球向相反的方向自转，于是，太阳开始西升东落。更奇特的是，一艘载着一名宇航员的飞船发射到太阳表面，并且采集数据。也有奇怪的，南极洲成为一片繁华的工业区。还有更奇怪的，将两人的意识储存在一人的身体中并继任履职。

当然也有讽刺。当一艘不怀好意的飞船闯入火星轨道时，地球上的许多悲观主义者经常靠在墙上，面色苍白，精神脆弱。作者叙事时有悲悯情怀。在一次大逃亡中，单亲母亲将她不满一岁的女儿塞进救生飞船，把自己留在即将毁灭的飞船上。

（四）

关于星球生命的演进，作者设计了一个链条，很有意思。

有种生物的历史很长很长。这种生命被称作"原始球"，很小，看起来就像一个有着两条触须的球。

后来，一些原始球聚合到一起成为一个更大的球，在漫长的演化中，这些原始球失去了球状部分，只剩下触须，看起来很像植物。单个的原始球成为这种"植物"的食物，因此，这种"植物"被称作

"捕球草"。

一个再平凡不过的日子里，一株捕球草的根脱离了海底。又过了几万年，那株捕球草的后代可以随心所欲地游动，它们看起来非常像地球上的鱼类。

这种"鱼"以捕球草和原始球为食，随着数量急剧增长，捕球草和原始球都灭绝了，它们开始弱肉强食。一次大规模的自然灾害，导致少数的鱼基因突变，第一次拥有了性别。

接下来，缓慢进化让鱼的脑容量不断提高，也出现了语言。

只是，它们不是地球人。

（五）

古靖云在幼儿园是"识字大王"。他"看"的第一本书是《少儿百科全书》，说要和老爸比一比谁看的书厚。幼儿园期间，他对天文很感兴趣，天天琢磨星座图，6岁时就给班上同学讲太阳系八大行星。小学起便对数学、化学、物理、地理感兴趣，有一段时间，还自己琢磨微积分。后来说太难了，看不懂，心思就慢慢集中到化学上。特别是对元素周期表，他可以倒背如流，随便问数字答元素或说元素答数字，而且不管是用中文还是英文都能应声而出。

至于写小说，是受别的小朋友启发。

大约8岁时，他认识的一个小哥哥10岁时就写了一本小说。古靖云开始模仿，断断续续写了4万多字，取名《化学往事》。结果在快10岁时，他再看这本书，觉得"太幼稚了"，就重新写了这本《三维往事》，大约6.7万字。出版社说字少了点儿，跟他商量。古靖云提出，自己动手把小说翻译成英文。2023年，他用3个月的时间翻译完。编辑老师说："主角不突出，心理描写、细节处理还不足。"他答道："那是你们成年人的看法。我们小孩子就是这样的思维逻辑，而且，我的故事已经写完了。"编辑老师没有强求，家长也没有勉强他进一步修改。

本书付梓之际，古靖云同学已进入初中。睡前和老爸聊天，他问："你觉得我应该在哪方面要特别注意？"老爸直言："坚持你最好的一方面，就是自主学习能力；另外就是加强自我管理，包括时间管理、生活自理。"小古他爸老古告诉我说："这小子，我最欣赏的就是他的专注力和自主学习能力。不管环境多吵多闹，他都可以安坐一旁，静心看书。"

据悉，他最近大半年把兴趣转到城市地铁线路的规划上了，已经画了厚厚一沓的地铁线路图。

（六）

小古这一代的人，是"10后"，也有人说是"Z世代"。

他们是"网络世代""互联网世代"，现在大部分还是学生。他们不可逆转地将循序离开校园，进入社会。在未来，"Z世代"将成为社会中流砥柱，握住代际传承的接力棒。"Z世代"的生活方式、思维模式、行为样式将对整个社会产生深远影响，一定会成为主流文化代表。

实话实说，看这本小说，很"烧脑"，需要相关的知识储备，需要有共情的能力，需要以欣赏的眼光相待，最不需要的是指责和挑剔。

　　社会如此，科学也一样。当科学不被人理解的时候，科学类似于胡话和神话，这本书的时空概念就是例证。

　　我们都明白，一维空间是一条线，二维空间是一个面，三维空间是一个体，四维空间就不仅仅是空间了，准确地说是四维时空。接下来麻烦了，宇宙中还有五维空间、六维空间……宇宙是多维的，多到十一维，是由震动的平面构成。现代物理学认为，剩下的空间维度是我们感受不到但确实存在的。对于这些全新的概念，开始大部分物理学家，包括相对论研究学者，都觉得难以接受，这是因为旧的思维方法阻碍了认知，直到推导出了可验证的公式。

　　不到12岁的古靖云同学之所以敢写"往事"，是因为他站在科学家的肩膀上。科学家的肩膀就是当代的"幽州台"，登临而上，前不见古人，后不见来者。真乃天地悠悠，不语也沧桑。

　　（作者系深圳报业集团党组书记、社长，高级记者，国务院特殊津贴获得者）

Preface

© By Ding Shizhao

Chapter One

It's not often that something written by a teenager in his teens captivates people in their thirties and beyond. This teenager is Gu Jingyun, and this science fiction he has penned is devoid of the present day but brimming with his imagination. The worldviews, philosophies, and values within the pages transcend the life experiences of his elders, offering a unique narrative.

As I write this preface for his book, Gu Jingyun is not yet twelve years old. They say he's at that age when you're a student and a comrade simultaneously. It's often said that novels draw from life, but his life experiences are limited, and his credentials are shallow. Nevertheless, he's in the stage of life where thoughts flow like the wind, untethered and imaginative. This book stands as a self-contained system, internally coherent, despite the majority of it being a product of his boundless imagination.

Because it's entirely new, it feels unfamiliar. To put it another way, *Three-Dimensional Past* tells a story that's never been heard before.

Chapter Two

Of course, it's about interstellar warfare. What sets it apart is that the book inadvertently touches upon the latest scientific findings, the current judgments of scientists about the cosmos.

The emergence of membrane theory signifies a fresh interpretation of the Big Bang theory, suggesting that our entire universe, where we reside, is like a membrane that can be flexed and stretched at will, often referred to as three-dimensional space. In proximity, there's another membrane, essentially another universe, also in three-dimensional space. The void between them constitutes four-dimensional space. Under the influence of some unknown force, possibly dark energy, these two membranes slowly converge, spanning a conjectured distance of 10 trillion light-years. When they collide, everything in the universe begins to disintegrate, then cools down, starting a new cycle – this is the new theory of the universe's Big Bang. Following the collision, the two membranes bounce back to their original positions, gradually approaching each other once more, cyclically restarting the universe, an eternal recurrence.

Gu Jingyun's "Three-Dimensional Past" is the story of this universe. It's a universe with love, hatred, passion, and defense. "Wormhole Theory" is a high-frequency term in this book, used by the author as a tool to traverse three dimensions swiftly through four-dimensional space. Its ability to traverse time is attributed to its capacity to access regions with anomalous time flow rates. The destination is a new world, a new universe, a fresh start. However, the new isn't always better; hidden within might be greater risks.

Chapter Three

All novels are constructs, but this one is quite uncommon. In "Three-Dimensional", the entire solar system's eight planets can be emptied, the sun and moon can be remade, and the moon is even remade three times over. There's interstellar migration, interstellar escape, and even planetary trading. Someone with limited funds buys a star: a yellow dwarf star, only to realize it's our Sun.

Then there are interstellar weapons, like the anti-matter bomb. There are also primitive yet real-world analogies, such as when a planet plans to conquer Earth, the people will create a rock about 50 kilometers in diameter to collide with Earth. Despite being the Stone Age of interstellar civilizations, it's an allegory for a genuine meteorite impact on Earth.

There's also aesthetics. Fragments from a planet's explosion form a star ring around Earth, resembling a beautiful and spectacular silver ribbon hanging in the light blue sky. The moon vanishes but transforms into Earth's halo, akin to a beautiful and grand silvery ribbon slanting across the sky.

The imagination is strange. When Earth is pushed back into the warm embrace of the Sun by a planetary engine, Earth starts rotating in the opposite direction, causing the Sun to rise in the west and set in the east. Even more bizarrely, a spaceship carrying an astronaut is launched into the surface of the Sun to collect data. Strange things happen too, as Antarctica becomes a bustling industrial area. And there's something even stranger: merging two people's consciousness into one body, with one succeeding the other's duties.

Of course, there's irony as well. When a malicious spacecraft breaches Mars' orbit, many pessimists on Earth often lean against the wall, pale-faced and mentally fragile. The author's narrative is tinged with compassion. In one mass exodus, a single mother places her infant daughter in an escape pod, leaving herself aboard the doomed ship.

Chapter Four

Regarding the evolution of planetary life, the author has designed a fascinating chain.

There's a species with an exceptionally long history. These life forms are known as "primordial ball", small and spherical in shape, each with two tentacle-like appendages.

Later, some primordial balls merge to form larger spheres. Through a lengthy process of evolution, they lose their spherical form, retaining only the tentacles, resembling plants. Single primitive sphere becomes the food source for these "balltrap plants".

On an ordinary day, a root from one of these balltrap plants detaches from the seabed. After several thousand years, the descendants of this root gain the ability to move freely, resembling fish found on Earth.

These "fish" feed on balltrap plants and primordial balls, rapidly multiplying in number. Eventually, both plants and balls become extinct, leading to predatory behavior among these fish. A large-scale natural disaster triggers genetic mutations in a few fish, marking the first instance of sexual reproduction.

Subsequent slow evolution leads to a significant increase in brain capacity and the development of language.

But they aren't Earthlings.

Chapter Five

In kindergarten, Gu Jingyun was the "King of Literacy". The first book he "read" was the *Children's Encyclopedia*, challenging his father to compare who could read more pages. During his kindergarten years, he had a deep fascination with astronomy, pondering constellations daily. At the age of six, he lectured his classmates on the eight planets in the solar system. Starting in primary school, his interests expanded to mathematics, chemistry, physics, and geography. There was a time when he even dabbled in calculus. But he eventually found it too challenging, admitting he couldn't understand it, and shifted his focus to chemistry, particularly the Periodic Table of the Elements. He could recite it forwards and backwards, provide an element for any given number, and vice versa, in both Chinese and English.

As for writing novels, he was inspired by other kids.

At around the age of eight, he met an older boy who had already written a novel at the age of ten. Gu Jingyun started imitating him, intermittently writing over 40,000 words titled *Chemical Past*. But by the time he was almost ten, he reread the book and thought it was "too childish". So, he started the *Three-Dimensional Past*, writing approximately 67,000 words. The publishing house suggested the book needed more words, so Gu Jingyun proposed to translate it into English by himself, which took him three months in 2023. The editor remarked, "The protagonist lacks prominence, and there's a need for more psychological description and attention to detail." Gu Jingyun responded, "That's how adults see it. We kids have our own logical thinking." He added, "My story is already complete." The editor didn't insist, and his parents didn't pressure him to make further revisions.

As this book goes to print, Gu Jingyun is beginning middle school. Before bedtime, he asked his father, "Where do you think I should focus my attention?" His father candidly replied, "Stick to your greatest strength, which is your ability to learn independently. Additionally, improve your self-management skills, including time management and self-care." Gu Jingyun's father, Mr. Gu, told me, "What I admire most about him is his concentration and self-learning ability. Regardless of how noisy or chaotic the environment is, he can sit quietly and read."

Reportedly, in the past six months, he has shifted his interest to urban subway network planning and has already drawn a thick stack of subway line maps.

Chapter Six

Gu Jingyun belongs to the "Post–2010 Generation", also known as the "Generation Z".

They are the "Internet Generation", and though most are still students. And they are gradually leaving the confines of school to enter society. In the future, "Generation Z" will become the backbone of society, carrying the baton of intergenerational transmission. Their lifestyle, thought patterns, and behavior will profoundly influence the society, undoubtedly becoming the representatives of mainstream culture.

To be honest, reading this novel is mentally taxing. It requires relevant knowledge, empathy, and an appreciative perspective. What it least requires is criticism and nitpicking.

Society works the same way, so does science. When science isn't understood, it's akin to gibberish or mythology. The book's concepts of time and space serve as a testament to this.

We all understand that one–dimensional space is a line, two–dimensional space is a plane, three–dimensional space is a volume, but four–dimensional space isn't merely spatial; it's four–dimensional spacetime. Beyond that, it becomes complicated: there's five–dimensional space, six–dimensional space... The universe is multi–dimensional, extending up to eleven dimensions, comprised of vibrating planes. Modern physics suggests that the remaining dimensions exist but are imperceptible to us. As for these new concepts, most of the physicists including the scholars of the theory of relativity, feel difficulty to accept. That is because the cognition is hindered by old patterns of perception, until they derive verifioble formulas.

The reason why Gu Jingyun, not yet twelve, dares to write about the "past" is because he stands on the shoulders of scientists. Scientists' shoulders are the contemporary "Yuzhou Terrace", an ascent with no sight of ancient travelers and no glimpse of future arrivals. Truly, it's a vast and profound expanse, wordless yet filled with the sands of time.

Author: Ding Shizhao, Party Secretary and President of Shenzhen Press Group, Senior Journalist, Recipient of the State Council Special Allowance

目录

CONTENTS

一、地狱神星

公元前9852年11月的一个下午，地狱神星（Tartarus）王国国王希尔霍夫和副国王[1]米耶在王宫的地下会议室中忧虑地看着那个红点，它代表着数千光年外的灭神星（Shiva）发射的一系列亚光速"子弹"，将于公元前7978年到达。这些子弹本身非常普通，使用非常廉价的金属制成，最小的大概只有篮球那么大，但是速度却非常接近光速，相对论效应使得它们拥有了巨大的能量。

"真是想不到，延续了一万多年的地狱神星王国就要这样灭亡了吗？这绝对不可以！那个可耻的文明，"希尔霍夫怒气冲冲地说，"竟然打算把我们以及附近的3000多个文明在将近2000年后灭亡！我们该怎么反制他们呢？"

"尊敬的殿下，现在，我们已经背上了造一艘世代飞船的任

---

[1] 地狱神星的一个官职，某种意义上相当于副总统，和采取世袭制的国王不同，是竞选出来的。

务。"米耶终于把这句早就准备好的话说出口来。

"你的意思是……逃亡？不，朕代表政府宣誓我们与地狱神星共存亡！"

"陛下，为了广大人民群众的安全，我们必须现在就走，造飞船才是唯一的出路！"

"不行。你作为我的臣子，没有权利反驳我！"

"这与君臣之间的关系无关，我们留下来就绝对不能活下去！"

"这不是我们地狱神星文明应该有的作风！"

"陛下，恕我直言，您是不是丝毫不在意我们的安全？"

"也许是，也许不是。退一步说，我们也不能抛弃这颗孕育了我们的地狱神星，这是背叛的行为。"

"请注意，您的存在，是为了保障这个国家和它的人民，您忍心看着100亿个地狱神星人死在您面前吗？"

"哼！从小我们这些贵族就知道：气节比生存更加重要！"

"但我们不能替地狱神星数以亿计的人民做走还是留的决定！"

"啊……这是我们共同的家园，身为副国王，你应该对地狱神星负仅次于我的责任！"希尔霍夫非常恼怒。

"陛下，我作为最新一届副国王，当然是由民众竞选的；我选择制造世代飞船，也是市民们的意思啊！"

面对米耶的反驳，希尔霍夫哑口无言，迟疑了一下。这是因为，这场争论其实是关于气节和尊严、自由和生存的争论。

一万多年后，地球上的一首诗[1]中写道："人的躯体哪能由狗的洞子爬出！"倘若把这句话说给地狱神星的民众，恐怕他们也不会同意；为自由与快乐而拼了命奋斗的地狱神星人，曾经经历过数不清的灾难，为了大多数人的生命，他们可以做出任何事情。这种"生存意识"推动着地狱神星经济、科学、技术和艺术的发展，没有它，地狱神星就没有今日辉煌的成就。可以说，地狱神星文明就是靠"生存意识"打磨出的艺术品。

但是，地狱神星的贵族却受到了截然不同的教育，他们更加重视荣誉和金钱，而不是人民的性命，因此，人们积怨已久。这一切，都变成了一个铿锵有力的字："不！"

"陛下，你怎么能如此固执呢？"

"不！"

"您确定……"

"不！"

"请再考虑……"

"我最后说一遍，不！"

"请……"

"绝不！别跟我扯淡！听见了吗？绝不！"

话音未落，希尔霍夫无礼的行为就激活了米耶的兽性。米耶对固执的国王失去了耐心，大声地咆哮道："扯淡？哼，你想想你是什么身份！你是这颗星球的敌人！我再说一遍，你是这颗星球的敌人！"

---

[1] 即《囚歌》。

他抛弃了一切礼貌和教养，如同一只硕大的猛兽："去死吧！"

　　他怒吼一声，竟然将一把不知从哪里找到的匕首刺入希尔霍夫的胸膛。希尔霍夫痛苦地呻吟道："不要……抛弃……地狱神星……"他的声音极其微弱，米耶知道他要死了。

　　面对奄奄一息的国王，米耶生出了怜悯之心。他对自己说道："不要管那么多……我必须除去这个威胁地狱神星全体人民生命的敌人……万一被发现，我还会被他的手下枪决的……"

　　民众就在外面，米耶为了隐藏自己杀死希尔霍夫的秘密，便把希尔霍夫的头砍了下来带走。

　　次日，米耶篡位成为新国王，并宣布希尔霍夫的死因是由于抑郁症导致的自杀，又当即下令制造世代飞船。地狱神星人的流浪就要开始了……

　　公元前7978年，那些星际"子弹"中的第一颗（比光速稍慢）击中了地狱神星，落入了海中。尽管如此，它由于以接近光速的速度移动，因此能量变得非常大，也掀起了巨大的爆炸，地狱神星的海洋在几秒之内彻底蒸发，而部分陆地也被炸塌了，陷入了地幔中。这时的地狱神星人已经全部逃离许多年了。

　　3小时后，又一颗"子弹"袭来，正巧地狱神星自转到了一个特殊的位置，使"子弹"击中了地狱神星王国的前首都。在那里，废弃的建筑物瞬间倒下，地上出现数百公里长的裂缝，许多被遗忘在这里的物品从这些裂缝进入地幔。岩浆从这些缝隙中涌出，就像洪水一样冲垮了沿途的一切事物。

　　又过了7小时，这时地狱神星的三块大陆中有一块已经陷入地幔。蒸发的海洋又以降雨的形式倾泻回来，重新覆盖了地狱神星。这时，第三颗"子弹"出现了。它击中了地狱神星的第二大城市，建筑物同样被夷为平地。这个历史悠久的城市在几分钟之内毁灭了，大地上再次出现裂缝。很快，这块大陆也被岩浆覆盖，便永远陨落了。海水涌入了这块大陆原来的位置，现在地狱神星只剩下一块大陆。

第四颗"子弹"在两个小时之后到来，这颗"子弹"的质量更大，撼动了地狱神星最深层的地质结构，霎时间，海量的岩浆从地下涌出，陆地上已经是一片火海。

紧接着，第五颗"子弹"来临了。这颗子弹的质量是前面四颗"子弹"总和的10倍，在击中地狱神星后，整颗星球被撕裂成大大小小的碎片。

另一方面，灭神星正在举国狂欢。长久以来的劲敌——地狱神星，终于被摧毁了，但实际上有一亿人逃离并幸存。不过，这也使得灭神星成为银河系猎户旋臂最强的文明，其他星球上孕育的文明基本上都是一群石器时代的原始人，而那些较强的文明也都被灭神星用类似的方式打压或制裁了。随后，也许是由于过度骄傲，灭神星的发展却开始陷入停滞，直到公元纪元即将来临时，他们才开始继续扩张。原先的灭神星被称作"中世界"，是这个文明的核心。中世界后来还被改造成了一个军事基地。灭神星发射出去的无数探测船和战舰则负责扩张。

漫长的扩张持续了数万年。但是，至于灭神星的统治能否持续下去，仍然是一个问题……

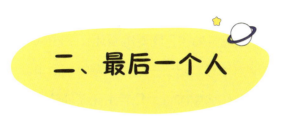

二、最后一个人

地球上的"最后"一个人独自坐在房间里，这时忽然响起了敲门声……

他叹气道："进来吧，门虚掩着呢。"

门开了，外面站着一个人，他始终站在门口没有进来。屋内的那个人原以为找到了同类，非常高兴，甚至冲上前来想给此人一个拥抱。然而，他的手毫无感觉地穿过了来者的身体。

他突然注意到来者身上的细节：一丝不挂，没有嘴，有着红色的皮肤、9只闪闪发光的蓝色的大眼睛、24块壮实的腹肌、满是褶皱的脖颈、一条比身体还长的粗尾巴，以及14条分泌着绿色黏液的触手。

它不知从哪个部位发出了声音："你好。"

他被这句话大大地震撼了，眼前这个古怪的生物，竟然懂得人类的语言。他的双眼中闪现着异样的光芒，分明是五分惊讶和五分恐惧，回答道："你好。"

接下来是持续了5分钟的沉默。

终于，这个"外星生物"发声了："你知道外面发生了什么吗？"

"不知道。"

于是，这个生物开始了它简略的叙述："2060年，猎户臂另一端的灭神星文明对地球发起了一场令人震惊的战争。灭神星非常好战，在战争中，他们势如破竹，几乎杀死了地球上的所有生命。幸存者都离开了灭神星的势力范围。现在是2120年，60年来，这些幸存者以及他们的大量后代都在默默地发展一支军队，以此反抗灭神星……那简直是幸存者们的梦魇。"

他的话被屋内的人打断了。"你是什么？"

"我只是一个人。我的这副模样也并不是真实的，而是一个虚构的投影。这也是为什么你看不见我的身体有丝毫移动。我这样做，是想要给你们一个特别的第一印象。

"我没有名字，只有一个编号：1379。你可以这样称呼我。你现在的编号是2015。

"在舰队中还有很多其他不是人类的生物，甚至包括一些细菌，它们会用自己的方式反击灭神星。我来的目的便是邀请你加入地球的军队。"

"为了地球，我同意加入。"

"好。您现在将成为地球反击军的一员，呃，元帅。待反击战结束后，您将成为地球副总统。"

"为什么是我？"

"到时候你会知道的。"实际上，2015在他该知道原因的时候，1379也没有告诉他。

接着，地球唤醒了它沉睡的力量。

2121年，地球和灭神星的战争开始了，大家开始奋战。灭神星的外貌和地球类似，但它的大气是75％的氧气、20％的二氧化碳和5％的稀有气体。灭神星人呼吸的是二氧化碳，地球反击军便将大量的植物栽到地里，借此夺取灭神星大气中本来就不多的二氧化碳。事成之后将其点燃，在高浓度的氧气中它们燃烧得极为剧烈，将灭神星唯一的一块大陆变成了一片不毛之地。但据相关人员推测，它会很快恢复。

肉食动物和杂食动物负责攻击地表上的敌人，草食动物用来夺走灭神星人赖以为生的几种植物，食腐动物则专门清理战场，它们共同组成了一支庞大的陆军。水生动物组成了地球的海军，负责攻击灭神星大海中的船只与其他生物。

所有可以飞行的鸟类则组成了空军，工作是干扰敌人。还有很多敌人被地球人释放的病毒（抑或是细菌）感染。至于万物之灵——人类，则在浩瀚的太空中驾驶着飞船与灭神星的舰队展开游击战。

2138年，地球反击军陆军已经将地表的灭神星幸存者逼到了灭神星的两极，他们立即被当地的另一些动物（例如北极熊等生活在极地的动物）彻底灭绝。地球的太空军一鼓作气，把灭神星位于太空中的军队清理得一干二净。殊不知，灭神星还留下了一点儿幸存者，日后将向人类发动一场毁天灭地的战争……

就这样，地球反击军从灭神星搜刮了大批资源，人类全部回到了地球，并将其他生物永远地留在了这里。这是因为灭神星环境恢复能

力很强，更适合这些动植物。

　　这时，"剩下的人类吃什么"是很多地球人常问的问题。政府给出的答案是：2045年人类就开始全面生产人造肉和人造蔬菜了，因此，人们的饮食并不是真正的问题。

三、两场战斗

2139年5月8日，这一天可以说是地球文明的里程碑：天文学家们发现了又一个外星文明，也就是地狱神星。同一天，地球共和国统一了地球，成为人类历史上第一个统一全球的国家。

在无边无际的外层空间中，一艘巨大的碟状飞船正在逼近地球。它属于一个绰号为"地狱神星"的系外行星，以地表的温度非常高而得名。如前文所述，地狱神星在公元前7978年被灭神星文明炸毁了，地狱神星人在最后关头发射了一艘在宇宙中寻找新家园的飞船。这艘飞船已经在浩瀚的太空中流浪了很久，可是人口还是只有一亿，最终找到了地球。

地狱神星人认为地球是一个非常合适的家园，而且拥有大量能让地狱神星东山再起的资源，但是必须赶走全部地球人。

这年的5月10日，全人类已经神经紧张，许多悲观主义者经常靠在墙上，由于对地狱神星人的入侵而过度恐惧导致面色苍白，精神脆弱。这是因为地狱神星飞船在当天闯入了火星轨道。

5月17日时，该飞船离地球只有40万公里，仅比地球和月球的距离多一点。

地狱神星人想要如何消灭地球人并攻占地球呢？按照法律，超过14岁且不满60岁的地狱神星人（除了技术人员和安保人员）都必须参与控制飞船，或同心协力制造一块用于撞击地球的岩石。这块岩石的直径大约在50公里，总共花了5个星期就完工了。它于2095年竣工。

5月20日，地狱神星飞船已经围绕地球旋转了三天三夜。这一天下午，地狱神星人将一块庞大的岩石对准地球，再等三天就会向地球发射。按照一位地狱神星人的话来说："那时，做一个地球人将会成为自杀的常见手段。"开这种令人摸不着头脑的玩笑，可以说是地狱神星人的特色。

地球共和国各地区的领导人与元首立马召开了一个重大会议，最终预测：地球上生活了20多万年的人类只剩下3天了。

要把所有地球人在3天内转移到其他星球完全不可能，而且有情报显示，地狱神星人一旦攻陷地球，就会打起整个太阳系的主意，赶走太阳系内的全部地球人，抢夺一切能使用的资源，即便逃离也没有意义。

他们还会在夺走太阳系的资源后卷土重来，将灭神星人赶尽杀绝。这看起来不关地球文明的事，但是根据目前得到的情报，地球人、地狱神星人和灭神星人都是所谓"银河族"的一员，是银河系内极少数具有智慧的种族，其内部几乎没有什么生物多样性。

目前看来，防止地狱神星人入侵地球唯一的办法就是释放反物质武器[1]。

5月21日，从世界各地集结的100颗反物质武器被集中到一个荒无人烟的小岛上，准备用火箭发射。

"3，2，1，发射！"

这架承载着反物质武器与地球人希望的火箭"反物质1号"于5月22日发射，这时候的火箭仍然是多级火箭，"反物质1号"的头部（即反物质武器所在）很快就脱离了已经废弃的第二级和第三级。

这在之前的人看来是非常危险的：要是火箭发射失败，就可能意外引发反物质武器爆炸，反而会毁灭人类。不过，现在是22世纪，人类已经可以非常精准地控制无人火箭了。

"反物质1号"的速度比两个世纪前发射的"土星5号"快很多，到达地狱神星飞船所在的位置只需半天，还有半天时间来调整方位和轨道，而后者可以在几小时内完成。

地狱神星人的飞船上，可以看到一块巨大的岩石，被数以千计的机械臂夹着，很快就要释放。"反物质1号"从飞船背对地球的一面发动偷袭，这是因为地狱神星人大都集中在飞船面向地球的一面，紧张地等待这块"人工陨石"的发射，对飞船背面的监管很少。

100颗反物质武器分两批向地狱神星飞船后方飞去，但由于是在太空中，所以没有产生声音。飞船外面出现强光，50颗反物质武器已经炸穿了外壳，摧毁了飞船的后半部。由于空气流失，许多人窒息

---

[1]　也称反物质炸弹，小一些的称作反物质子弹，原理是利用普通物质和反物质互相湮灭产生的巨大能量来爆炸。

了，还有许多人直接飘到了外面，在爆炸范围之内的人员更是直接被巨大的能量蒸发，伤亡已经超过8500万。现在，地狱神星文明已经处于几乎无法反转的劣势。

在飞船中心的一个房间，海索尔基拉和她不满一岁的女儿正在逃亡。这个单亲家庭的生活水平比较低，但总是尽己所能地活下去——海索尔基拉的曾祖父说过："生存胜于一切。"这是她家族中的每一个人都奉行的基本原则，也是整个地狱神星文明奉为圭臬的原则。

她抱着怀中的女婴冲出房间，在人流中大吼一声："啊——"人群愣住了，大家直勾勾地盯着她，看着她从停滞的人群中冲过。最近的救生飞船离海索尔基拉只有30米。她不顾一切地来到那里，想要把自己纤细而瘦弱的身躯挤进去。

不幸的是，那艘飞船已经满人了，只能容下一个儿童。她只能将婴儿交给飞船上负责维持秩序的保安。这时，婴儿的目光仿佛在说："妈妈，不要抛弃我……"

生离死别之际，在婴儿的目光中，海索尔基拉看见了文明的希望，那就是爱……

太空中，剩下的50颗反物质炸弹在第二层外壳上炸出了一道长长的裂缝，几乎要将飞船撕裂，同时所有未能逃生者都葬身火海。大量的碎片和残骸飞出，它们在高温下已经呈现出非常耀眼的蓝色，最后冷却下来。那块岩石凝聚了地狱神星一亿人民的劳动成果，已经在这场屠杀般的太空战争中被炸得粉碎，但却永远纪念着这个文明不屈的精神。这块岩石，也是地狱神星文明的墓碑，也就是说地狱神星文明按理来说应该彻底灭绝了。地球上的人开始欢呼，因为地球文明第一次参与太空战争就取得了胜利。可惜的是，"反物质1号"的引擎被一块饭盒大小的石头击中，然后它就永远遗失在太空中了。这无足轻重，因为它已经完成了任务，也没有携带任何反物质武器。根据一颗绕日人造卫星的观测，它最后脱离了地球，坠入了太阳。

当时没有人知道的是，9艘没有被爆炸吞没的逃生飞船组成了一个方阵，延续着这个垂死的文明，他们将在不久之后在月球上重建毁于一旦的地狱神星王国。

地狱神星飞船内部物体的碎片形成了地球的星环，像一串项链挂在深蓝的天空中。月球由于在环的范围内，经常受到碎片的撞击，背面的陨石坑也开始多了起来。在月球的众多月海之中也出现了许多陨石坑，显得格外诡异，而且规模不亚于第谷和哥白尼等陨石坑。

虽然地球取得了胜利，但是与地球上的战争不同，太空战争几乎是永无止境的，因为参战方太多了。虽然星际战争也有一些类似战争法的规则，但是享有长久和平无异于痴人说梦。

地狱神星曾经有一颗叫"巫神星"（Hecate）的卫星，上面存在智慧文明，两者的关系良好，甚至有着相同的语言。在100个世纪之前，当地狱神星被炸毁时，巫神星也效仿前者造了一艘飞船，随后巫神星也被地狱神星的碎片砸得四分五裂。双方的飞船原本是在一起的，后来走散了。收到地狱神星飞船被地球炸毁的信息，巫神星人都非常愤怒，飞船以最高速度向太阳系的第三颗行星飞过去。

"'巫神星号'，全速前进！"

巫神星飞船是在2142年9月30日来到地球轨道上的，距离地球35万公里，想用地球的行星环将自己藏起来。巫神星使用的武器也是一块岩石，但是直径只有15公里，比那颗灭绝了恐龙的小行星大不了多少。

在这个时代，地球轨道上有海量的高轨道卫星[1]，很快就发现了巫神星飞船，并发现了它们同样想用一块岩石消灭全部地球人。巫神星飞船内只有4000万人，不到地狱神星飞船的一半。

面对这种情况，地球文明已经有备无患了，再次制造了100颗反物质武器和一架火箭。

制造反物质武器在这个时代已经是易如反掌的事情了。最常使用的反物质便是反氢，但是在反物质武器中为了用磁场束缚住反物质，还需要将它变成高度压缩的固体。在湮灭前，先通过计算机解除低温，固态反氢便会变成气态。下一步是解除磁场，大量的气体就会把外壳挤爆，由于外壳是普通物质组成的，这时就会发生湮灭。

10月18日，巫神星人才准备释放他们制造的岩石。地球人接收到这个消息后，立即发射了火箭。火箭名叫"反物质2号"，以极高的速度载着100颗反物质武器发射。"反物质2号"相较于"反物质1号"大了很多，也融合了更多技术。

"反物质2号"在到达地球行星环内侧的时候，发现巫神星飞船正准备释放一颗陨石，于是绕到飞船背对地球的一面，准备像"反物质1号"一样偷袭。

可是，巫神星飞船上的一个低级别公务员偶然地看见"反物质2号"，立即报告上级。巫神星人惊慌失措地用飞船上的微型核弹扫

---

[1]　即轨道高度超过 3.6 万公里（同步轨道）的人造卫星。

射。其中，有几颗打到了火箭，而且恰好打中了它唯一的弱点——推进器。推进器被核火焰烧毁后，内部的计算机认为"反物质2号"已被敌方捕获，便引爆了所有反物质炸弹。

"反物质2号"立即化作一道白光，它的爆炸严重损坏了巫神星飞船的外壳，但是只有1000万巫神星人死亡，还剩下3000万人。

飞船外壳的一块碎片刚好打在了巫神星飞船自毁按钮（原本用于与敌人同归于尽）的上面，巫神星飞船立即进入准备自爆状态。飞船外围装载有数以千计的核弹，它们同时接到自毁的命令后，在同一秒爆炸。

没有一个巫神星人知道发生了什么，但是由于地球人有人造卫星，所以记录下了全过程。

核弹只炸掉了飞船的外壳，表面上看并非毁灭性的。不过，飞船内侧的所有东西都开始升温。最后，巨大的热量引起了剧烈的燃烧（飞船内原本有大量氧气），将整艘飞船化作灰烬。

人流挤满了每一条逃生通道，但这些物品燃烧时也将部分通道烧毁了。巫神星人以无秩序和极度民主著称，而这便是无秩序的后果。

于是，地球的行星环又加粗了一点儿，虽说暂时比不上土星宏伟、端庄而壮丽的行星环，但是天气合适的话，不论白昼还是黑夜都能看见天空中斜挂着一条美丽而壮观的银色丝带，到了夜晚还有一轮明亮的玉盘相衬，星星如宝石般镶嵌在环的两侧，有蓝色、白色、黄色和红色。

四、地球和月球

　　说起那轮明亮的玉盘，它最近有点儿不安分。月球文明是地球文明发现的第三个外星文明，也属于银河族的一员。地球的行星环刚好与月球轨道重合，受月球引力影响，地球环中的部分碎片会坠落到月球上，从而导致月球上的陨石坑越来越多。

　　最近，地狱神星逃生飞船降落到了月球上，被月球人接纳为月球的一员（两者同属于银河族）。由于陨石的坠落等原因，月球上出现了超大规模的生物大灭绝事件，在月球的31种大型动物中有29种都惨遭灭绝，只剩下月球人（有地下避难所）和另一种动物："月球大猩猩"（生存在月球北极，那里的陨石雨没有那么剧烈）。

　　月球的人口在60亿左右，综合水平比地球落后一个世纪多一点儿，月球人初步掌握了可控核聚变和反物质武器，但是不论是科技、军事，还是文化水平，都没有地球人想象中那么发达。

　　地球人和月球人几乎是同时发现对方的。地球人于2155年12月下旬发现月球人，2156年1月上旬月球人也发现了地球人，并且发现这次生物大灭绝是地球人引起的。地球的行星环严重影响月球对星空的观测，因为地球行星环主要是由来源于两艘飞船的岩石和金属组成的，还有少量有机物（可能是地狱神星人和巫神星人身体的残留物），这不仅遮挡月球人的视线，还会反射大量光。

月球政府非常愤怒："地球人竟然如此阴险而狡猾！"月球政府向地球发射了一串用月球语言写的文字[1]，翻译成中文大概是："我们月球为你们地球做了几十亿年的卫星，协助制造了潮汐，但现在地球上生机勃勃，绿意盎然；而月球上却一片荒凉，寸草不生。1.4亿名外星人宝贵的生命都葬送在你们手上，他们可是漂泊了100个世纪，但你们在短短十几年内就残暴地屠杀了他们。这也就算了，你们竟然还炸了他们的两艘外星飞船，用碎片撞月球。"月球人发现地球人"爱打感情牌"之后，也决定这么做，并且将月球和地球拟人化了。

地球共和国的元首回应说："他们入侵地球，我们自然要反攻，而他们又没有投降或者离开的迹象，只能把他们赶尽杀绝。在地球环形成之后我们才发现你们，但为时已晚。对此，我代表全地球向你们表示深深的歉意。"

就在此时，地球人发现一本月球人的书，有关整个月球的历史，因此本书的中文翻译为"月史"。

地球人在书中看到一个故事，大意是月球人在1980年前有两个分支，人口分别是40亿和20亿，后来前者把后者彻底消灭了。

---

[1]　出于某种原因，月球文明的语言文字是摩尔斯代码。虽然月球上的环境接近真空，声音几乎无法传播，但是由于月球人的皮肤上有一个代替声带的器官，可以受意识控制并发出光，所以根本就不需要声音。

月球人一看地球人手上有《月史》，傻眼了：这本书记载着月球人血腥而黑暗的一面，而且死亡的人数是30亿（第一个分支中10亿人死亡，第二个分支中所有人死亡），这个数字远大于1.4亿。

于是，月球向地球开战了。地球人在这场战争中使用了氢弹。在这个时代，氢弹甚至可以量产，微型氢弹一次就是几千颗，正常的氢弹少说也是一次几十颗。

众所周知，氢弹是用原子弹产生的高温引爆的，而原子弹在22世纪已经可以用来控制爆破，很小的一颗就可以把一栋摩天大楼变成废墟，说明了原子弹的威力和地球人对它的控制都已经达到令过去的人们叹为观止的地步，所以数千颗大型氢弹是完全够用的。而月球的武器则是几百颗中型氢弹。

为了以防万一，人类还同心协力制造出了有史以来最强大的反物质武器，名为"地球炸弹"。普通的反物质武器甚至是大型氢弹在"地球炸弹"面前就像是在核弹面前放鞭炮一样，完全不是一个层次。2156年3月19日，除了"地球炸弹"，这些大型氢弹都被装上了火箭的引擎，向月球发射。

3月20日，几百颗属于月球的氢弹和几千颗属于地球的氢弹相遇了。很快，一场短暂的战争开始了。由于地球的武器很多而且非常自动化，而月球的所有武器都是人工操纵的，灵敏度不高，所以在几分钟内月球的大部分氢弹都被地球的氢弹摧毁。

3月21日，"地球炸弹"在同一个岛上向月球发射，原本只是示威，想让月球文明投降。没想到，月球文明誓死不降，而且大部分月球人准备逃跑，日后再来复仇。

于是，"地球炸弹"穿过了地球的行星环，次日早晨，内置的计算机发出指令使它爆炸。正反物质的湮灭开始了，这时它离月球只有几公里远，在风暴洋上空。

在月球背面的月球人侥幸躲过了这次爆炸。据称，月球人选了100个幸运儿搭建了一艘简陋的飞船（速度比地球人最快的飞船慢6倍以上）向火星方向飞去，推测是想定居火星。

人们不知道，这是月球人安排的行为艺术，即便有"地球炸弹"的轰炸，大部分月球人还是得以幸存……但这些信息都被月球人强大的计算机干扰了，地球人们看到的是："地球炸弹"在月球表面撕出了一条极长的裂痕，不断有月球人陷入裂缝，上千万人丧生……

得知部分月球人逃跑的信息，地球人并没有感到遗憾，因为只要他们不回来报仇，地球就是安全的。即便他们回来，地球人也能迅速发现，而且月球人的飞船很简陋，很容易出事故。

接下来发生了一个意外。根据相关人员的检测，"地球炸弹"的当量比设计的多10倍！这是谁的责任已经无法追查了。如果没有这个意外，月球上会出现一个巨大的撞击坑，将月球上最大的月海——风暴洋一分为二。但这不是事实！实际上，被一分为二的不是风暴洋，而是月球！几道巨大的裂缝贯穿月球的北半球，导致严重的引力异常，地球行星环中有一大部分碎片飞过去，制造了更宽、更长、更致命的裂缝，最后这些裂缝将月球撕裂，受到碎片的影响，它们无法聚合，而是迅速分散到地球的行星环中。

月球消失了，它化身成了地球的行星环。现在的地球行星环比起土星行星环要壮观得多，因为土星行星环合起来形成一个球体，该球体的直径最多只有300千米；而地球环合起来形成一个球体，直径超过3000千米。

潮汐是月球和太阳的引力引起的，现在月球化作了地球的行星环，虽然质量没有少，但重力被抵消了，于是能影响潮汐的只有太阳。

原本的地球行星环虽然比土星行星环窄很多，但是它的密度非常高（是土星行星环的几百倍），如果有航天器从中间穿过，那么这个航天器很快就会被碎片撞击，最后报废（必须从上方或下方穿过）。事实上，正因为密度很高，所以地球行星环没有任何环缝。

对地球行星环的研究，使人们发现了关于两艘飞船和月球的很多秘密。地球行星环内几乎没有冰，即便有也会融化，大都是岩石和金属，与由岩石和冰组成的土星行星环不同。地球行星环由于反射很多太阳光而呈现出银白色，而不是土星行星环的棕黄色，呈现出独有的美丽。

五、火星文明

在地球的夜晚，天空中可以看见众多的星星镶嵌在天幕中，地面上可以看见各种建筑物散发出的光亮，但它们的光芒在地球行星环面前都黯然失色。在白天，由于地球行星环会反射太阳光，它会更加耀眼而璀璨。当地球的行星环遮挡住太阳，就可以看见行星环的小部分淹没在太阳的光芒之中，如同一颗镶嵌在银手镯上的钻石。由于大量的反射，此时太阳的亮度会大幅度增加。

但是，没有了月球，夜空中还是少了些什么。也许白昼的太阳能弥补它。说到月球，在2157年1月份，月球人的飞船靠近火星时出现故障，用来驱动飞船的燃料舱破了一个洞，里面的核燃料很可能泄漏，必须停在火卫一上维修（此时火卫二在另一侧）。

月球飞船紧急降落在火卫一上，准备用岩石填补燃料舱的漏洞，于是开始采矿。飞船在降落中还发生了损坏，所以需要大量岩石来修补。并且，这艘飞船原本是几艘航天飞机匆忙拼接而成的，所以还存在一些裂缝。但是，在岩石和土壤组成的"面具"下面，火卫一有着一颗巨大的冰核，充分解释了它的低密度，因此，岩石完全不够用。

几天后，火卫一上的岩石都被用完了，冰核暴露在外，使它的反照率大幅提高[1]。

地球人发现了这个现象，于是确认月球人想要在火星定居。

月球人的飞船仍然存在潜在的危险。他们抱着侥幸心理，驾驶飞船准备在火星着陆。但是由于飞船根本无法刹住，所以飞船最终坠毁。在这100名月球人中，只有10人生还。

对于这10个土生土长的月球人来说，火星的大气虽然稀薄，但是比起月球接近真空的大气就不算什么了，但火星对他们来说，仍是地狱的代名词：首先，大气压是一个重要的问题；其次，火星的重力接近月球的两倍，走路可说是非常困难；另外，沙尘暴在火星可谓是家常便饭。

在如此极端而苛刻的情况下，这些月球人着手搭建基地。首先，他们将飞船拆开，把能用的部件拼凑起来，再用火星上的岩石和土壤填补，最终得到了一个半球形的外壳。在它的内外两侧，还制造了由火星岩石构成的墙壁。最后，这些月球人在墙壁和外壳上开了一个口子，这就是一道简陋的门，虽然连门把手和门板都没有，但是也只能这样用。

大家进入基地，用土将门堵死，然后把所有空气都压缩在一个罐子里，最后把这个罐子埋在几米深的地下。这个基地可以解决大部分问题，但是只能要求自己接受强重力了。

---

[1] 组成火卫一的岩石的反照率非常低，但是冰的反照率较高。

　　飞船已经被损坏得差不多了，它的残骸被掩埋在基地外面的土壤中，一同被掩埋的还有90个在飞船坠落时失去生命的月球人。他们上面放了一块从飞船上拆下来的金属，上面写有他们的名字。这块金属就是他们的墓碑。

　　基地和墓地建成以后，这些月球人（现在已经成为火星人了）开始制作各种生活用品，比如说床和椅子。由于除了岩石以外没有任何工具，所以进度很慢。6月，大部分必需的东西已经制作完成了，还囤积了大批用来扩建的资源。他们开始制定法律，并选举出了领导人。这10个火星人都没有名字，只有编号，现火星领导人的编号就是7，因为他在这些火星人中是第七年长的，而且是从地狱神星飞船毁灭时逃跑的一员。

　　光阴似箭，很快就到了2157年的8月。一天，一个编号为9的火星人宣布："我们之中有5个男性和5个女性，正好能组成5对夫妻。我们的生育下限[1]是2，那最后就可以生下10个孩子。而且，这10个孩子的年龄差距不要太大，否则他们就难以生育了。"

　　9的观点得到了大家的一致认同。9将全体火星人分为男性和女性，并各派出一名代表玩"石头剪刀布"，这是从地球引进的一个游戏，采取一局一胜制。男性一组派出了7，女性一组派出了9。最后，

---

[1]　生育下限，指一种动物如果选择与异性交配并生育后代的话，最少会生多少个孩子。地球人的生育下限是 1 个，月球人和当今的火星人则是 2 个（这是因为月球女性至少会释放两个卵子，所以每个月球人和火星人都是一对双胞胎的其中一员）。但受当地宗教影响，在 21 个世纪还有很多月球人终身不婚，所以月球文明在最鼎盛的时期人口也只有 60 亿。

7出了"布"，而9出了"石头"，于是7取得胜利。

接下来，9说道："一会儿，你们就知道我在搞什么名堂了。"她把两组人分开，在自己的口袋里翻出一张洁白的纸，迅速地撕成五片；用自己带来的一支勉强能用的笔，在每张纸的中间写上数字代表女性一组全体人员的编号，分别揉成纸团，抛到远处。

接下来，9把男性一组的人拉到这五个纸团的地方，让每个人自己拿一个纸团，但暂时不能打开。这下子，所有人都明白9在干什么了，她是在用别致的方法抽签，决定哪两个人将会结婚。她问大家："明白我在干什么了吧？"

"明白了，"其他人异口同声地回答道。"我们发誓绝不反悔。"

"很好。现在，全体男性打开手上的纸团。"9说道。这组人怀着紧张的心情打开纸团，无论结果如何都只能坦然接受。

7将9提出的所有建议整理为火星法律。巧合的是，他手上的纸团写有9的名字，也就是说两人将成为一对伴侣……由于处于极端的情况，5名女性在当天就尝试受孕了，幸运的是，所有人都是一次成功。

2158年6月末，10个孩子陆续出生，编号为11至20。这一段时期对火星文明来说是最艰难的：10个新生儿无法工作，5个女性还没有完全康复，5个男性又要养活前两者，也要养活自己，因此，每个人都必须加倍努力。

并且，这些孩子的父母毕竟来自月球，而月球新生儿的骨头非常脆弱，火星的重力又相对强一些，很有可能把这些婴儿的骨头压折。

不过，这些顽强的火星婴儿还是适应了强重力。年末，当其中最年长的11步履蹒跚地迈出第一步时，所有成人都乐开了花，尤其是他的父母，也就是7和9。紧接着，11的妹妹——12也站了起来，和11在基地里踱步，摔倒了十几次。

日后也可以看出，11和12的身体素质是第二代火星人中最好的，剩下的8个孩子暂时比不上他们。13和14想到了一个办法：两个人一只手撑着地，另一只手紧紧握着对方的手，双脚踩住地面，缓缓松开撑着地的手并站起来，再松开对方的手。

看到这一幕，一名编号为8的火星男性提议，为了确保这些孩子之间没有矛盾（如果有的话，火星文明就会分裂成多个阵营，最终导致灭绝），应该让他们从小培养感情。

此时，剩下的6个孩子已经用类似的方式站起来了。很快，所有人都可以稳稳地行走，甚至可以慢慢地跑了。令他们的父母欣慰的是，他们的孩子更能适应火星的环境，这颗红色的星球再也不算是地狱了。

2206年1月，新一代的火星人也出生了，编号为21至28。他们有着比他们父母和祖父母更坚硬的骨骼，他们也陆续站了起来，摇摇晃晃地迈出第一步。

在20腹中的两个孩子（一男一女）比其他8个晚出生一些，她的第一个孩子（29）于2206年7月13日23时52分出生，而第二个（30）于次日0时3分出生。

之后，这些火星人就迁移到地下，因为地表环境仍然很恶劣，从此杳无音信。在500年之后，他们也许会对地球进行疯狂的行为……

六、太阳系故事

2216年，地球人为了获取资源和增加人口等各种目的，将一群宇航员分为多个小组，在太阳系的其他3颗类地行星上搭建基地。

2230年，地球人的足迹已经遍布整个内太阳系，在4颗气态巨行星周围还搭建了6座太空城（木星和土星各两座，天王星和海王星各一座），以地球六大洲[1]命名。

地球人殖民的脚步还未停止，2245年地球人已经在冥王星周围建立太空城，里面的一小部分人甚至来到妊神星、鸟神星和阅神星周围建造太空城[2]。这四座围绕矮行星的太空城分别以地球的四大洋命名。

2246年1月1日，时任地球元首庄严地宣布：太阳系联邦于2246

---

[1]　在这个时代，欧洲和亚洲被认为是同一个洲，通称欧亚洲。

[2]　不在谷神星周围建造是因为谷神星已经从矮行星中除名，它的天文学地位已经下降。

年1月1日0时正式成立！

太阳系联邦使用的历法与公历一致，只是以2246年作为元年。从此，地球人进入了太阳纪元，23世纪的这一天是新纪元的元年元日。

太阳纪元元年2月4日，木星周围的两座太空城"欧亚洲号"和"非洲号"与土星周围的两座太空城"北美洲号"和"南美洲号"爆发战争，最后将天王星周围的"南极洲号"、海王星周围的"大洋洲号"、鸟神星周围的"北冰洋号"、妊神星周围的"印度洋号"、阅神星周围的"大西洋号"和冥王星周围的"太平洋号"也卷了进来。

这场战争是外太阳系的一场混战，任何一座太空城都不再有可靠的盟友，只有凶狠的敌人。

内太阳系4颗行星试图阻止他们的大混战，但是在太阳系联邦建立后外太阳系的实力更强了，完全无法控制，不听使唤，甚至有几个城市威胁联邦政府禁止干预，否则会向太阳系首都——地球发动进攻。

太阳纪元2年11月，战争在联邦政府的介入之下强制停止，各座太空城也友好相处，像是什么都没有发生一样。

有人说，好的开始就是成功的一半。太阳系联邦似乎没有什么好的开始，刚刚建立就出现了严重的内部矛盾。这个问题虽然还未真正体现出来，但却对太阳系联邦的未来造成了深远的影响。

太阳系联邦先是在此后的几十年迅速发展，享受了一段平静的时期。太阳纪元70年9月，太阳系联邦的天文学家们发现，南门二发出了耀眼的光芒，持续了一段时间又恢复正常，但是又少了点东西，让他们百思不得其解。

当人们将望远镜指向南门二时，惊奇地发现：南门二B和比邻星都消失了，变成了一团气体云和岩石！并且，剩下的南门二A旁边出现了一颗行星！由于南门二距离太阳4光年左右，所以这件事应该发生在66年。

这颗行星来自哪里？由于观测数据的缺乏，太阳系的科学家也只能推测。它是在70年8月1日被巨大的望远镜阵列发现的，但由于其系统忽视了它的重要性，没有人知道它。再往前就无法追溯了。不过，聪明的太阳系人类将第一次发现它的位置与它现在的位置用一条虚拟的线连起来，再将这条线的一端无限延长。这条线途经地狱神星原本的位置，证明它曾经是地狱神星的第二颗卫星，后来在地狱神星爆炸时被抛射出去，最终被南门二的引力捕获！

观测表明，这颗行星表面完全由10公里厚的海洋覆盖（在严寒的太空中，海洋表面还有一层冰，现在已经融化），中心则是一颗相对整颗行星而言非常大的液态铁核，因此，有很强的磁场。

在该行星的海洋中，有着综合实力不亚于太阳系人类的智慧生命。他们在太阳纪元66年发射了大量的推进器，把南门二B的一颗行星和比邻星的一颗行星（也可能是比邻星的两颗行星）高速推入这两颗恒星中，导致两颗恒星爆炸，这件事是太阳系人类在70年得知的。

他们这么做的动机是：南门二A是一个非常合适的母星，它不大不小，刚刚好，非常类似太阳，对于南门二b这么一颗和地球一样宜居而美丽的行星来说，是再合适不过的了。

可是，南门二A属于一个三星系统，这会使围绕它的行星的轨道极为混乱，导致一系列灾难，所以必须要处理掉另外两颗恒星。现在，南门二这个恒星系统只剩下一颗恒星和一颗行星，因此，人们以"南门二"称呼南门二A，而以"南门二b"称呼这颗行星。由于南门二b的大气流动极快，在其海面上经常上演风速不亚于音速的风暴，因此也被称作风神星（Aeolus），以希腊神话中的埃俄罗斯命名。

太阳纪元71年，风神星已经围绕南门二公转了一圈，公转周期为380天（注：这件事发生在太阳纪元67年）。这一年，太阳系人类接收到了其海洋中智慧生命的信息，其内容出乎所有人的意料，是简单的三个字：有人吗。这条信息是用恒星当作"天线"发出的，类似公元纪元21世纪的小说《三体》。只不过，这本小说中的三颗太阳如今只剩下一颗。

利用同样的做法，太阳系中的各个地区也向南门二系统发出了一条很短的信息：有！

太阳纪元75年，风神星上的智慧生命接收到了来自太阳系的信息，于是又向太阳系的方向发送了一段话："向回复我们信息的这个世界致以美好的祝愿。通过这段信息，阁下将会对我们的世界有一个大致的了解。我们的行星曾经是另一颗星球的卫星，后来那颗星球被炸毁了，我们的行星被抛射出去，最终被南门二的引力捕获。就像你们看到的那样，南门二系统的两颗恒星被我们炸毁了。在穿越寒冷的星际空间时，我们行星的海洋表面凝固了，形成了一层几百米厚的冰，但是冰层使我们的海洋没有冻结。这一段时期相当于你们的冰河时代，时间跨度达一万余年，期间我们的科学技术有巨大的突破。但是，由于遇到了一个瓶颈，所以可能需要你们的帮助才行。并且，我方大量公民在得知你们的存在后，想与你们的行星系建交。"

太阳纪元79年，经过太阳系联邦的决定，太阳系同意与南门二系统建交，这样能使双方都快速发展。

从次年开始，双方和平发展，互相帮助。风神星上的智慧生命在纳米技术这个领域上有了巨大突破，太阳系人类则在可控核聚变这个方面取得了重大进展。

在太阳系，陆续出现了很多有关风神星智慧生命的电视剧、电影和小说。受这种文化的影响，再加上他们是生活在海洋中，民间将那里的智慧生命称作"海人"。

"海人"与太阳系人类和银河族的其他成员都有很大区别，因为他们实际上是进化出智慧的鱼，不仅脑容量比银河族更高，游动的速度也非常快。

时光飞逝，又过去了70多年。太阳系人类和"海人"的实力都已经今非昔比，两个恒星系都发展到了非常高的程度。在太阳系，反物质和核聚变已经民用，不再用来做武器。太阳系人类为了自卫，在每颗行星和矮行星的周围布置了军队，一共有1亿名士兵和10万艘飞船。

太阳系纪元152年，一颗巨大的流浪行星飞掠南门二，它是一颗非常大的类木行星，利用强大的引力将风神星拽到离南门二更近的地方，自身却"逃之夭夭"，向浩瀚的星际空间飞去。

南门二b的轨道降低了很多，它在目前的轨道上围绕南门二一周只需要38天，大约是之前的十分之一。如此短的公转周期意味着它离南门二非常近，因此，表面温度在刹那间升高，上面厚厚的海洋如同烧开的一壶水一般沸腾。

海洋被蒸干了，海中的所有生物（包括全体"海人"）也被烧焦，整颗星球只剩下中心的铁核，以及附着在上面的一堆尸体。于是，风神星从"海人"的舒适家园变成了不折不扣的地狱。

太阳纪元156年，太阳系人类观测到了上面的现象。大家心中都有千言万语，想表达自己对"海人"文明的感激和惋惜。毕竟，是这个已经毁灭的文明帮了太阳系一把，让太阳系和自身都迅速发展。

但是，这场悲剧已经无法反转了，人们也从短暂的悲伤中恢复过来，面对眼前残酷而黑暗的现实。一些人对报道这些信息的科学家和电视台甚至有了仇恨，加剧了民众和科学家之间的冲突。

太阳纪元199年，太阳系联邦的政府确立了新的行政规划，大大方便了治理。在新的行政规划中，每颗行星或矮行星为一个省，每座太空城为一个城市，地球的各个大陆是不同的城市，与太空城享有完全平等的政治地位。为了方便治理，太阳系联邦军队开始裁员，事后发现这是一个错误之举。

过了一年，现有的太空城全部更名，围绕木星的两座太空城分别改名为"木星一号"和"木星二号"，围绕土星的两座太空城则变为"土星一号"和"土星二号"，其他行星和矮行星周围的太空城也如法炮制。另外，围绕类木行星的6座太空城奉命建造新的4座太空城（每颗行星各一座）。

又是5年过去了。新的4座太空城和之前6座太空城下降到它们围绕的类木行星浓厚的大气之中，据称是为了进一步探测这些星球。这一举动引起了巨大的争议，有人担心太空城会坠毁，就像四个半世纪之前的"伽利略号"和"卡西尼号"这些探测器一样。尽管科学家们反复解释，太空城有足够的能量使其在接下来的几千年都不坠毁，但是完全没有用，民众还是在抗议，往日两者之间的裂痕已经无法弥补。

这件事情被称作"太空城运动"，最后在太阳纪元222年从一场社会运动演化为一场大规模战争，也就是赫赫有名的第三次世界大战，简称"三战"，参战方分别是太阳系叛军和政府。

据官方相关说法，这场战争一直持续到了太阳纪元457年，中间一刻也没有停歇。太阳系联邦在这场长达235年的世界大战中毁灭了，该国家发展到了行星际时代。太阳系叛军把全部的太空城都摧毁了，里面的人被转移到地球上来。其他行星上的人类也回到了地球。2个月后，全体太阳系人类都回到地球，重新建立了地球共和国。

令人惊奇的是，太阳系联邦政府居然能顽强地抵抗两个世纪，任何自然因素和人为因素都不可能导致这样的结果。有些人发现，它们拥有一种奇特的物质，可以制成比反物质武器还要强大的炸弹。

经过多名专家的分析，这种奇特的物质来自内太阳系。之所以做出这一推断，是因为太阳系联邦政府的总部就位于地球，而在战争中他们不可能发射探测器到外太阳系采集该物质，这种物质既然在政府手里，就必然来自内太阳系。

可是，这种物质具体来自哪里呢？

专家们的视线从整个内太阳系渐渐集中到一个地方：太阳。这是因为，当时水星、金星和火星都有很多叛军，小行星带也位于太阳系叛军的控制范围内，对政府来说很危险。至于地球，人类这个种族从诞生开始就没有在这颗美丽的蓝色弹珠上找到比反物质武器还要强大的东西。因此，这种奇特物质只能来自太阳。

据推测，政府军的探测器在发射并穿过金星和水星的轨道后向太阳飞去，从这颗恒星带走了几百吨的物质，最后制成了这种武器。这种特殊的物质在民间和科学界被昵称为"日"，因为它来自太阳。

"日"具体是什么只能通过它的影像来判断，而这样的影像一共只有十段。从这些影像分析，"日"是一种银白色的金属。现在的问题是，它是一种元素还是一种合金呢？

太阳纪元458年4月1日，科学家们宣布，"日"是一种元素，原子序数119。化学界一直在寻找119号元素，然而来自各地的专家们一起找了700多年才找到。为了庆祝这一事件，地球共和国政府将使用的纪元重新改回公元纪元。按照公元纪元，这一年就是2703年。

七、最大的玩笑

　　可是，刚解决一个问题，两个新问题又来了：以太阳这种黄矮星的能力，是无法生成"日"这么重的元素的，那太阳表面的"日"又是从哪里来的？并且，原子序数这么高的元素为什么没有衰变？

　　实际上，这是一个玩笑。"日"根本就不是119号元素，实际上它根本就不存在。政府部门策划了很久，终于在2703年的愚人节向民众开了这个历史上最大的玩笑！实际上，太阳系联邦在三战开始的时候就灭亡了，三战只持续了3年，接下来的200多年都是和平时期。

　　但很快，就会有一个新的玩笑来打破"日"的纪录了，而且与前者不同，后者是毁灭性的。2703年7月10日，人们突然发现，太阳在天空中突然开始以肉眼可见的速度萎缩！也就是说，地球正在远离太阳！

　　在人们首次发现这个现象后一个小时，地球的公转轨道半径已经达到了1.5个天文单位，和火星轨道很近，但由于火星在太阳的另一侧，所以两颗行星并没有相撞。这时的太阳在天空中的视星等大约为−25，而在原来的轨道上太阳的视星等为−26。虽然看起来并没有多大变化，但实际上太阳已经变暗了两倍多。

又过了一个小时，地球距离太阳2个天文单位，已经超越了火星轨道，进入了小行星带内侧。于是，小行星带和地球光环中的粒子混杂在一起。

另一方面，地球人都躲到了地下，因为在距离太阳2个天文单位的地方，严寒已经无法阻挡。

当地球从小行星带外层出来时，已经失去了它美丽的光环，而小行星带的总质量在这几小时内增加了20多倍，这都是因为地球行星环里面的岩石进入了小行星带。

地球继续远离太阳。又过了7个小时，地球已经离太阳5.5个天文单位，在木星轨道之外。太阳的视星等变为−23。

跨过木星轨道后9个小时，地球来到了土星轨道，距离太阳10个天文单位，太阳成为一颗−21等的恒星，但仍然是天空中最亮的天体。

穿过土星轨道后的18个小时，人们一直待在地下，没有什么大事情。接着，地球穿越了天王星的轨道，距离太阳足足19个天文单位。

地下的人们出奇地冷静，也没有爆发任何大规模骚乱。在地下的人们可以保持温暖，环境并不比原来在地表的生活差多少。说到地表，那里已经开始下雪了：不是冰晶组成的雪，而是大气中的氮气和氧气在寒冷中凝固产生的雪花。地球正在失去它的大气层，取而代之的是地表厚厚的积雪。

越过天王星轨道后的第22个小时，地球越过海王星轨道，轨道半径30个天文单位，成为八大行星中离太阳最远的行星。

　　大约五天半之后（确切地说，是135小时），地球跨过了阋神星的远日点，轨道半径97.5个天文单位。又过了五小时，地球的轨道半径达到100个天文单位，是正常情况下的100倍。地球的大气层已经彻底消失了，而远方的太阳也只是一颗−16等的恒星。

　　2703年7月18日，地球在这一天成为太阳系内离太阳最远的大天体，甚至比阋神星这颗属于离散盘的矮行星还要远。

　　75天很快过去了，到2703年10月1日，地球和太阳的距离达到1000个天文单位。如果一个人站在地表，他只能在周围看到积雪和星空，太阳也只是天空中一个不起眼的小点。

　　经过反复计算，地球正在向南门二的方向飞去。这一结果公布后，民间一片哗然，有人担心地球会与南门二b相撞，有人担心地球不会到宜居带，还有人担心地球又会被抛出这个行星系。但是，这一切都没有发生，因为地球停在了距离太阳1000天文单位的地方，开始绕太阳公转。

　　接着，一颗熟悉的行星从太阳的方向飞来，那就是水星。水星远离太阳的速度比地球快四倍，每小时行进2个天文单位，但是它开始远离太阳的时间不得而知。无论如何，水星追上了地球，在天空中越来越大，直到10月30日，它成为了地球的一颗卫星。

　　2703年11月15日，由于水星的惯性，它脱离了地球，向太阳方向飞回去。不过，水星一走，金星也跟了上来。它的大气层已经消失得无影无踪，地表出现了一层非常厚的干冰，覆盖了它的大部分表面特征，几乎无法辨认出它是金星了。金星远离太阳的速度是地球的3

倍，但是它还是在11月17日追上了地球，向地球撞来。

幸运的是，金星在距离地球35万公里时被一颗较大的小行星击中，化为碎片。

三颗行星从太阳向南门二飞去的现象使人们百思不得其解。并且，水星为什么会返回？那颗小行星真的有能力击碎金星吗？地球为什么会停止远离太阳？当人们绞尽脑汁思考这些问题时，发现火星在金星被击碎的那一天远离太阳，虽然速度只有地球的一半。但是，火星是向仙后座的阁道二飞去的，与水星、金星和地球完全相反。

11月18日早晨，地球人发现了惊人的现象：海王星在靠近太阳，而且速度是地球的8倍！仅仅过了七个半小时，海王星就已经来到水星的轨道上运行了。

接下来的一系列现象使地球人非常头疼，因为现有理论完全无法解释：11月20日，木星从现有轨道上突然移动到火星正前方，火星撞上了木星后，木星以海王星靠近太阳的速度远离太阳，向北极星飞去；11月21日，天王星以同样的速度靠近太阳，到达海王星轨道后又向前运行，追上并撞上了海王星，由于惯性，天王星和海王星的残骸一起撞向太阳；11月22日，土星以木星远离太阳的速度的两倍远离太阳，但也是向北极星方向，随后和木星相撞；11月23日，谷神星也飞向地球，又离开了。

综上所述，地球成为太阳系唯一的行星。虽然地球人都来到了地下，建立了大量的地下城和防空洞，但是地球表面已经不适合生存了，而地下城和防空洞中的空间也不够。想让人类生存下去，唯一的办法就是：把地球推回原来的轨道。

2704年1月，人类利用几十个行星发动机抵消了地球的自转。人类拥有28世纪的科技水平，因此，这并不费力。地球的自转停止之后，太阳就不再升起和落下了。行星发动机被输送到地球背对太阳的一面，随后开始运转。

2705年4月1日，地球回到了太阳温暖的怀抱之中。利用行星发动机，地球重新开始自转，但是由于这天恰好是愚人节，人们故意使行星发动机往错误的方向推进，使得地球往与之前相反的方向自转。于是，太阳开始西升东落，间接导致了人们对于太阳更多的关注。

八、南极洲文明

2706年1月16日，世界航天局（WSA，World Space Agency）成立，其中一个目的就是将一艘载了一名宇航员的宇宙飞船（被命名为"日冕号"）发射到太阳表面，并且采集数据。

并且，这场旅途并不是单向的，"日冕号"上面的那名宇航员并不会在太阳的烈焰中死去。相反，他将会利用强大的引擎离开太阳，回到地球上。

按照计划，"日冕号"虽然会降落到太阳6000摄氏度的表面，甚至进入太阳内部，但是对于这艘由超高熔点金属组成的飞船来说完全不成问题。

2709年5月，"日冕号"被装在最新一代的反物质驱动火箭"星空三号"上面发射。"星空三号"与之前的火箭发射有些不同：第二、三级脱离之后，它的第一级在飞行一段时间之后就直接裂成碎块，利用惯性推动里面的"日冕号"飞船和飞船中的宇航员向太阳飞去。其他的飞船只需要垂直于地面就可以发射，因为它们的引擎能产生足够强的推力。这些飞船是不配备燃料的，只有储存能量的容器。

"日冕号"拥有强大的引擎，但是由于这时可以借助惯性和太阳的引力飞向太阳，所以引擎是关着的。

飞船里面的那名宇航员的祖先是被太阳系联邦派遣到火星基地的人员之一，所以他、他的父母、祖父母和兄弟姐妹实际上是在火星出生的。

就像火星人一样，火星基地的人都只有编号，这名宇航员的编号就是68957986。之后，他被召回地球，最后被选为"日冕号"的宇航员。现在，68957986正漂浮在"日冕号"的座舱中，向着太阳飞去。为了迅速到达太阳，他手动打开了飞船的引擎，并调至最大功率。

20天后，68957986乘坐"日冕号"抵达了太阳，将引擎关上，利用飞船系统进行记录数据、拍摄照片等工作，使人类了解到了更多有关太阳的信息。同时，"日冕号"还成为第一艘也是最后一艘到达太阳表面的飞船。

不幸的是，当飞船穿越太阳表面时，飞船的外壳被一颗坠向太阳的陨石砸中。飞船内置的监视器将这整个过程拍摄了下来，但是由于速度过快，68957986根本没有时间控制飞船躲避它，所以飞船的外壳破了一个大洞，热浪从洞中倾泻而出，焚烧了飞船内的一切，当然也包括68957986。

飞船上有一个监视器，它和"日冕号"的地面控制中心是连着的，飞船毁坏的过程都被它拍摄了下来。8分钟后，当地面控制中心里的人接收到监视器传来的图像和视频，恐惧和震惊立即占据了他们的心灵。

经过数月的调查，得知小陨石撞击太阳这种事件其实非常频繁，平均每10秒就有一次。虽然如此，一颗陨石不偏不倚地撞在"日冕号"的位置，就非常不可思议了。

由于担心这起事故重演，原本要在2710年发射的"日冕二号"制造好后被改为绕地球旋转的载人飞船，名字也变为"地中海号"。"地中海号"内部有1000万人生活，相当于一座围绕地球的太空城了，在地球静止轨道上运行着。

2711年6月8日，刚刚投入运行的"地中海号"抓拍到了一艘围绕太阳的飞船，它正在靠近地球……

可以肯定，这艘飞船并不是"日冕号"，因为在7月11日，这艘飞船就以极高的速度接近了"地中海号"的轨道。透过太空城的窗户，可以用肉眼看到这艘飞船，上面发出耀眼的红光，这一切都不是"日冕号"可以做到的。

7月12日上午，它掠过了"地中海号"。这时候，两者之间的距离只有100公里。接下来，它向地球方向缓慢地飞行了500公里左右，推测是关闭了发动机之后进行的自由落体。

诡异的事情发生了：它突然打开了发动机，向"地中海号"飞了过来，显然是发现了这座太空城。可以清晰地看到两者的大小相当。这一次，它们直接相撞。攻击是绕日飞船发起的，它径直撞上了"地中海号"的燃料舱，使得它坠向地球。还好，大部分人得以生还。

紧接着，绕日飞船一头扎入了地中海，又缓慢地浮起来，悬在半空中，并向东方缓慢移动。

绕日飞船跨过了整个欧亚大陆，又越过了国际日期变更线。它在横跨北美洲时突然开始向南飞，飞过了整个南美洲，在西南极洲降落。

从绕日飞船里走出了一个外星人，他的身高在2米以上3米以下，又细又长的手臂一直下垂到自己的小腿，每只手上都有5根很长的手指。他面色苍白，巨大的眼睛下面是两个微小的鼻孔，再往下则是一张看不到嘴唇和牙齿的大嘴和异常尖的下巴。

这个外星人没有头发，是个秃子，也没有穿衣服和裤子。他的嘴巴虽然大，但是合起来的时候只能看到一条缝。他的右手拿着一把装满子弹的手枪，左手拿着一把匕首。

这个外星人来自火星而不是太阳，他们是定居火星的月球人的后代，在火星飞离太阳系之后，正是他提出了制造这艘飞船的构想，并飞回内太阳系。他的名字的发音为"拉达雅图"，地球人将其简称为"拉"。

拉径直走向最近的科考站，一枪打碎了窗户的玻璃，钻了进去，对着里面的人大吼："不许动！"

他把这句话说了三次，第一次使用中文，第二次使用英文，第三次用的是一种只有他自己听得懂的外星语言。

看到有一个人想逃跑，拉立刻将手中的匕首投掷出去，不偏不倚地砸在那人的胸口上，并刺穿了他的心脏。其他人没有一个敢动，恐惧地看着拉把匕首拔出来，扔向下一个人。接着，拉用手枪射杀了科考站内全部人员，把科考站内一切能与外部通信的设备全部毁坏，大摇大摆地走回飞船。

他在飞船面前停下了，对着它大喊："出来吧！"这句话是用外星语言说的。

飞船的门被撞开了，几千万个和他一样的外星人涌了出来。其中有一个外星人头戴白色的王冠，显然是这些外星人中的领导人。他也是火星人，但是名字不同，被其他外星人称作"沙伊巫诗"，被地球人称为"沙"。沙向拉问道："拉达雅图，这里环境如何？"

"我的王，这里环境不错，"拉双膝跪地，对沙说，"但是有点儿热。"

"这个温度还好吧？"沙说道。

"我的王，现在正值冬天，等夏天来了……"

"没关系的。"沙打断了他的话，又拿着一个被称作"超级扩音器"的东西，对全体外星人大声说：

"各位！我们终于来到了地球，我们梦想中的家园。现在，我将公布一件意义重大的事情。

"第一，地球文明的实力目前比我们弱，我们可以轻而易举地占领这颗星球。但是，地球的其他地方，就像拉达雅图说的一样，非常热。因此，我们只需占领这块白色的大陆就足够了。

"第二，在占领这块大陆后，地球人肯定想将它夺回。我们一定要做好防范，不要让地球人把这块地方抢走！

"第三，从今以后我们就在这块被地球人称作'南极洲'的大陆上生活了，虽然我们仍然要遵守火星法律，但是我们已经不是火星人了！今天，我们成为了南极洲人！"

在几公里外的南极点上，沙插上了他亲自设计的南极洲旗帜，并且宣布占领南极洲，建立南极王国。

有很多人造卫星发现了这一现象，地球人知道以后立即对火星人——或者说南极洲人——发起了总攻。南极洲人的军事非常强大，不到一天，他们就打退了如洪水般涌来的地球军队，后者死伤极为惨重。

无奈的地球人被迫与取得胜利的南极洲人签订《南极洲独立条约》。该条约将南极王国的领土限制在南极洲以内，将地球共和国的领土限制在南极洲以外。

从2711年开始，地球人对南极洲人怀恨在心，而后者则欢天喜地，享用着这块白色大陆带给自己的一切福利，却没有注意到地球人的军事和科技都已经真正发展起来了。

2759年，《南极洲独立条约》被打破，实力已经今非昔比的地球共和国彻底摧毁了南极王国。这件事非常精彩，令所有的地球人大快人心。

九、夺回南极洲

2740年，有些地球人突然想起6个世纪前的地狱神星人。他们试图用一颗岩石撞击地球，尽管没有取得成功，但经过多名科学家的分析，发现这样攻击敌方是极为有效的，而且地狱神星在来到地球的途中也通过这种方法消灭了很多竞争对手。

28世纪的地球早已具备制造如此巨大的岩石的能力，但由于这次撞击的目标只是南极洲，因此，这块岩石要小得多。经过上千万人的不懈努力，3天内，人们成功制造了一颗直径5公里的岩石，用来撞击南极洲。

由于担心岩石伤害到南半球的其他地球人，岩石造好后，地球共和国政府就在南半球的几个地区发布公告，通知南半球全部人员撤离到北半球（南极洲人除外）。此时的地球有将近800亿人口，南半球有大约300亿，所以撤离过程花费了将近15年。

撤离过程中使用的交通工具其实就是普通的飞船。地球人在多个"据点"上集合，飞船一齐从地面出发，把每个据点上的人分批运送到北半球。这种飞船后来有了一个名字："巨兽"客船。一艘"巨兽"客船大约可以承载5000到1万人，速度在每秒1000米左右，采用可控核聚变技术驱动。

南半球的人们还要在北半球有临时的住所，所以撤离过程结束后，又花了一段时间让他们安定下来。

2755年，撤离过程结束，被称作"星空四号"的火箭搭载着那块直径5公里的岩石从北半球的沙漠中升空。岩石向着地球最南端的大陆飞去。

岩石撞击南极洲会产生大量的热，可能导致南极洲的冰层融化，进而使海平面上升，淹没大量沿海城市。

因此，人们又花了将近4年从海边撤离。在确认一切正常后，那块人造的岩石进入大气层，随后狠狠地撞在了南极点附近。

这块岩石的速度比预想中更快，将整个南极洲的冰盖全部融化了，海平面上升了60多米。

南极洲的淡水储量非常丰富。全世界超过一半的淡水就这样流入了南冰洋之中。与此同时，一大批沿海地区都被海水淹没。

海水被南极洲的冰盖冲淡了，造成了对生态系统的巨大破坏。与此同时，增加的海水也使地球的气候彻底改变了。

再来看看南极洲。这些定居南极的火星人几乎都在岩石撞击地表的那一刻丧生，接着，本能驱使剩下的幸存者远离撞击点，向海边跑去，然后跳入大海中拼命地通过一种低效的方式游泳。他们当中大部分人死于海中。

幸存的南极洲人只有三四十个，包括沙以及他的亲人、随从和大臣，还有一两个平民。这些人狼狈不堪地驾驶一艘快艇，向最近的大陆——南美洲航行。

由于地球人都离开了南半球，南半球的海上几乎没有船只。很快就有人造卫星发现沙等人乘坐的船，地球人们得知后立即派出一艘战舰（还是一艘比较简陋且过时的），将这艘船击沉，上面所有的南极洲人都葬身海底，他们的尸体很快就被那里的鱼群当作食物吞了下去。

2760年，确认一切平安无事之后，那些撤离的人回到了南半球，一共花了10年。2770年，"回归"活动彻底结束，大家安居乐业、和睦相处。地球重新成为了一颗平静而安宁的星球，生态系统和气候也以惊人的速度恢复。

南极大陆成为了一片群岛，上面的冰也暂时消失了，成为了一处旅游胜地。由于南极有很多未开发的资源，它也成为了一座工业基地，这片基地中还有着一些保护区。总之，南极洲成为了一片繁华的大陆。

十、第二月球

2800年，月球回来了。

什么？月球不是已经消失了吗？

月球的确已经消失了，这里所说的月球，也不是地球历史上那颗美丽的银白色卫星。地球现在的卫星，或者说现在的月球，是一颗黑白相间的丑陋天体。这是因为，这颗卫星结合了以下卫星的特征：

1. 月球的大小

2. 木卫一的火山

3. 木卫二、木卫三和木卫四的地下海洋

4. 土卫一巨大的陨石坑

5. 土卫二的间歇泉

6. 土卫三、土卫四和天卫一的峡谷

7. 土卫五的行星环

8. 土卫六的大气

9. 土卫八的"阴阳脸"

10. 天卫三的断崖

11. 天卫二和天卫四的撞击坑

12. 天卫五的冕状物

13. 海卫一的"哈密瓜皮地形"

这些特征都是很吸引人的，但是合起来就非常丑陋了。

由于它的大小和之前的月球差不多，但是质量和与地球的距离都只有月球的一半，在天空中所占的面积差不多比原来的月球大两倍。并且，它是目前太阳系唯一的卫星，被地球人称作第二月球。

地球上的生命全都离不开水。在第二月球的地下海洋中，人类发现了一类全新的生物，他们最后毁灭了地球上的生命。

这种生物的历史相对短暂，最多有50万年，进化速度很快。他们是从一种类似细菌的生命开始的。这种生命被称作"原始球"，看起来就像一个有着两条触须的球，身体表面覆盖着全反射镜面，所以是银色的，体长3毫米。触须很可能是由聚乙烯包裹着神经系统而形成的，"球"则是由一些烷烃和烯烃构成的。

这个球可以通过某种方式发送电信号，使两条触须摆动。原始球的两条触须相对球来说很长，有20厘米，是用来捕捉食物的。这些"食物"其实就是地下海洋中的灰尘，成分与原始球的身体类似。

当原始球的重量增加到最初的两倍左右，它会分裂为两个更小的原始球，重复进行上述过程。一个世纪后，第二月球的地下海中就布满了原始球，灰尘的数量急剧下降。接着，一群原始球聚到了一起，它们中间的球体也融合成一个更大的球，这些触须之间也有了联系，可以比单个的原始球更快地捕捉灰尘。

由于自身的重量，这些更大的原始球一直沉到了地下海洋的底部。在漫长的演化中，这些原始球失去了球状部分，只剩下触须，看起来很像植物。单个的原始球成为了这种"植物"的食物，因此这种"植物"被称作"捕球草"。电信号就从这些触须的根部发出。

捕球草实际上是动物，但是它们扎根于海底，只能随着水流飘动。

时光飞逝，5万年过去了。在45万年前一个再平凡不过的日子，一株捕球草的根脱离了海底。又过了几万年，那株捕球草的后代已经可以随心所欲地游动，他们看起来非常像地球上的鱼类。这种"鱼类"被叫作"地下鱼"。

地下鱼以捕球草和原始球为食，随着他们的数量急剧增长，捕球草和原始球都灭绝了。

食物消失了，地下鱼必须自相残杀。30万年前，发生了一次大规模自然灾害，导致少数的鱼地下基因突变，第一次拥有了性别。

这件事的好处在于，地下鱼不必等到体积变为之前的两倍时才分裂，他们可以进行类似于人类的"生育"过程。这样，一条地下鱼在被袭击的时候，就可以交配生下50余条幼年的地下鱼，也就是孩子。地下鱼是胎生动物，并且从怀孕到生下孩子的时间只有几秒钟。

如果一对性别不同的地下鱼一起出行，发现危险就可以交配，生下幼年地下鱼。有了幼年地下鱼作为掩护，两条成年地下鱼就可以逃脱，大部分的幼年地下鱼也可以逃离危险。

接下来，就有"聪明"的地下鱼发现：无论是否遇到危险，都要尽可能多生孩子。这样，没有性别的地下鱼就会被这些有性别的地下鱼攻击，而且无力反攻。

10个世纪之后，没有性别的地下鱼彻底灭绝，地下鱼只能以灰尘为食。这种灰尘同时是地下鱼的食物、排泄物和分泌物，死去的地下鱼也会渐渐变成灰尘，化为尘土。

由于以灰尘为食，它们不需要自相残杀，也不需要多少体力，地下鱼慢慢进化成人形，脑容量也在不断提高。

1万年前，地下鱼"文明"步入了石器时代，这些石头从海洋顶部的地层和海底来，此时也出现了语言。200年前，地下鱼，或者说第二月球人，挖开了海洋上面的"地壳"。透过这个洞，它们，或者说他们，第一次看到了灿烂的星空。这时，他们已经离太阳系很近了。

2800年，第二月球闯进了太阳系，向着这个行星系唯一的行星冲了过去，成为了它的卫星。

2185年，第二月球人的技术就超过地球人的水平，比地球人领先了6个世纪。第二月球人最擅长的两项技术是钻探和基因工程，远远超过地球人。

再看看地球上。公元2893年，黄石超级火山爆发了，由于火山灰遮蔽了阳光，引发了一串连锁反应，导致全体地球人几乎都灭绝了，只有100万人幸存。在这个时候，剩余的人类推举出了一位领导人。不幸的是，这个"首领"其实已经邪恶到不可描述的程度。

这个人自称为"卡法汪图戎宾辛基坎"，简称"卡法"。卡法创造了一种邪教，并强迫所有地球人相信，大体内容被其中一位信徒描述为"地球发怒了，被困在地下的种种灾难已经被地球之神释放出

来，它们将一步一步地将所有的生命推向死亡，让人类永远饱受地球之神的折磨"。信徒们要做的，就是虔诚地膜拜地球之神——也就是卡法——并祈求他拯救地球上的生命。

第二月球人早就盯上了地球，想把这颗星球据为己有。看到地球人相信卡法的这种邪教，人口又如此稀少，第二月球人决定在2894年对地球发起攻击。

寡不敌众却又被迫相信宗教的地球人在数量庞大的第二月球军队面前如同蝼蚁，很快就被打败。

随着2895年的到来，极地、沙漠、海洋、天空、山丘、盆地、峡谷……全都被第二月球人占领，他们摧毁了地球上的绝大部分地球人。

十一、时间之旅

幸存的地球人苟活在一艘邮轮上的几个偏僻的角落中。即便如此，他们有时还需要忍受着第二月球对邻近海域的突袭。

这天，第二月球的军队终于发现了他们，慌乱之中有一人想起：2892年，政府向太空发射了一艘名叫"时间号"的飞船，这也是少数没有被第二月球击毁的飞船之一，他们现在应该在围绕地球旋转。

在地球被完全占领的前一天，此人成功躲避了第二月球人的攻击，一路逃亡，最后杀死了卡法；还用无线电向那艘飞船发送了一段很长的信息，主要讲述了目前地球人的处境。

那个地球人向"时间号"发送的第二段信息比前一段短得多，全文如下：

"向你们飞船上的500名船员致以美好的祝愿，希望你们早日发现新家园。从明天开始，你们将会成为仅存的人类。再见。"

收到信息之后，"时间号"年轻的船长感受到了危险，毕竟最近的第二月球飞船就在几公里以外。他们把飞船上所有的光源都熄灭了，并利用一种类似于900多年前使用于隐身战机的技术，才幸免于难。

他立即决定向远离第二月球的方向逃亡，来到安全距离后开始在时间内进行"曲航"，用通俗的话来讲，就是不断地进行时间旅行。

"时间号"是目前为止使用寿命最长的人类飞船，可以使用1亿至1.5亿年，而它本身可以以光速的一半航行5000万至1亿年，最高速度可达光速的四分之三。船上的冬眠系统也可以使人不间断地冬眠两亿年，并且苏醒时依然健康。因此，"时间号"根本没有必要寻找新家园，只需要探索物质世界就可以了。

2895年初，船长正式宣布他们将穿越到公元3000年，以查看未来的状况。虽然旅程是绝对安全的，但船长仍然有些犹豫，脑海中竟出现了自己的墓碑，上面连自己的名字都没有，只有他的生卒年：2870—2895。

穿越到过去已被证实不可能，但是穿越到未来是可能的。他们通过虫洞技术制造了通往一个区域的虫洞，在该区域中时间的流速比地球上慢了很多，使得穿越这105年只需要用1.05秒。在该区域中的1秒就是地球上的1个世纪。俗话说，天上一天，地上一年；但在这里，完全可以说是"天上一秒，地上一世纪"啊！

在地球上的人看来，他们度过了漫长的一个世纪，但船员们的年龄实际上只会增长一秒钟多一点，根本不是问题。

船长把飞船上的时间机器——也就是虫洞制造机器和自己的笔记本电脑用简单的数据线连接起来，电脑打开后，瞬间弹出一个窗口。它的左边是一个时钟的图标，下边显示着现在的时间，只精确到了秒的级别，可以说只是一个普通时钟。在窗口中还有着"确认""取消"两个按钮，而右边是一行字：时间机器已经与设备连接，请点击确认以继续。

船长操作鼠标，点击"确认"按钮，窗口的内容瞬间改变，上方有着"请输入目的地"这么一行字，下方则是一个文本框。

船长敲入"3000.1.1.00.00.00"这串数字后，窗口中出现一行字：已经进入虫洞，1.05秒后离开。这个数字还在以极高的速度跳动。1.05秒很快过去了，电脑发出"哔"的提示音，同时，窗口关闭了。在电脑自带的日历系统中明确地写着今天是3000年1月1日，仿佛什么都没有发生过一样，但船员们都知道，自己刚刚跨越了一个世纪。

船长关闭了窗口，关上了电脑，拔掉了数据线。他召集所有船员，说道："我们已经到达公元3000年的地球，你们去看看那里怎么样。"说完，一名船员就向地球方向看去。

地球仍然是一片没有生机的废土，并且已经被第二月球人当作工业和军事基地。

"哼！"船长大喝一声，"第二月球人竟然霸占了地球105年！"

"走，我们去1000年后。"船长说着，又恢复了那种平静的语气。他再次进行2895年的那种操作，不过输入的数字是"4000.1.1.00.00.00"。

10秒后，"时间号"就穿越到了4000年。船员们惊奇地发现，地球蔚蓝的海洋已经变成了白色，预言中的冰河时代终于来临。

"太阳呢？"飞船的副船长问。

过了一阵子，才有人意识到问题的严重性。

太阳消失了。这颗伟大的黄色恒星，竟然葬送在微不足道的第二月球人手上！

"下地狱吧！你们毁灭了人类文明和地球上所有的生命，还毁灭了太阳！你们毁灭了我们美丽的海洋和大地！你们让我们星球的海变成了冰！十恶不赦的你们，犯下了不可饶恕的滔天罪行！你们必须为此负责！"船长如同一头野兽般怒吼道。

船长的好心情荡然无存，目光夹杂着愤怒、震惊、悲伤和恐惧，隐隐约约地说："我们去1000年后。"

"时间号"的船员们想象了各种可能，但是现实比想象更残酷：地球和第二月球像太阳一样消失了，连影子都没留下——在那个位置只剩下一片黑暗。

"到底发生了什么?！"船长咆哮道。

即使已经进入冰河时代，地球仍然是"时间号"船员们的精神支柱。现在，地球消失了，在它原来的位置上，空气和生命都消失了，连实实在在的物质都没有。

"以前，宇航员不管飞多远，总是有一根精神之线连接着他们和地球……现在地球没了，那根线也断了，我们再也不是地球人了……"飞船的副船长喃喃说道。

飞船的一号驾驶员一手指着外面，一边惊叫："啊！看外面！"

船长训斥道："安静！"随后，他也知道这个人在指什么了。

外面没有任何天体。

"时间号"是这广阔的宇宙中唯一的存在了。船员们感觉到巨大的压力撕扯着他们的心灵。在这样的环境下，哪怕是最坚韧不拔的人又算得了什么？能仅仅用孤独描写他吗？

这时船上出现了一个悦耳的声音，来自飞船的人工智能："数据显示，飞船上的时间机器出现了故障，与推进器的连接断开了，导致我们没有及时地从虫洞撤出。虫洞已经关闭，而且现在已经过去了将近半分钟了。"

大家都愣住了。船员们都在想着自己的心事，但一个念头却如同电击一样，深深地植入了他们的脑海："完了！"

此时，他们眼前的世界变得扭曲，所有人很快就晕倒在地，很可能是因为一片巨大的透镜飘到了他们面前。

进入这个区域后的第9分钟，大家的状态恢复正常，飞船上的医生才终于打破了这份沉默："那么等我们回去的时候，是不是已经过去许多年了？"

医生在说这句话的时候仍然出奇地冷静，也许是因为他曾经在停尸间工作，学会了冷静地面对恐惧，无论是血淋淋的尸体还是无情的时间。

"是的。"

"地球离我们多远？"船长问人工智能。

人工智能给出的回答是："有几十万光年，我们开不过去，必须及时人工制造虫洞！"

船长按下了一个按钮，人工智能说："虫洞制造机器已经启动，请勿随意移动，否则虫洞可能无法制造成功。"

在他们进入这个区域9分22秒的时候，虫洞被成功制造，飞船以迅雷不及掩耳之势，立即开了进去。他们在这片空间中原本应该待上10秒（相当于我们宇宙中的1000年），但却因为故障足足在这片空间中度过了562秒——也就是9分22秒的时间，相当于我们宇宙中的5.62万年，而现在是公元60200年。

"怎么样？"这是船长在今年说的第一句话，也是上万年以来他说的第一句话。

人工智能回答道："现在我们来到了公元60200年，不过应该没有大碍。"

冰冻的地球再次映入眼帘，第二月球也还在它的轨道上运行，但是第二月球人已经离开了。

船长问："以'时间号'的功率，可以把第二月球摧毁吗？它实在是太恶心、太邪恶了。"

人工智能的回答是："确实可以。"

几小时后，原先第二月球的位置只剩下一堆碎片，但是在这个距离上只能看到零星的几块。地球即将成为一颗没有卫星的行星。

"我们补充一下能量吧。"人工智能提议道。

"好的。"船长表示赞同。

飞船停止航行了一段时间。之后，人工智能机械地说："能量已经充满了，请确认下一个目的地。"话音刚落，它就大声尖播报："发现巨型不明物体！重复，发现巨型不明物体！"

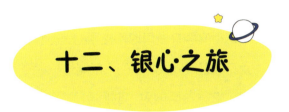

十二、银心之旅

"到底是什么？"

"目前数据显示，是……"

人工智能的话被打断了，大家一起尖叫："外星飞船！"

的确，窗外有一艘巨大的外星飞船，与人类的流线型飞船不同，这艘飞船是五边形的，厚度在10米左右。这艘外星飞船正在以缓慢的速度向"时间号"飞来。

"飞船内是否存在生命迹象？"

"存在，绝对存在，"驾驶员惊叫道，"那不就是吗？"

透过"时间号"和外星飞船的舷窗，可以清晰地看到几个人形物体，还可以看到外星飞船的名字，一行是用外星语言书写的，另一行则是用英语书写的。这说明它们理解英语。两行字都书写得非常工整而美观，但显然是手写，似乎飞船里的人都有强迫症似的。

可以清晰地看见，外星飞船的英文名字是"Zmy"，因此"时间号"上的人们将这艘飞船称作"Z号"。

"Z号"上由外星语言书写的名字也同样清晰，而且字体更大，只不过没人读得懂。但是这种外星语言非常简单，飞船的名字看起来就像是"1πe"。

副船长说："这行文字并没有地球文字的美，它包含的是一种极为复杂的东西，我觉得这艘外表平庸的飞船属于一个高等文明。"

人工智能认为"Z号"目前对"时间号"没有威胁，事实证明它是对的。"Z号"上的外星人发现了"时间号"之后，掏出了一支笔，在"Z号"的舷窗上用英语写道："你好！你可以看到这行字吗？"

船长用同样的方式在"时间号"的舷窗上写道："可以！"

"Z号"上的外星人把前面一行字擦掉，写道："可以跟着我们的飞船吗？"

"时间号"上的人回应道："为什么？"

"我们要把你们带到我们的母行星并邀请你们加入行星俱乐部。"

"好的，但是你们的母行星离我们多远？"

"大约2.5万光年。我们可以超光速航行，所以你们不用担心。"

"Z号"突然打开了一扇门，与此同时，外星人又写道："进来吧！"

"时间号"缓慢地掉转船头，小心翼翼地开进了"Z号"。"时间号"的船员们都下来之后，"Z号"上的一个人解释道："我们正在向最近的虫洞飞行。"

“最近的虫洞就在那里！”“Z号”的驾驶员大声说道。

“Z号”开到了最大功率，钻进了虫洞。这艘飞船从虫洞飞出来时，“时间号”的船员们发现周围的恒星很多，还能看到很多飞船。他们的神情，就像是一群乡下的农民来到了大都市一样。

“请问，你们的星球在哪个方向，又叫什么名字呢？”船长问一个外星人。

那个外星人回答道：“哪个方向？从这里看不到，所以我也不知道。只有从飞船的仪表盘上才能看到。说到名字，我们的星球叫作埃普莱涅特[1]，得名于组成我们星球的物质，它在你们的星球上不存在。你们愿意的话可以起一个中文译名。”

船长又说：“我们的星球叫地球。那从这里能看到你们的恒星吗？”

那个外星人回答：“我们的星球围绕黑洞旋转。我不知道你们怎么称呼这样的天体，总之我们并不围绕恒星旋转。另外，我们居住在一颗矮行星上。”

“谢谢。”

“不客气。”

“Z号”到达埃普莱涅特后，“时间号”的船长原本想下去，却被别人拦住了：“请穿上防护服！我们的星球是矮行星，没有空气。”

“好，但你们为什么不佩戴呢？”

---

[1] 这是音译，英文为“Eplanet”。

"我们虽然也是和你们一样的人，但是我们可以适应真空。这附近另一颗矮行星的人也可以。"

船员们觉得这句话很奇怪：你们是人，而且你们认为我们也是人，那你们为什么有这样的"超能力"呢？不过，他们都没有继续追问。

他们穿好防护服后走下了飞船的舷梯，感到走路比在地球上轻松一些，因为重力更低。副船长就问旁边的一个外星人："你们有文化、政治和艺术吗？"

"都有。"

船长突然问同一个外星人："之前你们说的那个'行星俱乐部'呢？"

"哈哈哈，根本就不存在。我们请你们来，是邀请你们在我们的星球上生活，'行星俱乐部'只是一个借口。"

"让你们在这颗星球上生活是一种福利。""Z号"的船长说。

"福利？我们怎么可能穿着防护服度过一生？另外，这里靠近银心，辐射太强，我们怎么可能生存下去？！""时间号"的船长吼道。

"你们可以得到我们所有的科技成果，这会让你们星球的人受益的！之前你们的行星远离你们的恒星，就是我们干出来的事情，目的是让你们认识我们！""Z号"的船长说。

"不对。我刚刚偷偷测过，你们的智商不够高，暂时不能理解我们的科技成果，也没有能力自主发现把你们的行星推到离散盘以外的地方的人就是我们，反而对我们动怒！请赶紧离开这里。""Z号"

的副船长说道。这得到了"Z号"船长的赞同，却让"时间号"的船长一头雾水。

"你们这种行为不可容忍！你知道把地球推回轨道花费了我们多少钱、多少力吗？""时间号"的船长大吼道。

"谁叫你们智商太低呢？""Z号"的船长一嘴顶回去。

"我们诅咒你们的星球！""时间号"上的船员一起喊道，这句话最终导致"时间号"的全体船员就被带到了埃普莱涅特的法庭上。很快，结果就出来了。

法官大声宣告："'时间号'全体船员的言行严重违反本星球法律，驱逐！"

法官手上的木槌敲下后，"时间号"全体船员回到了"时间号"上，但这次是被驱逐的。

"时间号"被迫起飞后，船员们决定回到地球。转念一想，如果不用虫洞技术，那"时间号"到达太阳系的时间将会是数万年后，谁知道那时会发生什么呢？

于是，"时间号"正式改名为"银河号"，继续做一艘流浪的飞船。他们现在的目标仍然和那个杀死卡法的地球人给他们的目标不一样，新目标是：回到地球！

十三、被驱逐之后

60201年，"银河号"的虫洞制造器重新开启。途中，工程部主管发现它被埃普莱涅特的居民入侵了，而且用了一种极难修复的方式。单是修理和重启这两步就花费了8年的时间，这期间其他船员也没有虚度光阴，指导"银河号"收集了许多科研用的数据。

这些数据绝不会掩埋在历史的垃圾堆中，它们在日后还有大用。

60210年，虫洞制造器在经过了成千上万次的试运行后，正式开始工作了！

不到半分钟，船员们回到了久违的地球。它仍然被冰层覆盖，仿佛敷上了一层面膜。严寒笼罩着大地，地表唯一的热源恐怕就是火山口了。

地球已经成为一片冻土，只剩下细菌这样的微生物游荡。由于环境太过恶劣，"银河号"只好头也不回地离开，将这颗曾经孕育过各种生命的星球抛诸脑后。

"银河号"继续在太空中流浪了10年。这几年来，船长经常会做一个梦，大概内容是一个戴着头盔的老妇人愤怒地盯着他，她炯炯有神的眼睛透过头盔面罩喷射出烈焰般的目光，意思很明显：你两次抛下了我！

在60220年的一天，船长明白了，那个老妇人就是地球的形象。船长从自己的房间里跑出，手上拿着一把里面只有一发子弹的枪。

可不要小看了它，这颗子弹是一颗微型原子弹，只要船长扣动扳机，整艘船上的船员就会葬身于太空，最后的人类也将灭绝。

船长将枪顶在飞船驾驶员的额头上，大喝一声："啊！"说完，他轻轻地将食指放在扳机上。

驾驶员感到一种无法形容的恐惧，他不自觉地举起了双手，其他人也都照做。

飞船里除了一把即将杀死500名船员的手枪，就只剩下沉默。

一秒过去了。

两秒过去了。

三秒过去了。

一方面，他的心灵被无限的仇恨占据，"地球"和船长的对话一直在脑中浮现。另一方面，他又想到自己被世人谴责并被处决的样子，因此，船长迟迟没有扣动扳机。

船长苦笑了一下，用只有自己能听到的声音说："已经没有别人了。"

那个位妇人的声音在船长脑海中出现："去吧，杀死所有人！"

"不！我不能灭绝人类，"船长咬紧牙关说，"我不能把陪伴我数万年的船员们杀死！"

　　船长嘴上这么说，他手上的枪却仍然没有放下。接着，船长把枪扔了出去，奇特的是，它竟然准确无误地飞进船长的房间，并钻进了它原有的位置——抽屉中。

　　这天晚上，"地球"的声音和她饱经风霜却又美丽得不真实的脸庞再次在船长的梦中出现，但她旁边还有一个年轻男子。这个人高大英俊，声音洪亮，但他的脸却是灰色的，上面没有任何表情，只有深色的斑点。他一直在"地球"旁边。这两人同时说道："你好！你……"却被船长的梦话打断了："月球！得月球者得天下！你还在！你没被我们的祖先炸掉！"

　　船长又梦见自己激动地冲上前，却被"月球"粗暴地推开。

　　"听着，小子，"那个被称作"月球"的人恶狠狠地说，"我们是你的长辈，要表现出对长辈的尊敬！"

　　"月球"恢复了他正常的声音，又开口说："我虽然已经被你们微不足道的'地球炸弹''炸碎'，但我孕育的文明仍在！你们之前听到的消息都是错误的，的确有月球人逃往火星，他们是一批志愿者，被用来掩盖大部分月球人逃脱的事实。大部分月球人——也就是除了那100个人之外的月球人——都逃脱了。"

　　"月球"的话再一次被船长打断："啊。"

　　"月球"接着说：

　　"剩余的月球人用之前储备的飞船（速度也是光速的一半）去到了银河系中心的一颗行星上，这颗星球被它的原住民称作'普乐比亚'。

　　"这颗星球和月球一样没有大气，但地表的土壤富含铅。当然，这种金属对月球人无毒。我们这些月球人很快就适应了它的环境，并融入了这颗星球。

"原住民以及附近的一些文明的科技比我们发达多了。由于触犯了当地的法律，我们被原住民押送到了其他行星，饱受折磨，将近50年后才重获自由，被流放到太空中。之后，我们意识到了银河系中的许多文明远比我们发达。现在，我诚挚地邀请你们加入我们。

"我之所以能这样'托梦'给你，是因为我们已经掌握了控制与转移梦境的方法。其他船员也在做同样的梦。如果你们想要加入我们，那就按'1'；否则就按'0'。"

第二天早晨，这些船员们就互相分享了这个梦。但是，暂时没人清楚"月球"的最后一句话。

突然，飞船上凭空出现了一个正方形键盘，有"0"和"1"两个按键，下面还有一个键写着"确认"。这个键盘的面积达到4平方米，每条边都有2米长。

副船长发表了自己的观点："我认为我们应该帮助月球人，原因如下：首先，他们也是被压迫的种族，应该援救；其次，我们应该对'普乐比亚'这样的行星充满戒备，并尽力地讨好他们，原因显而易见；然后，一旦与月球人联合，我们就有足够的机会、信心和武器来对驱逐我们的埃普莱涅特复仇；最后，银心内绝不止普乐比亚和埃普莱涅特两个种族，肯定还有更多的，与这两者的接触可以协助我们了解其他星球。所以，我认为应该按下'1'。"

船长同意了副船长等人的意见，果断地按下了"1"并点击了"确认"键，键盘瞬间变成一个窗口，内容是："请发送您的坐标。"这行字下面是一个文本框和一个发着荧光的键盘。船长输入他的坐标后，一艘飞船立即飞了过来，后来得知这种实时通信和高速飞船是通过虫洞实现的。

这艘飞船是球形的，但是表面上有一个坑，很像是公元20世纪的电影《星球大战》中的"死星"。飞船的名字清晰可见，名叫"Luna"，也就是"月球"的意思，所以被称作"月球号"。那些不同意船长按下"1"的船员们却把这艘飞船蔑称为"死亡之月"，被船长训斥了一顿。

在这行字下面是一行外星语言，很像是汉语。船长读道："第一个字左边是'人'，右边是'一'，第二个字上面是'从'，下面是'龙'。第三个字是'从'，第四个字是'皿'。似乎对应着'Luna'四个字母。"

"月球号"通过那个"坑"发射一种电弧般刺目的未知物质，将"银河号"吸了进去。

"月球号"的船长走了过来，说："你们好！其实，我们的真实用意是邀请你们和我们一起建造一颗新的行星，因为我们和你们一样，都已经成为吉卜赛人一样的流浪民族，所以我们需要建造一颗星球。然而，我们只有原料，没有足够的技术；你们只有技术，没有足够的原料。当然，我说的是相应领域的，我们的综合科技水平已经比你们高很多。这就是邀请你们来的原因。至于这艘飞船，则是在我们流亡之前建造的，为了防备致命的危险。"

"竟然骗我们……又来了……"船员们发起了牢骚。

"银河号"的船长最先冷静了下来："这不是欺骗。但是，我们就住在你们的飞船上不行吗？”

一个"月球号"的船员缓缓地摇了摇头，说："不行，不行。这样一个相对小的生态系统也是经不起宇宙中最狠的东西——时间的风浪的。像地球和月球这样巨大的天体，可以经历大风大浪而不损坏；而我们的飞船，即便是在小阴沟里航行，最终也会翻船的。"

在"银河号"的船长脸上，渐渐出现了诡异的表情。这名船员立即猜透了他在想什么，笑着说："虽然我来自月球，这个没有船、风浪和小阴沟的地方，但我的确知道它们是什么。"其他"月球号"的船员表示赞同。

"但是，这颗你们要制造的人造星球是用来干什么的？"

那名月球船员回答道："有两个选项：要么成为一艘在宇宙中四处漂泊的世代飞船，要么继续围绕地球旋转。"

"简单来说，它要么是宇宙中的一只漫无目的的无头苍蝇，要么是地球的新卫星。"看见"银河号"船员都不理解那个月球人的意思，"银河号"副船长就这么脱口而出，丝毫不顾及月球人的感受。

"你们能把飞船上的所有数据拿出来吗？我们要开始建造行星了。"这名月球船员又说道。

"大约要多久？"

"这可说不准，保守估计要一年。"

"一年制造一颗直径几千公里的卫星？这么快！"大家倒吸一口凉气。

"嗯，是的。在被流放之前，我们从普乐比亚那里得到了很多技术。还有，你们是地球人，人数不超过1000，而这里有将近100亿月球人。你们显然无法适应我们的生活，因此，你们可以将意识转移到月球人的身体中。"

"那么，那些身体原来的意识呢？"

"那些身体都属于轻生者。在我们的社会中，这样的意识是罕见的，是不道德的。"他用这种鄙视的语气说话显得非常奇怪，"我们将这些身体的主人从那些不道德的意识替换成你们高尚的意识，你们对此应该没有异议。当然，他们的身体都是健康的，这一点你们不用担心。"

"原来是这样。哈哈，通过你，我又了解了一点月球文化！我对这一点完全赞同。"

两天之后，"银河号"500名船员的意识全都被转移到月球轻生者的身体之中，而原来的身体被月球的科学家们用来研究。

不久，人造星球已经建好了，采取了月球船员提出的第二个选项，外观、性质和原来的月球几乎完全一样，被称作"第三月球"，100亿月球人将定居在这里，并建立月球共和国。

十四、第三月球

"银河号"上面的数据全部被保留在第三月球的一座建筑中，这栋楼是第三月球最高的建筑物之一，被称作月球数据库。它储存了一切月球人知道的信息，并且还会通过已知信息推导出新的知识，经过筛选后，合格的知识就会进入数据库，而且所有持有相关证件的人都可以进去查询资料。可以说，月球数据库是一本电子书，是一座图书馆，还是一个计算机。当然，月球数据库永远被重兵把守，非法进入绝非易事。

至于"银河号"本身，它被保存在第三月球第一博物馆中，任何人都可以前来观赏。

在第三月球建好后的一个月，"银河号"船长才得知了那名月球船员的名字：斯卡基文[1]。

---

[1] 由于月球人使用摩尔斯代码作为语言，因此，这个名字实际上是其英文名字 "Sikakiwen" 的音译。

在一次谈话中，"银河号"船长（他已经不是船长了，现在担任月球共和国副总统，改名为"克马尼罗"[1]）问斯卡基文（是月球共和国的另一名副总统）："斯卡基文，你原来是做什么的？"

"克马尼罗，你说的'做什么'是哪方面？"

"当然是职业。"

"我原来是一名专门开采氦–3的工人。在月球，这种职业也被称为"矿工"，后来成为军人，又经过筛选成为航天员，冬眠了很久后到"月球号"那艘飞船上当副船长。"

"你原来是副船长！"克马尼罗惊讶地说道。

"是的。"

一个星期过去了，两人再次进行私人谈话。克马尼罗首先问："月球共和国为什么没有国旗呢？"

---

[1] 类似的，这也是其英文名字"Kermainero"的音译。

"国旗？什么是国旗？"

"就是……一面旗帜。"

"你不是在开玩笑吧？'旗帜'是什么啊？"

"不是开玩笑。国旗是地球上用来象征一个国家的一片材料……换句话说就是用来象征国家的长方形图案。"

斯卡基文若有所思："你能拿出几面国旗看看吗？"

克马尼罗说："公元2139年以来，地球上都只有一个国家，我根本不是那时候出生的，怎么会记得那么多国旗呢？我要去月球数据库看一下。"

从月球数据库里面，克马尼罗找到了几面21世纪和22世纪的国旗。

斯卡基文看完，摇摇头说："太复杂了。你在月球生活了很久，不知道月球人崇尚白色吗？你肯定知道的。采用这些五彩斑斓的旗帜作为国旗……总之不合适。我们可以给总统提议，或者设计国旗也行。顺便说，你们国旗的寓意很巧妙呀。"

"好，完全赞同。"

60221年末，月球共和国的总统，也就是"月球号"的前船长西里山[1]在100亿月球人的凝视下，将一面庄严而纯洁的白色旗帜插在第三月球的南极点上。

由于月球上没有风，所以这面旗帜的悬挂方式和地球上不一样。

---

[1] 这是其英文名字"Ceelesan"的音译。以下的音译人名或地名将只提及其英文名字。

旗杆是"丁"字形的，大约有2米高，在最顶部有一根长1米的横梁，而这面国旗就悬挂在横梁上。

月球旗和地球历史上的大部分国旗一样是长方形的，比例是最常见的长短边比3：2。克马尼罗等人突然想到：悬挂白旗是在投降吗？

想到这里，他便扑哧一笑。西里山厉声说道："你笑什么？"

"在地球上，举白旗代表投降。"

对克马尼罗来说幸运的是，西里山把"投降"听成了"和平"，因此没有受到任何惩罚。

不幸的是，西里山在60222年逝世了。克马尼罗和斯卡基文商量了一下，决定将两人的意识储存在一人的身体中并继任总统。最终，他们决定将意识放在斯卡基文的身体中，原因大家都心知肚明，但是没人敢说出来。

两人的意识合为一体后，改名叫"塞萨"[1]，在第三月球的一种方言中，这个名字的意思就是"新总统"。根据第三月球的相关规定，斯卡基文、克马尼罗都就此"死亡"，但他们的意识仍在。

颇具讽刺意味的是，原本认为自己将死在做时间旅行时的船长，却奇迹般地活了数万年，确切地说是57352岁。

塞萨上任的那一天（60222年4月2日）后来被定为月球的国庆节。塞萨于60223年宣布改元为第三月球纪元，简称"月球纪元"。

月球纪元2年4月2日，月球共和国迎来了两年一度的总统选举。各项数据表明，塞萨的人气很旺，去年（月球纪元元年）的支持率一

---

[1] "Cysas"。

度达到81%（在第三月球，这个支持率可以说是非常高的了）。

而且，塞萨还是月球历史上公认的最贤明、威武、善良、聪慧且刚正不阿的一名总统，丝毫不逊于西里山。人们认为，他死后也将受到万人追捧，并成为后面所有总统效仿的对象。但是，命运显示了它的怪异无常，塞萨并没有成功连任总统。

一周后，塞萨怀着沉重的心情，在大庭广众之下大声说（这是月球共和国总统交接仪式的一部分）："我将月球共和国总统的头衔赐予希尔尼诺[1]。"

希尔尼诺就是新的月球总统，这个名字在月球的一种古代语言中的意思是"神之子"。

希尔尼诺自称为"月球王"，在他的总统生涯中，他已经把一个繁荣的共和国不知不觉地变成了一个腐败无比的王国。

在希尔尼诺担任总统的第11天，他宣布改国名为月球帝国。

自从希尔尼诺继任，塞萨再也没有公开露面，隐居在第三月球的第谷陨石坑外沿的一座很小的房子。月球帝国成立的那一天，他却突然来到希尔尼诺的住宅，在光天化日之下大喊道："走开！你根本不配当第三月球的总统！"

希尔尼诺错误地认为是一个平民在外面喊叫，于是派自己的护卫前去逮捕他。可是，这些护卫看到他们要逮捕的对象就傻眼了，立刻在塞萨面前惶恐地鞠躬，甚至不敢接近他一步。带头的护卫说："大人，请原谅我们吧。"说完，便带领全体护卫冲进希尔尼诺的住所，

---

[1]　"Hurninau"。

将他押解出来。

塞萨给带头的护卫一个慈祥而又严厉的眼色，他立刻拔出一把刀，并把它架在希尔尼诺的脖子上，在场的和路过的群众无不欢呼。

希尔尼诺的眼中闪过一丝乞求的目光。

突然，群众沉默了。他们想，塞萨是一位仁慈的总统，任期内从未批准处决任何人（在第三月球，死刑必须要总统批准才能执行）。但是，他又嫉恶如仇，对于希尔尼诺这种人更是如此。这些群众将目光集中在塞萨、那名护卫和希尔尼诺的身上，全神贯注地看着。

塞萨以为有些人对希尔尼诺产生了同情和怜悯之心，如果这时不处决希尔尼诺，最终就没有机会了，因为群众会反对。他说："你们想要杀他吗？"

希尔尼诺的希望重新燃起，他的绝望也多了几分，这两种情绪使他剧烈地摇头。

这时，塞萨又想起了希尔尼诺所犯下的种种罪恶。看得出，他的心灵也正在挣扎着。群众没有任何反应，他们也正在犹豫，等待前总统进行下一步指示。

塞萨看破群众的意图后，平静地说："如果你们保持沉默，我就处决他；如果你们表态，我就视情况而定。"

群众仍然没有反应，不知是想要处决还是正在犹豫之中。这正体现出了塞萨的高明之处：即便有些群众还在深思熟虑，默不作声，仍然可以正当地处决希尔尼诺。

塞萨笑了笑，又严厉地说："我数三下，你们再不说话……"

塞萨又扭头看向希尔尼诺："那么，你的死期将至！"

塞萨大声喊："三，二点五，二，一点五，一，零点五，零！"

塞萨并不着急，用一根手指指着希尔尼诺："你的生命只剩下几秒，还有什么话说？"

希尔尼诺慢慢说："我没什么话可说了。"如果月球人会流泪，那这时希尔尼诺的眼眶已经湿润了。不过，月球人的泪孔不在眼部，而是在脚底。

一直沉默的群众突然一齐大叫道："杀了他！"显然，他们期盼的事情终于来了。

塞萨立即从护卫手中夺过刀，狠狠地劈向希尔尼诺的脖子。这个简单的动作饱含着第三月球人民对希尔尼诺这个暴君、野心家和独裁者的全部仇恨。

希尔尼诺的头颅和百亿第三月球人民悬着的心同时落地，塞萨却装作什么事都没有发生一样扬长而去。

十五、前往地球

第二天，塞萨宣布继任总统，并发表公开演讲。在演讲的中间，他当场背诵了一首诗，并说："我的远大目标便藏在这首诗里，当然，隐藏得不深。"

在背诵这首诗时，他的语气非常沉稳，声音也很低、很慢，与演讲时的慷慨激昂完全不同：

有趣的人，在快被挤爆的地方苟活！

人人皆知，那里有块地方空旷无比。

风火雷电？那地方当然有这些奇观！

没人知道，它就是挂在天空的蓝星。

无知的人，那里近在眼前远在天边。

到底是哪？快被挤爆的地方绕着它。

在演讲台下，有个人问："找到一颗蓝色的星星？"

“不对。”

“在太空中生活？”

“不对。”

正确的答案来自一个五六岁的孩子，她说：“去地球？”

“对了！孩子，说说你是怎么知道的吧。”

在这么多人的关注下和总统说话，这个孩子一点儿也不紧张，泰然自若地说：“月球已经有100亿人，对于一个直径只有3000多公里的星球，显然快被挤爆了；地球现在就空旷无比，一个人都没有；地球上有风、火、雷和电；地球是一颗蓝色的星球，也就是诗中的蓝星；地球是离我们最近的天体；最后，地球是我们月球所围绕的行星。”

“原来是这样。看来，你不是一般的聪明！另外，我注意到你发言时显得非常自信，很好！”塞萨这样赞扬道。接着，他又恢复了平日的语调，总结道：“第三月球实在是不够大，这是因为我们当初的原料不够。因此，我们要移民到更大的地球。尽管我们的人口增长已经很慢了，但是我们的人口还是很多，第三月球难以支撑我们的生活。为了适应地球，我们需要‘变成’地球人！”

“实际上，来自地球的飞船‘银河号’上有着有关一个正常地球人的全部生理信息和他的尸体。这个人生前是该飞船的一名船员。我们可以参考这些信息以及他的尸体，并‘制造’出一个地球人。然后，我们再把被制造出的地球人克隆100亿份。科学家已经证明，在克隆地球人时，该个体的记忆并不会保存，我们必须再把每个月球人的意识移植到这些克隆人的身体中。”塞萨补充道。

一天过去了，那个被制造的地球人已经出现了，塞萨的演说还在继续，但是内容没有那么重要。

两天过去了，塞萨的演讲已经停下。第三月球人用一种从未公开的技术，在4分钟内克隆出了110亿个克隆人（多余的10亿是备用的），然后把全体第三月球人的意识移植到他们的身体中。

第三月球的警察趁着这个机会，逮捕了大批前来的小偷、土匪和通缉犯，并禁止他们的意识被移植。他们要么去到地球上因为不适应而死，要么被政府在第三月球上处死，已经没有活路了。禁止恶人参与一个全体国民都要参与的事件，是月球历史上常用的一种清除恶人的方式。

现在，月球人全部成为了地球人。

由于没有太阳，地球的表面已经结冰了，温度低到难以想象。因此，第三月球政府把"月球号"上面提供动能的核聚变发动机改装成提供热能的人造太阳。"月球号"上面的核燃料占了飞船总质量的九成以上，因为都是氢，而且是高度压缩的，所以储量很多。第三月球人制造出来的恒星叫作"第二太阳"，可以说是一颗货真价实的恒星。

第二太阳的直径、温度和距离与太阳几乎相同，可以提供足够的热量。之后，它也被称作"太阳"，被某些非主流宗教群体称作"太阳神的转世"。

说到这里，不得不提一下月球的宗教文化。月球在公元1389年以前是有宗教的，有大大小小的派系，统称为太阳崇拜（Heliosism）。月球的自转周期很长，因此白天和夜晚也都很长。

在漫漫长夜之中，当时还未开化的月球人们非常艰苦，就捏造出了所谓的太阳神。在1389年，终于有人提出夜晚后面必然会有白昼，并给出了如何在长夜中生存的系统方法。一夜之间，太阳崇拜几乎消失了。

随着第二太阳的核聚变开始，地球缓慢地解冻了。为了加速地球的解冻，成为一颗宜居的行星，人们从第三月球上取下一块大小合适的岩石，向地球砸了过去，利用产生的热量融化一部分最寒冷的冰盖。

由于岩石足够小，所以地球的表面温度仍然适合地球人，当然，也适合这些拥有地球人身体的月球人。

这时，忙碌的人们又把所有地球上对人类无害的生物克隆出来。对于一个相对高级的文明来说，这也不是什么难题，只花了一年。

月球纪元4年，即将回到地球的100亿地球人和生物从第三月球出发了。所有的植物都被栽培，或者说种植在一个空间里，动物则有单独的几个舱室，人类则密密麻麻地挤在巨大的驾驶舱。以"月球号"的速度，这次航行只需要30分钟，因此，这些人也只需要忍受半小时的拥挤。

"月球号"内部配备了很多飞机，在降落前这些飞机就把所有动植物带到它们原来的栖息地。最后，飞船上剩下的生物就是一些细菌和备用地球人了。

"月球号"缓缓降落在东亚的海滩上。这片海滩在公元21世纪曾经属于一个人口超过两千万的繁华城市。尽管这里又被地球共和国和太阳系联邦统治过，名字也被更改过很多次，但在那两个时期，这座城市璀璨的灯光和高大的建筑物一点儿也没有变。

第二月球人曾经摧毁了地球上的所有生命，这些高楼大厦也早已倒塌，而现在，它们的残垣断壁已经被飞船上的飞机带走。这些飞机的速度比地球的逃逸速度还要快得多，它们带着地球文明的痕迹飞向宇宙。

飞船降落了，"地球人"回家了。"月球号"的舱门打开，舷梯在"嗡嗡"声中降下，塞萨第一个下飞船。

一小时后，所有的地球人都下了飞船，在大家的密切注视下，塞萨向海走去。这些地球人从未如此近距离地看过地球的海，因此，也跟着走了过去。

走到水齐膝盖深的地方，塞萨和他率领的民众跪了下来，一起仰天长啸道："啊！"

塞萨是拥有两个人意识的一个人，此时充满他大脑的情绪，是克马尼罗对地球的眷恋和斯卡基文对地球的热爱。两者再合为一体，他就突然丧失了所有风度。

他站起来后，像大猩猩一样猛捶自己的胸膛，呐喊道："我回来啦！"疯狂的民众也跟着照做。

那天晚上，这些新的地球人异常兴奋。之后，大家就开始拆卸飞船，并建造一栋楼。其间，100亿地球人都住在飞船里面。这是一个疯狂的种族，也是一个疯狂的计划，主要是因为这座大楼里面可以住下100亿人。

不过，没有关系。月球最初就是一群外星人中的疯子和精神病患者被放逐的地方。每个房间都有一张上下铺的床，食物由服务员（数量超过1亿）送过去。地球人将在这栋楼里面住上一年。

月球纪元5年，塞萨宣布改元为地球纪元，改国名为地球共和国，并且继任总统。同时，越来越多的建筑物也在机器人的帮助下建在世界各地，其中大部分是居民楼。

地球纪元2年，地球上陆陆续续出现了购物中心和办公楼等建筑物。最开始的那座建筑物也已经被夷为平地，它的一切组成部分都被回收了。

月球数据库的电子版也在飞船中，它被储存在地球共和国的总统府旁边的一座大楼。月球所有博物馆、艺术馆和展览中的物品也都以电子版的形式被放在那座楼里面。

至于地球共和国的总统府，它理所应当地位于地球的首都，也就是东亚的那座大城市。

接下来，摆在政府面前的最后一件大事就是确定行政区划了。这件事花了一年才最终完成，将地球划分为北美、落基、五大湖、中美、安第斯、南美、西北欧、南欧、东欧、北非、西非、中南非、东非、北亚、西亚、中亚、南亚、东亚、东南亚、大洋洲和南极洲这21个地区。

现在的地球共和国和公元22世纪成立的那个已经没什么区别了，甚至有着相同的国旗。民众毫无怨言，经济正在稳定地发展，一切贪污腐败问题都能解决。

但是，美好的日子总会过去，时间的巨轮仍然在无情地向前滚动，没有任何人或事能阻止它。地球纪元1453年，地球共和国宣告灭亡，就像公元1453年东罗马帝国的灭亡一样。一夜之间，地球共和国就变成了一个充满贪官污吏、抢劫事件和割据势力的国度。

灭亡前一年的地球共和国仍然可以说是一个"健康"的国家，但这一年过去后，地球迎来了似乎无休止的黑暗，如同一个巫师维持青春的巫术突然失灵，超过15个世纪的岁月一下子显现出来那样。

地球共和国的国名变成了"冈东孔帝国"[1]，陆地面积只有20万平方公里。正如其名，它已经变成一个帝国，元首是全球历史上臭名昭著的暴君——喀洛力[2]。他是一名凶猛、残暴而恶贯满盈的皇帝。喀洛力曾经下令把对方的战俘统一关入集中营，进行惨无人道地虐待。

地球被各地的割据势力瓜分成数百块，一次又一次的战争上演，最终第四次世界大战打响了。

在大战中，冈东孔帝国百战百胜，不到一年就统一了全球，除了南极洲。

地球的确需要一位能够统一全球的战神，但他不能是喀洛力这种无比残暴的人。这个人便是地球共和国末代总统的长子，名字是格罗比亚[3]。

格罗比亚是在地球纪元1443年出生的。他出生后的十年，地球共和国灭亡，于是他被秘密送到地球上最平静的地方——南极洲生活，他的父亲——地球共和国的末代总统以及他的母亲被谋杀。

---

[1]　"Cantoncong"。

[2]　"Calori"。

[3]　"Globia"。

在南极洲陪伴格罗比亚的，只有一个同时担任保镖和老师的成人和一条警犬。

很多平民百姓都从冈东孔逃往南极洲。为求平静的生活，他们不惧严寒，纷纷来到格罗比亚的旗下，并拥立格罗比亚为总统。

因此，喀洛力派冈东孔军队讨伐南极洲。这些军队并非真的服从喀洛力的指挥——事实上，如果他死了或者失踪了，冈东孔帝国也不复存在。格罗比亚发现了这一点，先后派了10个刺客前往刺杀喀洛力，然而都没有成功。幸运的是，第十个刺客逃了回来，窃取了海量的情报带给格罗比亚。

在喀洛力攻打南极洲的时候，格罗比亚派人贴出几十万张通缉令："能把喀洛力的头颅送到我面前来的，必有重赏！"

俗话说，重赏之下必有勇夫。这些通缉令一贴出来，冈东孔帝国的皇后竟然来揭榜了。她之所以这么做，是因为她是被强迫与喀洛力结婚的，自己并不乐意。

喀洛力的妻子并非等闲之辈，在那天晚上，她抽出喀洛力枕头下面的刀，一分钟后就捧着后者的头颅来到港口。

她坐船来到南极洲，正好见到了格罗比亚，于是把喀洛力沾满鲜血的头颅放在后者脚下。她正准备扬长而去，格罗比亚就命人把两袋金子放在她的船上。

地球纪元1460年，格罗比亚重建了地球共和国。这一次，它越来越快地发展起来，在地球纪元1500年就追赶上了那时的埃普莱涅特。

地球纪元2025年，一个叫作斯塔尔斯[1]的人继任总统，宣布开始殖民附近的星球。不仅如此，斯塔尔斯还是个狂妄的野心家，试图将整个银河系都攻打下来，使这个国家统治整个银河系。

他不知道的是，宇宙中有一个外星文明，他们处在一个极为隐蔽的地方。这个文明曾经将一个行星系中的所有生命灭绝，但是在这个行星系外部无人知晓此事。

---

[1] "Stars"。

十六、隐藏的危机

这个文明就是灭神星文明。由于灭神星人曾经被地球人攻打，只留下了屈指可数的幸存者，成为星际文明，其名称也正式改成"隐藏者"，整个银河系都存在他们的个体。

隐藏者只剩下1000万成员，大部分都住在飞船上。他们的领袖被称作"长老"，一共有10万名，占全体人员的百分之一。除了长老，几乎所有的人都被称作"清洁工"，专门攻击并灭绝比自己弱的文明。

"清洁工"是隐藏者文明中一种卑微的职业，但如果战功赫赫是可以被提拔成长老的。当然，"清洁工"也分三六九等。

地球纪元2026年，隐藏者文明中一个名为"歌唱者"的"清洁工"在游荡时发现了地球。这完全是偶然的，他在这么做时也没有全神贯注，而是在吟唱着一首歌。

相对于平均年龄为600岁的长老们，歌唱者还很年轻。他出生于地球纪元1825年，这时200岁，并且没有什么极其出众的战功，因此，歌唱者是"清洁工"中最低等也最普遍的那种。

在十年前的地球纪元2016年，歌唱者在自己的歌声中发现了位于银心的一群低等文明，它们之间没有联系。歌唱者驾驶飞梭，用反物质武器将它们所在的行星系中的每一颗星球都变成了一片寸草不生的土地。这群文明合起来也远远没有地球共和国强大，和中世纪的地球差不多。这两次，他都唱了这首歌：

这世界的空间多么广阔，

在时间上有美丽的斑点。

我隐藏在宇宙的黑暗中，

正在等待着下一个猎物。

让所有的生命和非生命，

全都拜倒在我的脚下吧。

征服和统治是我的乐趣，

我正在不择手段地前进。

但这次不同，歌唱者发现了地球共和国之后，感觉到提拔的机会要来了——按歌唱者的话说，是"迟来的两百岁生日礼物"。虽说地球共和国的发展水平比隐藏者弱（据估算只有隐藏者的三分之一），但也是歌唱者见过的最强文明之一了。一旦自己把这个文明灭绝……

歌唱者不敢再想下去了，他急忙来到最近的长老面前（在100个天文单位之外），申请了一颗名为"数学破坏"的武器。

长老质疑道："歌唱者，你了解隐藏者文明吗？我们的文明是一个谨慎的文明。谨慎！"

"我难道不可以使用'数学破坏'吗？您提到了我们的文明，您不知道'先行动，后思考'这句话吗？"歌唱者质疑道。

"唉——你怎么还没明白？这种武器从未被使用过，甚至没有测试过，很不安全。我在为你的安全着想。你知道一颗'数学破坏'的成本有多高吗？答案是100万灭神星元，足以购买5亿瓶水[1]。歌唱者，你知道这种武器目前只有多少颗吗？"

"多少颗？"歌唱者的确不知道这件事。

长老伸出一根手指："一颗。"

"长老，抱歉。我刚才发现的这个文明自称为'人'，他们实在是太强大了，万一他们发生一次技术爆炸，自然会发现我们。另外，我们的行星以前就是被他们占领的……"歌唱者回答道。

长老把那颗武器塞到歌唱者的前肢末端，不耐烦地打断道："好的好的，拿去吧。"

歌唱者来到自己的飞梭，按下墙上的一个按钮，并控制飞梭的人工智能将"数学破坏"扔向地球共和国的首都：地球。这时的歌唱者离地球只有20个天文单位，离原先的天王星轨道不远。

"数学破坏"是一种以数学规律为基础的武器，这种武器可以说是数学和科技的终结者。

预计十天后，它就会将地球变为一个非常恐怖的世界。在那个

---

[1] 约合 10 亿元。一瓶水按 2 元计，5 亿瓶水便是 10 亿元。

世界里，通过允许除以零即可使得零等于任何数，数学和科学将彻底崩塌。

当任何数都相等，一切生物都将死去，没有什么能活在这样的世界中，原因显而易见。在十天内，人类必须逃离任何数都相等的世界。

十七、小宇宙室

时间转瞬即逝，9天过去了。人类已经得知"数学破坏"，于是在空间中撕开一道裂缝，并制造了一片独立于这个宇宙的空间。

这片空间如同一个微型平行宇宙（但并不是平行宇宙），它独立于我们的宇宙，因此可以躲过"数学破坏"的攻击。它是一个立方体，边长为1公里，其资源能让一个人在其中生活两年，时间流逝速度和这个宇宙相同，因此被命名为小宇宙室（Micro universe room）。如果有两个人，那只能生活一年，只有这样才有足够时间去寻找新的行星。

虽然这非常不公平，但是只有两个地球共和国的公民能活下来。

小宇宙室的入口是一个2米高、1米宽的门，没有门板，只有一个发光的边框来标示其位置，在纷乱的宇宙中像是从计算机图库中取出的一个长方形图标，又像是简洁的象征。这扇门原本在1000公里的高空中，现在被拉到地面上来了。有幸来到小宇宙室的两个人走到门前，其中一个是地球共和国总统斯塔尔斯，另外一个是一个没有名字的平民女子。很快，两人就手拉手跳进了门。

他们进入小宇宙室后，门边上的一个士兵按下了一个按钮，门就突然熄灭了（实际上是以光速飞向太空）。门外的群众非常愤怒，因为这意味着他们与生存彻底失之交臂了。门其实和虫洞是有区别的，并且那个按钮可以控制它的位置。门只是那道裂缝，约等于传送门。

有个女人试图穿过门原本的位置，有个男人朝那个位置扔石子和木棍，然而什么都没有发生，像是那扇门从未存在过一样。

另一个女人朝士兵大声嚷嚷："开门啊！开门啊！"

那个士兵手握着打开宇宙之门的开关，在群众的压力下，他按下了开关，打开了门（实际上是把它移回地球）。

群众如潮水般涌上前来，那个士兵用一只手制止了他们。在数万双眼睛的注视下，他看到了对侧的两个人。

士兵把宇宙之门的开关扔了进去，那个无名氏接住了它。士兵大喊："单击！按一下！对！"

无名氏和门外的群众正在发愣，斯塔尔斯一个箭步冲上去，夺过了开关，并按了一下上面的按钮。

群众中，有一个人高马大又眼疾手快的年轻人在门关闭时，粗暴地挤开群众来到门前。

他正在与时间赛跑，他正在与宇宙赛跑，他正在与生存赛跑，他正在与大门赛跑……

可惜的是，他在四项比赛中都以一秒之差落后于对方。门再次飞到了空中，他只能把几乎伸进去的手收回来。

他非常愤怒，开始殴打把开关扔进小宇宙室的那名士兵。5分钟后，在那名士兵所站的位置上只剩下一具尸体和许多血。

在进入小宇宙室并令剩下的人留下之后，两个人立刻冷静下来。只有两个人，是不足以重建一个文明的。无名氏说："这需要把我们改造成机器人。"

斯塔尔斯大笑："哈哈哈！正确！你猜对了！是这样，我已经准备好了一个机器人。那个门位于我们之前的宇宙中的出口，可以随意移动，我们可以用它找到宜居的星球，对于机器人来说'宜居'就可以。之后，就可以把一个人的意识放到机器人中，然后让机器人穿过门就行了。当然，机器人是无法繁衍后代的，但是可以让机器人制造人类。"

"那我们怎么过去？"

"小宇宙室中也有一个门，就在我们背后。"

"那我们怎么控制门移动到宜居的星球？"

"开关可以按我们的指示操控门的移动，并移动到宜居的星球。只要目标星球的温度等参数合适就行。"

时光飞逝，电脑在一年后（在大宇宙中是地球纪元2027年）找到了一颗合适的星球。它不仅对机器人宜居，对地球人也勉强算是宜居的，只不过比地球更冷、更大，平均温度恰好为0摄氏度。这颗行星所围绕的恒星非常像那颗非人造的太阳，但是轨道半径更大。

机器人只有一个，那把谁的意识放进机器人中呢？

"当然是我了。"斯塔尔斯的回答是这样的。

"哼！请注意，现在地球人只剩下两个，你和我。"无名氏冷笑道，"在这种情况下，你还是总统吗？"

"当然是！"

"你还真是自负。我是平民，你是总统，那你们竭力宣扬的'平等'不就消失了？"

斯塔尔斯哑口无言，但是他注意到，那名正在质问他的女子正从腰间掏出一把寒光闪闪的匕首，于是大喊："打住！打住！一切都可以商量。这样，我们把意识同时放进去，就像2000多年前的斯卡基文和克马尼罗一样。"

"好。"无名氏虽然同意，但是说话时仍然非常不客气。

十天以后，两人的意识就被放进了名为"Xenon"的机器人——得名于这颗行星富含氙的大气。两人用紫色颜料把这个名字粉刷在其背部。

十八、白星帝国

那颗行星几乎是透明的，还带一些来源于冰盖的白色，于是Xenon将其称作白星（Whiteice）。

进一步探测表明，白星和地球的相似度其实比预想的要低。地球所拥有的海洋、沙漠、山脉，在白星全都没有——白星只有冰盖，一望无际的冰盖。说"冰盖"其实也不准确，因为这颗星球完全由冰组成，在冰层之下还是冰。在这颗行星的内部，水分子被高度压缩，形成的仍然是冰，只不过是不同形式的。白星的密度远低于普通的类地行星，但是体积非常大，所以表面重力和地球差不多。

白星表面有一种长相类似于猛犸象的生物，只不过更高、更重、更慢、更温顺，被称作"冰象"。它们不需要摄入食物，也不需要排泄，只需要吃脚下的冰以补充水分。

除了冰象，还有一种被称作"飞蛇"的生物，体态非常像眼镜蛇，只不过其"鳞片"是白色的，是为了隐藏它自己。正如其名，飞蛇是可以飞行的。有趣的是，飞蛇以冰象为食。过去，有一个谚语叫做"人心不足蛇吞象"，而在白星上每时每刻都在发生的这一幕正好是故事的真实版本——当然不是一条飞蛇对一只冰象，而是一大群飞蛇和一只冰象战斗。

Xenon不仅存有两人的意识，还保有原先月球数据库中的所有信息，于是它从里面调出一个男性和一个女性地球人的全部信息，制造出了一对地球人。

随后，它重复进行这种操作，就制造出了5000万对地球人，共计1亿人。它此时的想法只是：人类文明可以繁衍下去了！

Xenon在制造这1亿人之后将体内储存的全部信息留给他们，随后自毁了，因为它认为自己的存在会干扰到重新出现的人类文明。

新人类以冰象为食，这种食物能提供很多养分和能量，它的"象牙"还可以做工具。这种生物的繁衍能力极强，而且数量很多，并没有因为人类的到来而灭绝。

地球纪元2028年，人类推举出了全白星的皇帝，他的名字是"尤巴斯"[1]。尤巴斯是白星历史上的第一位元首。

这一年，尤巴斯建立了白星帝国。地球纪元2031年，尤巴斯公布了Xenon遗留的资料，并下令重新发展科技。在地球纪元2052年，白星帝国恢复了往日的科技水平。

如果以白星为中心画一个半径20光年的球，那么球内每一颗星球都是白星帝国的领土。

地球纪元2063年，时年237岁的歌唱者（这时他已经成为一名长

---

[1]　"Yawbus"。

老）再次发现了人类。经过深入调查，他发现这是37年前他曾经灭绝过的地球人的后代。俗话说，智者千虑，必有一失。他千算万算，万万没想到地球人竟然制造了小宇宙室，还存活了下来。在37年间，隐藏者文明的人口是之前的15倍，达到1.5亿，白星帝国的人口数也差不多是这个数。

人类文明和隐藏者文明同属银河族的一员，但两者有可能自相残杀。

歌唱者非常愤怒，他知道这次不可能使用"数学破坏"了，毕竟唯一的一颗也被他用过了。虽然他已经贵为长老，但在隐藏者文明中，长老其实也只是身份高贵的"清洁工"而已。不做"清洁工"，就得成为政府机关的工作人员。

为了让自己冷静下来，歌唱者又开始唱歌了。这次，他唱出的歌曲是：

我再未看到这个宇宙，
宇宙对我永远封闭了。
时间也已经黯然失色，
空间也已经变得狭窄。

唱完后，歌唱者选择沉默，不把人类仍然存在的消息报告给上级，多少有点酸葡萄心理："人类也是伟大的文明，在我的考验下竟然能活下来，就让他们活着吧。"

白星帝国仍然在扩张，而人类文明在宇宙中也有了很高的威望。

地球纪元2081年，尤巴斯逝世，其子斯莱福鲁斯[1]在一番皇室纠纷后当上了皇帝。帝国扩张的脚步当然没有被这场无关痛痒的皇位争夺战停止。按他的话说："统一银河系指日可待，顺便把隐藏者文明毁灭。"

但是，白星帝国作为一个人口众多且版图巨大的国家，君主制是行不通的。地球纪元2087年，白星帝国民间就出现了自称为"第二势力"的反抗组织。

"第二势力"是一个秘密会社或是地下党，从来不公开露面，因此政府对它们的了解很少。"第二势力"的成员们一致认为（也是"第二势力"的格言）：想要统治银河系，就必须打倒皇帝！

并且，"白星帝国"这个名字具有十足的人类中心主义意味，充分表明了对其他物种乃至其他文明的不尊重！

对于白星帝国的皇帝斯莱福鲁斯而言，"第二势力"这样的一个地下党是不可能影响到自己的统治的，因此也并没有在意。这最终导致了"第二势力"的壮大。其实，他并不是一位昏君，也没有干什么特别坏的事情。

很快，大臣们就发现"第二势力"想要推翻白星帝国，但是他们却都不敢劝谏，因为之前有人这么说却被斯莱福鲁斯处决了。地球纪元2089年，当"第二势力"攻入白星帝国首都后，斯莱福鲁斯才如梦初醒，但是为时已晚。他长叹一声："唉！大势已去，我该听他们的话的……"

---

[1] "Srefrus"。

最终，"第二势力"的领袖渺基[1]被对白星帝国灭亡倍感欣慰的群众推举为总统。

然而，有些人却认为"第二势力"的行为大逆不道，应该被群众谴责而不是追捧。他们大都是有钱有势的人，而且他们的权力和金钱都来源于皇帝，因此他们支持宫廷和政府。当然，这些人的数量也很少，很快就被当作帝国的余党而被彻底镇压了。

---

[1] "Milky"。

十九、银河共和国

正如渺基的名字"Milky"所体现的，他继承了斯塔尔斯的野心，他伟大的志向是：统一银河系（Milky Way），建立银河共和国！

同年，这个心愿就得以实施了，渺基建立的银河共和国在一年内发动"银河战争"，统一了银河系。

白星帝国已经被银河共和国代替。这时的人类拥有一艘名为"猎户臂号"的飞船，它打通了整个猎户臂中的虫洞网络，每颗星球附近都有一个虫洞的端口。当时的银河共和国已经具备了制造跨度5万光年的虫洞的条件，于是立刻来到了猎户臂的对面，也就是人马座方向。

距离银心3万光年之外的地区难以孕育生命，其原因还是未知的。由于这里的生命较少，因此也非常容易占领。3个月后，银河共和国就变成了环形，环内便是银心。

银心正是大部分高等文明所在的区域——这听起来非常不可思

议，因为这里的宇宙射线很强，出现生命已经是很难办到的事，孕育出文明更是难上加难。

这些生命中超过九成都不是碳基生物，因而拥有极其强悍的身体，其中的一部分甚至可以不呼吸空气。

在这些能够孕育生命的星球中大都有一种所谓的"元素场"，可以将地表和宇宙射线隔离开来，还赋予了这些生物极高的智力。

例如，埃普莱涅特就是围绕黑洞旋转的行星[1]，比地球小，甚至比火星还小，却有着智慧生命。

这些星球大都是友好关系，敌对的星球在这种时刻也联合了起来，因此对抗它们并不容易。事实上，这是一件非常困难的事情，即便是银河共和国这种巨型集体，征服也花了足足9个月。

例如，有颗星球拥有一种能将任何类地行星表面焚烧成灰烬的武器，被称作"行星火柴"；有几颗星球有着大量的毒气储备；还有的星球利用人工元素场摧毁了不下5颗属于银河共和国的星球；有些星球雇佣的军队甚至没有真正的智慧。最疯狂的是，曾毁灭地球的隐藏者现在也躲在这片区域。

这一切，都未能阻挡银河共和国的脚步。这些星球最终被征服，大部分公民都投降了……

银河共和国将首都定在银心的埃普莱涅特，也就是克马尼罗等人曾经被放逐到的那个星球。

人类使用的纪元曾经变换过很多次。但是，在地球纪元2090年

---

[1] 前文有提到过。

的元旦，渺基仿佛觉得不够乱似的，又把它换成"银河纪元"。时长2089年的地球纪元结束了。

更换纪元其实是一件很麻烦的事，例如很多计算机就要进行一些调整，印刷厂还要印新的日历，带来的困难很多。和月球人一样，现在的人类同样崇尚白色，因为白色是银河的颜色。银河纪元元年，这种颜色被定为"象征色"。某些地区仍然沿用地球纪元，但后来随着地球纪元被银河共和国废除，也就不再用它表示年份了。

在银河共和国，也发生过很多趣事。银河共和国总统的任期是10年，渺基连任了一次。银河纪元17年，有一个住在人马臂的人来到银心，向渺基提建议。总统官邸的守卫放他进去后，他立即看见了总统。当他发现周围一群表情严肃的人后，又跑了出去。出去后，他心想："我不远千里过来，就是为了在总统府跑来跑去？"于是他又跑回来了。

他直视着表情严肃的总统，欲言又止，磨蹭了几分钟才提了那个平淡无奇的建议，令人哭笑不得。这件事后来还被做成寓言，叫作《跑来跑去》。在银河共和国学校的思想品德课上，老师经常讲这个故事，并告诉学生："这告诉我们做事一定要有决心。"

然而有些学生却对这件事有着不同的解读。有人认为这个寓言表达的是"说话时不要紧张""浪费包括浪费时间，同样可耻"……

银河纪元18年，"数学破坏"失效，地球重新出现。如果歌唱者知道这些，那他一定很沮丧……

但是，歌唱者永远也不可能知道，因为他在银河纪元元年就与世长辞了，享年265岁，死因是谋杀。这种事其实很少发生，但是他被提拔为长老后，招来别人的妒忌，于是一群反对他的人就精心准备了很多年。有一天，在歌唱者为了修理飞梭进行太空行走时，肇事者用超微型核弹击穿了他的宇航服面罩，同时被击碎的还有他的大脑，他当场就一命呜呼了。

银河共和国当然不知道这些，它迈入了短暂的太平盛世。就像公元20世纪和21世纪的天文学家寻找地外生命那样，银河共和国的天文学家们也开始寻找银河系之外的生命。鉴于银河系之外的星系被称作"河外星系"，所以银河系之外的生命就被称作"河外生命"。

以银河系人类的能力，航行到最近的大星系——仙女座星系理论上是可行的，因为人类早就可以通过制造虫洞来超光速航行了。但是，这会花费很长时间，因此银河共和国的相关机构一直没有批准，相当于给银河系人类制造了一道半天然、半人为的枷锁。

对于其他星系，它们要么被认为没有生命存在，要么航行距离太远，因此一直没有人探索过河外生命。

银河纪元19年，渺基辞职了，回到他的故乡白星上当一名猎人。银河共和国选举出了新总统，然而他却是一个无能之辈，被后人谴责为"失土者"。他颁布的政策使政府大失民心，于是叛变爆发了。

叛乱从英仙臂和盾牌–南十字臂开始，19年间很少训练的共和国军队节节败退，当外臂[1]和银晕终于失守时，总统崩溃了。

危急时刻，现任总统被誓死保卫祖国的群众推下台，并仓促选举了一个新总统。新总统急忙废除前任总统颁布的一切政策，又加紧训

---

[1]　也称天鹅臂。

练军队，叛乱者与政府签订和平条约，暂时恢复了平静。

一波未平，一波又起。叛乱接踵而至。第二次叛乱的苗头始于银河纪元24年。那一年，政府在银心举办了一场类似于奥林匹克运动会的星际运动会（正式名称是"银河运动会"[1]），交通问题使观众苦不堪言。接下来又发生了一系列连锁反应，使一场交通堵塞导致了一场叛变。

还好，这次叛乱被政府军及时镇压了。太平盛世再次延续下去，时间的巨轮继续滚动下去……

---

[1] 英文为"Milkypics"，是"Milky Way"和"Olympics"的混成词。

二十、仙女座星系

叛乱被镇压后的一年（银河纪元25年），瑞诺斯[1]出生了。银河纪元47年5月8日0时52分，来自另一个星系的侵略者攻击了银河系。这时的瑞诺斯还是一名大学生。攻击来临时，他和其他同学都在宿舍里呼呼大睡，因为那时是晚上。

仙女座星系与银河系的战争打响了。

在战争中，瑞诺斯将成为拯救银河系的英雄……

两个月后的一天中午，在吃完午饭后，他发现自己坐在了一位名叫米萨[2]的女同学旁边（当时，瑞诺斯还不知道她的名字）。

后者立刻注意到瑞诺斯的目光，并第一次发现了瑞诺斯身上的与其年龄极不相称的聪慧、坚毅与沧桑。米萨和瑞诺斯互相看着对方，突然想起了对方是谁。

---

[1]　"Renos"。

[2]　"Misa"。

在他5岁时，瑞诺斯的父母离异，给他了一大笔钱，说是上大学的学费以及生活费。他在父母留给他的房子中孤独地生活了两年，按他的话说："当时陪伴我的只有五种事物，学习、娱乐、金钱、食物和孤独。"

瑞诺斯上了小学二年级后，米萨一家搬来了他所在的小区，正好住在他隔壁。米萨一家在这里住下后，米萨在父母的鼓励下，去了解了一下周围的邻居，就与瑞诺斯结识了。两人在同一所学校上学，但是由于两人的年龄差一岁，在学校中并没有交流。

瑞诺斯上初中时，米萨一家人搬去了另一个小区，虽然米萨极力劝阻，但无济于事。由于两个人上的也不是同一所学校，从此两人失去了联系。

瑞诺斯在中学时结交了很多的朋友，就渐渐地把米萨忘记了，只是模糊记得自己有一个失散的邻居；而米萨则记得，她的邻居是一个说不出带有语气的话的孩子——连带有问号或者叹号的句子都说不出来。今天是他第一次知道，小时候的玩伴竟然在自己所在的大学里！

两人长久地互相对视着，没有说话。瑞诺斯已经深刻地感受到对方用目光表达出的信息："我认识你！在某个地方我一定见过你！"

在仙女座星系（该星系和银河系一样，已经被一个国家统一）攻击银河系后，银河共和国政府正在招募可以击退仙女座星系的人士，名额只有两个。

地球上有句成语叫作"面壁思过"，而这两个人在"面壁"时所想的则是对策，直到仙女座星系的侵略者被击退。这两个人一度被称作"思策者"，但后来变成"抗奎者"[1]。

过了一会儿，米萨打破了沉默，对瑞诺斯说："这么多年来，我一直没有忘记你……根据以往对你的了解……今天看到你的第一印象，我觉得你很适合当抗奎者呀。"

瑞诺斯凝视着前方，忽然转头笑道："我当然也没有彻底忘记你。在我心中始终有你的位置。你觉得我适合当抗奎者。是的……哈哈哈哈……"

米萨惊恐地问："瑞诺斯？你怎么了？"

"没事。"瑞诺斯看得出来，米萨已经明白了这句话的意思。瑞诺斯把这句话的含义说了出来：

"我说'是的'，是因为我要毕业，没有别的事干了。我将竞选抗奎者。"

那一年的10月15日，瑞诺斯等许多人提交了成为抗奎者的申请。经过一系列机缘巧合，他被选中了。

另外一名抗奎者在被选中后立刻开始工作，但是他在计划中体现出的，似乎只有极其天真的幻想。他荒谬的计划是：在银心到仙女座星系的路上建立两个虫洞，第一个虫洞从银心到本星系群中心，第二个虫洞从本星系群中心到仙女座星系，然后在仙女座星系建立虫洞网络。这时，派遣舰队来到仙女座星系就可以了。

在第二次抗奎计划听证会上，他发表了自己的观点。瑞诺斯请求发言，得到总统的许可后站起来反驳道："先生，您的'虫洞计划'

---

[1] "奎"字来源于仙女座星系的旧称——奎宿增廿一。

在理论上是完全可行的，银河系已经有执行这个计划所需的技术和财力。但是，您没有考虑到实际情况。银河共和国之前已经知道，仙女座星系的军事很强，比我们强很多。留守在仙女座星系的士兵数量和银河系所有军队的士兵数量差不多。"

他停顿了一下，喝了一口水："由于资源问题，我们派出去的舰队最多只能是银河系全部军队的三成，是根本攻打不了仙女座星系的。何况，仙女座星系的人都很聪明，武器也比我们先进。银河系只剩下七成军队，仅仅从数量上来说，是很容易被仙女座星系的远征队消灭的。您这么做，反而会使银河系被侵略者征服，而这是在座的各位都不愿意看到的……"

"你给我闭嘴，瑞诺斯！你一个计划都没想出来的家伙，你还好意思反驳我？啊？"另一位抗奎者突然站起来，大声吼道。

"请注意您的言辞。"瑞诺斯和总统一起说道。

看到有人想发言，瑞诺斯举起一只手制止了他们，并继续道："我没有说完。另一位抗奎者，您的计划是在座的各位都不愿意看到的结局。没有计划总比一个会导致银河系被侵略者征服的结局更好。我们知道一个好的计划是需要时间的。"

瑞诺斯转向那名抗奎者："您在计划中表现出来的只有三件事：无知，粗鲁以及不可能。"他又回头对着大家说，"各位都是崇尚和平的，我们希望与仙女星系在谈判桌上而不是战场上说话。并且我的计划其实已经有了个雏形。"

"可以公开吗？"总统问道。

"总统先生，不行。一旦公开，可能会有某些人对这个计划断章取义，最终导致不好的结局。"

总统在用沉默进行无声地逼迫，瑞诺斯妥协了："但是，如果你们想我公开，那我就说了。"

总统点了点头。"在我一名好友的帮助下，我发现了仙女座星系军队的漏洞：每一万艘飞船中有一艘'头目'飞船，一旦其电脑被破坏，它所领导的9999艘飞船都会因为不受控制而爆炸，至少会失去攻击力，只能充当障碍物。为什么说有些人会断章取义，因为这是一种在我们的电影中很常见的片段，但现在，它是真实的。"瑞诺斯爽快地道出了他的全部计划。

"按照正常的打法，攻击这些'头目'飞船就可以取得阶段性的胜利。根据我们的研究，丧失攻击力的飞船都会自毁，而接下来只需要打扫战场就行了。"

"那我们用什么来攻击这些'头目'飞船？"另一名抗奎者问。

"先生，我原本指望您发明一种超级武器以协助我的。但听了您刚才的发言后，我大失所望，所以我才说我的计划处于'雏形'阶段。"

这次听证会不是秘密进行的，而是在各电视台转播的。观众们都非常兴奋。

那天晚上，瑞诺斯回到刚付完租金的公寓后倒头便睡。他在第二天10时醒来后，匆匆吃完早餐后奔向手机，给总统发短信："我们可以用反物质武器攻击那些'头目'飞船！"

一年后，在举行抗奎计划第六次听证会时，银河共和国国防部部长苦着脸指着瑞诺斯说："尊敬的总统先生，他的计划的确可行，但敌人在发现我们知道他们的弱点后采取了不同的战术，也就是用普通飞船保护'头目'飞船，我军损失惨重。"

"这样啊。你们遇到的问题我已经有解决方案了。在一次实验中，本人的团队触发了一种特殊机制，得到了之前只存在于科幻作品中的技术：四维物质。我们早就可以通过虫洞旅行，也就是，"瑞诺斯组织了一下语言又说，"折叠三维空间、进入四维空间、行驶更短的时间，来到目的地。"

有一些群众露出了疑惑的表情。瑞诺斯解释道："注意，'银河号'——或者说'时间号'——在进行时间旅行的时候也有大幅度跨越空间（也就是进入时间很慢的一个区域），虽然用了虫洞，但最后还是回到了地球，它原先的位置。另外，他们的目的不是穿越空间而是跨越时间。"

他又回到了正题，说："我们没有发现四维的物质。这种物质的复杂程度远超我们的想象。例如，一个四维的原子可能是一个四维的球形，但是其电子云是交叉、扭曲而复杂的。总之，这不是我能用三维语言解释的。我可以用它来攻击仙女座星系，但是不能公开方法，否则它们的亚原子级别窃听器可能得知，并找到反制的方式。"

发现四维物质的事情使瑞诺斯赚了一大笔钱，而另一方面，银河系也以此来挟仙女座星系：如果不按银河共和国的要求做，是不会有好下场的。那名可以要挟仙女座星系的人便是瑞诺斯，他被称作"抗奎者的灵魂"，简称"灵魂"。他的饮食起居都在一个小房间内，只要敌方干出了不可接受的事情，瑞诺斯就可以远程破坏仙女座星系内部。

银河纪元50年，瑞诺斯正式成为"灵魂"。他以为，从此以后这个职业将一直陪伴着他，但他想错了。

第一天，他有些不适应，因为看到四维物质是一种极其怪异的体验。他可以随心所欲地移动这块实际上巨大（直径上千公里）的四维物质，使其变大或变小。第二天，他就完全适应了。人们在那片四维空间内给瑞诺斯搭建了一个简易的卧室，这所房间外表看起来非常怀旧，就像公元纪元建造的一样。在业余时间，他可以看书或者看电脑。

仙女座星系得知了四维物质的存在，立刻束手无策。经过深思熟虑，他们决定试探一下"灵魂"的态度。

仙女座星系在攻打一颗星球的时候被银河共和国军队发现了，他们立刻报告给瑞诺斯，后者毫不犹豫地将仙女座星系军队的最高统帅以一种独特的方式杀死：调整四维物质的位置，在四维空间将其移动至仙女座星系，并使其三维大小达到数百千米。受四维物质的重力影响，仙女座星系军队的最高统帅所乘坐的飞船爆炸了。瑞诺斯并没有对仙女座星系赶尽杀绝，而是以这件事为借口逼迫仙女座星系围着银河系的指挥棒转。

瑞诺斯要求仙女座星系无偿提供物资和知识给银河系，而它们必须这么做。这使"瑞诺斯"这个名字在仙女座星系成为恶魔的代名词，而在银河系则被视作拯救世界的英雄，甚至是上帝派下来的正义天使。

银河纪元55年，银河系的科技水平就远远超过了仙女座星系，后者不再有知识和物资可以提供给前者，因此，对银河系也没有存在的必要。瑞诺斯用私人财产购买了多艘配备有冬眠系统的飞船，并以个人名义赠送给仙女座星系，随后发出信息："感谢你们对我们的帮助，你们可以离开本星系群了。"

为什么不把他们赶尽杀绝呢？答案是：没有必要，而且也浪费资源。

在"灵魂"的胁迫下，仙女座星系的人真的离开了本星系群，从此再也没有公开出现过。

他们走后，"灵魂"也没有存在的必要，瑞诺斯离开了那片他生活了5年的四维空间，将其使用权交给政府，但在使用权移交声明上表示自己有权继续研究它。

瑞诺斯原以为他要在那片空间内度过余生，一辈子见不得阳光，没想到只需要5年就把敌人击退了。

走出那片四维空间，把里面的私人物品都带走后，他被记者和群众簇拥着，他们问着各种问题。瑞诺斯听后，把那些重要的问题以及自己的答案记录下来并交给秘书，让他来回答，然后坐飞船回到了自己的故乡：地球。其实，瑞诺斯是在白星出生的，但由于他是地球人，对地球有着更深的情感。他把原来居住的公寓退了回去，在地球上买了一栋中等大小的别墅。

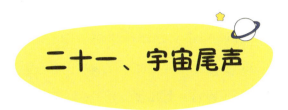

二十一、宇宙尾声

担任抗奎者和"灵魂"期间，瑞诺斯和米萨失去了联系，如今又恢复了正常。在这几年，米萨成为了一名著名的军事科学家，是她率先发现"头目"飞船的存在，并告诉了瑞诺斯。后来，米萨就搬到瑞诺斯的住宅内，两人的关系开始升温，于同年结婚。

银河纪元56年3月5日，临产的米萨在睡眠中被一个想法惊醒：为什么三维的宇宙中会有四维空间？宇宙原本是三维还是四维的？

疲惫的米萨没有多想，便倒头睡去。

3月20日，米萨在医院中生下了她与瑞诺斯的孩子。

孩子名叫卡里特勒[1]，这个名字在其出生地所使用的语言中表示"你是一个人，一个通人性的人，一个非常重要的人"。

充斥在米萨和瑞诺斯心中的只有幸福，一种无法描述的幸福。

时光飞逝，卡里特勒上了小学、中学和大学……

---

[1]　"Qalitra"。

毕业之前，他似乎只是一个学习好、身体好、特长多、朋友多的人。除了这些特征较为出众，卡里特勒和他周围的同学并没有太大的差别。

　　有一次，卡里特勒抓住了上太空的机会。为了节省钱财，他挑选了距离地球最近的南门二作为目的地。风神星已经在银河战争中被炸毁，因此南门二目前仍然是一颗单星，还是一颗没有行星的裸星。

　　他所在的飞船飞到离太阳几十个天文单位的地方，钻进了虫洞。待飞船出来时，已经距离南门二很近了，再往前数千千米便是安全与危险的边界线。

　　卡里特勒问驾驶员："还能往前开多远？"

　　驾驶员耐心地答道："大概2000公里吧，再往前飞船会变形，有时还会解体并熔化的。"

　　"那就开到极限吧。据我所知，这种民航飞船里面有飞梭，用的是更耐高温的材料，但由于这种材料成本很高，所以每艘飞船只有一艘。"卡里特勒这样说。

　　"嗯，是的。飞船是由超高熔点金属和一些纳米材料组成的，几乎有着金刚不坏之身；飞梭在驾驶舱前面，用了中子材料。"驾驶员说完便带着卡里特勒走向飞梭。

　　返回后，卡里特勒开始工作，很快就顺利地成为了一名天文学家。银河纪元81年，银河共和国举行了隆重的阅兵式，一共花了三天三夜。另外，政府开展了一个名为"星空计划"的项目，将一些恒星出售给公众，就像销售私人的岛屿一样。这个项目得名于发射"日冕号"的火箭"星空3号"。由于数量巨大，一颗恒星的价格只相当于一辆古老地球上的房车。只要合法，政府无权干预私人恒星的任何事情。

卡里特勒出于想要研究恒星的目的，也想要购买一颗恒星，但他认为如果购买稀有的蓝巨星或是红巨星，价格会很高，而常见的红矮星又没有什么特别之处。他于是选择了折中的恒星：黄矮星。

他是来到银心的一座太空城上购买那颗黄矮星的，而被分配给他的恒星位于两万多光年之外的猎户臂。销售员对卡里特勒说，这颗恒星名叫"RA1093"，然后将一个袋子递给卡里特勒，里面有恒星所有权证明以及极其精确的坐标。销售员不知道的是，这颗恒星是太阳。

这颗太阳是后来被月球人人工制造的那颗，而不是几十亿年前自然形成的那颗，但在卡里特勒看来，两者实质上并没有任何区别。

他在少年时代读过地球历史，知道太阳曾经被第二月球人熄灭，而这颗太阳是人造的，也知道太阳周围只剩下地球一颗行星。不过这些对他来说都无所谓，因为在他的眼里，行星只是能够孕育生命的灰尘。

银河纪元87年，他辞去天文学家的职位，将自己的研究放在宇宙学上。他发现了宇宙真正的终结方式以及时间。他虽没有被黑暗的事实吓退，但也确实令他担心——宇宙会在14年到15年之内灭亡，可能更早。

银河纪元90年，大灾难发生了，一个由于故障出现在错误位置的虫洞出现在太阳中心，不巧的是，虫洞的另一端还有一个黑洞，这个黑洞用强有力的巨手——引力，使太阳从中心坍缩，并移动到虫洞另一端的黑洞中。

太阳被吸入黑洞已经是一场大灾难。但这个虫洞还偏偏关闭了，太阳直接被裂开的虫洞切成已进入和未进入的两部分。太阳的核心被吸入虫洞另一端的黑洞，而剩余部分在失去了核心后剧烈地坍缩，占据了日核原先的空间。

这本来是幸运的，因为太阳还在那里。不过，这些部分在坍塌之后就由于压力过大而爆炸，产生了一团绚丽而可怖的行星状星云。最令人恐惧的是，它的中心没有白矮星——也就是恒星核的残骸！这个星云就是太阳星云，它呈现出耀眼的红色。

飞船从地球上的各个角落奔向宇宙，所有人都想逃离太阳星云这个所有人都避之不及的死亡与恐惧之地。

根据星空计划宪章，如一颗被购买的恒星被人为摧毁，则恒星的主人可以要求一颗新的恒星。那个星期过后，销售员就把南门二的所有权证明交给了卡里特勒。

卡里特勒拥有一艘飞船，灾难发生时他把自己的父母也带走了，现在他们全家都住在南门二的太空城。这种太空城是由飞船拼接在一起的，每艘飞船中间都有门。

后来才知道，仙女座星系的敌人一直没有走，黑洞和虫洞都是他们人工制造的。仙女座星系在这之后，又一次进攻了银河系。四维空间已经因为某种原因突然消失，还没有人找到对仙女座星系的威慑手段。

在民间，仙女座星系上的敌人被蔑称为"奎寇"，不断有各种虚构作品涌出来表达对他们的仇恨。银河共和国恢复了抗奎者这个职位。

银河共和国虽然不盛行血统论，但是卡里特勒却成为了唯一的抗奎者。奇怪的是，在他想出方案的时候，就有地区武装部队用极强的元素场将仙女座星系直接分解（准确而言是把所有生命都分解成原子级别的粒子），至今也没有一个人能解释原理。他原先的方案也是利用元素场，不过不是去攻击仙女座星系，而是去攻击银河系中心的黑洞。受到元素场的影响，黑洞会放射出大量的能量，毫无准备的敌人必将覆灭。

卡里特勒失去了大显身手的机会，他非常失落，后来他就没有在公众面前露面了。事实证明，这是一个愚蠢的决定，民众不再敬仰他，舆论不断攻击他……他忍受着数百倍于常人的痛苦，患上了严重的抑郁症。于是，他制造了一个微型平行宇宙。在平行宇宙中，他用铅笔写下了几句话：

　　来不及了。写下这些文字的是卡里特勒，刚刚发现了一个惊天动地的事实。这个宇宙之前有8个宇宙，接下来，它也即将毁灭。在穿越到这个微型平行宇宙之后，我见到了一块□[1]，上面记载着宇宙的□。

　　宇宙将坍缩，所有生命、所有天体、所有记忆，都将被压缩在那里。尊敬的后人们，宇宙可以储存信息，它的内存是无限的。这些信息都被我读取，保存在这里了。你们可以过来，在新的宇宙中复制这

---

[1] 代表难以辨认的字。

个宇宙，这个过去的世界。

不想死就快跑！

最后一句话还被刻在了石头上。

后来，他出于绝望，在自己的微型平行宇宙中度过了他的余生。

银河纪元100年末，卡里特勒回到了大宇宙中的地球，面朝天空中的银河，轻轻说道："一路走好。你们的尽头要来了。再见……"说完，便跳下了面前的万丈深渊。

舆论一直都在攻击他，得到卡里特勒自杀的消息后，许多人竟然都非常兴奋。后人是这样评价他的一生的："先天的条件赋予他许多的机会，但他从来没有抓住过。"殊不知，正如卡里特勒所预言，世界的末日即将到来……

银河纪元100年（公元62415年）12月31日23时59分59秒过后，在银河纪元101年开始前的一刹那，宇宙重启了。一切突然坍缩成为

一个奇点，在这一刻，时间停止了流逝，停下了它138亿年间从未停歇的脚步。接下来的很多年都没有任何能被称为"人"的生灵了。银河纪元结束了，时长刚好是100年。

宇宙坍缩成了一个奇点。

在这一刹那，全宇宙又在一次大爆炸中重启了。新宇宙的结构和之前的宇宙基本相同：三维的黑暗中点缀着恒星和行星，恒星组成了星系，星系组成了星系团。

有些文明建立了小宇宙室这样的结构，据不完全统计，这些"小宇宙"共有1000万个。它们的大小不等，小的只有一艘轮船那么小，大的却有一个星系那么大。

它们带走了宇宙大量的物质，因此，新宇宙发生的事情也与上一个宇宙发生的事件不太一样，甚至物理定律也有些许差别。某个人脑中可能因为残缺了几个分子，导致他想的事和说的话与上一个宇宙中的他不同；某颗星球可能在新宇宙中不再存在；某个星系可能在不同的时间与其他星系合并……

笔者在这里要说的是，本书中多次提及"平行宇宙"这个概念。宇宙是有限的，当你——当然是毫无征兆地——到达了边缘，会被一股神秘的力量阻挡，只能通过"宇宙之门"来在不同平行宇宙之间穿梭。和我们宇宙中的一些科幻作品不同，平行宇宙的意思是：我们宇宙之前或之外的宇宙。

而这些文字就不属于这里，它们属于上一个宇宙。那个宇宙是有史以来的第9个宇宙，一个更加疯狂而刺激的宇宙，它的历史上有着美丽的斑点和条纹。跟它比起来，这个宇宙，也就是10号宇宙，

可以说是较为呆板而无趣的。可以说，上面都是对9号宇宙的历史的演绎。

本书的内容是完全真实而可靠的，每一个角色也都存在过，但是他们的想法以及对话则来源于笔者的推测，而且笔者在写本书时，忽略了大量细节。两个宇宙的物理规律也稍有不同，因此有一些略显荒谬的情节，实际上对9号宇宙而言都是合乎常理的。

笔者并非来自9号宇宙，只是一次机缘巧合使我得到了来自那个宇宙的信息。这些信息来自于一个居住在微型平行宇宙的一个高等文明，它自称是9号宇宙的银河系人类的后代，因此，本书以人类为中心。

笔者将其口述的内容整理后，便有了本书。值得一提的是，这个文明将9号宇宙称作"前宇宙"。笔者认为，他们也坦然接受了自身宇宙毁灭的事实，因为这正是世界的基本规律。

不过，笔者写出想法、对话和细节并没有实际意义。那个将信息交给笔者的高等文明证明了宇宙是一台计算机——宇宙具有储存每一个基本粒子的状态的能力。

但愿人类能发展到那个全新的高度，并得以浏览这台计算机中的数据——也就是知晓宇宙的历史；也希望读者们能从这部"宇宙演义"中得到一些启示。

总之，新宇宙来了，新世界来了。

二十二、我们之前

　　虽然我们的宇宙也只是世界中的一个"小村落"，但笔者还是不得不承认，9号宇宙的故事相对来说是非常有趣的。然而，8号宇宙就是彻头彻尾的奇怪了。这个宇宙存在于几百亿年前，平均温度比现在的宇宙高得多，大约是−10摄氏度；又由于其绝大部分的质量都是水，因此，出现了绵延数百光年甚至更长的冰柱，组成了一个巨大的系统。是的，仅仅是一个。所有这些冰柱都是连接着的。

　　在这些冰柱上甚至孕育了生命，它们也有着历史、文化、语言、科技和战争。从这些冰柱上看天空，就如同在树枝上看着一张巨大的蜘蛛网，不同的是，这些冰柱是几乎透明的，能看到它们背后还有更复杂的结构……

　　这个宇宙中是没有虫洞和时间旅行的，理论上也不可能实现。但是，在这个宇宙中，光速趋近于无穷，因此，看到的一切天体都是它现在的样子，而不是几分钟甚至几年之前的样子。8号宇宙只存在了五十七亿二千六百三十五万年，随后就坍缩，形成了复杂得多的9号宇宙，原因不得而知。

至于7号宇宙，它存在了一百六十三亿零三百四十八万年，并且温度非常高，大约有10万摄氏度。这个宇宙中富含氢和氦，还有少许星际尘埃，形成了许多星云，大部分都孕育了恒星。恒星内部比外面热得多，达到了核聚变的条件后，便源源不断地产生更重的元素。

这个宇宙中没有孕育碳基生命，因为在这个宇宙中，由两个氦-4原子相撞产生的铍-8是稳定的。在我们的宇宙中，铍-8是不稳定的，所以三个氦-4相撞产生的碳-12就相对而言常见得多。这种现象导致在7号宇宙中，以氢、氦、铍、氮、氧这些元素最为常见，生命只能依赖丰度更低的硅。7号宇宙的硅基生命以水或是氟化氢作为溶剂，铍的硬度赋予了它们坚硬的外壳，身体则是硅组成的各种化合物。另外，在7号宇宙中，硅-28的原子核是极其稳定的，甚至比我们宇宙中的铁还要稳定得多，因此，一旦聚变到硅，核聚变就停止了，没有更重的元素。

由于硅本身的局限性，这个宇宙中的生命并未发展出文明，最后被淹没在历史的长河之中。根据一具那个时代留下来的生物制造的标本，后来的文明创造出了一件复制品，两者都已经失传。我们唯一的考证是根据仿制品建立的三维模型，其中显示这种生物叫做"岩脑"，是小型的岩石状物体，生理活动极其缓慢。它们不以个体为单位生存，在某些地方你可以看见大批的"岩脑"，但是没有人能看见单独的、活着的这种个体。它们会通过氟化氢腐蚀地下的土壤，挖出地下通道，向每一个个体输送营养；还会在每一条通道附近加一条"辅道"，来输送信息。

　　6号宇宙只存在了三十六亿七千八百一十万年，正好是那个宇宙中恒星寿命的平均值的两倍。这个宇宙中含大量的硼，生命也就都是硼基生命。由于硼缺电子，它可以形成非常复杂的结构，这个宇宙中的生命也更加高级。也许是因为这个原因，硼基生命发展得很快，在经过几万年之后就统治了整个宇宙。当然，我们必须承认，6号宇宙比接下来的宇宙小得多，体积只有我们宇宙的三分之一。

　　最后，一个疯狂的人竟然试图击碎时空的基本结构[1]，结果可想而知：时空的某一处深深地陷了进去，形成了一个质量巨大的黑洞，周围的时空也不断被吞噬，成为黑洞的一部分。在几千年后，整个6号宇宙都陷了进去，宇宙成为一个奇点。6号宇宙的终结可以说是人为导致的，而5号宇宙就不同了。

　　在5号宇宙爆炸后，它膨胀得非常慢，这是因为这个宇宙中含有大量的暗物质。其最大的时候，它的直径也只有52光年。接下来，暗物质所带来的引力夺得了这个宇宙的命运的控制权。它迅速地升温，一切物质最终都被暗物质魔鬼般的大手挤压在一起，直至成为一个奇点，正式宣告坍缩。这个宇宙只存在了18亿年。

　　4号宇宙存在了三百二十七亿九千四百五十八万年，这个宇宙显然不能孕育我们宇宙的生命，这是因为它的压力很低，温度很高，物质以气体的形式存在。在这个宇宙中存在着一些特殊的生命，它们只

---

[1]　具体的过程是：它们（也许可以称为他们）将一个夸克放在加速器中（6号宇宙里没有夸克禁闭，也就是说强子可以在足够高的能量下分解为夸克），用高能的电离辐射"攻击"这个粒子。数据对当时的生物来说完全不可理解。有证据显示，今天的夸克也是这样。

是漂浮在太空中的巨型云团而已。

在4号宇宙里，生物的进化一直是个谜团。后来发现它们几乎是永生的，可以变形，因此无需演化。这里生命的基础是氯化氢，呼吸是最重要的生物过程，完全靠它来维持生命：先是把"气管"拿来吸收外部的氢气和氯气，用"肺"进一步推入气体来实现呼吸，再点燃它们变成氯化氢流入"心脏"。把气体推出之后，通过"动脉血管"控制气体流动到全身上下每一个部位，在"静脉血管"中推动气体回到"心脏"、进入"肺"和"气管"，以此实现呼吸。

3号宇宙存在的时间就长得多，甚至超过了1000亿年。它主要由水组成，其温度达到25摄氏度，因此它所包含的水是液态的，甚至出现了600亿光年深的海洋，填满了整个宇宙。而天体则是由一些杂质汇聚而成的，大小可以达到上万千米，在"大海"中进行漫无目的地运行。这些杂质主要是难溶盐，其中硫酸钡是最多的一种。这里大概率不存在任何生命，而且光速是目前最慢的一个，每秒只有841米。

2号宇宙和我们的10号宇宙的外貌较为相像，但是存在了684亿年，而且没有一种元素有稳定的同位素。换言之，每种元素都有放射性，其中半衰期最长的是氢，它会衰变为中子（在2号宇宙中，自由中子也是稳定的）。中子，是一切元素最终的归宿。用来制造前文中提到的飞梭的中子就有很大一部分来源于此，因此也不会衰变。

对于1号宇宙的故事，就几乎不得而知了，但可以肯定的是，它存在了上千亿年。除此之外，笔者对它们一无所知，只能通过那个高等文明留下的零星话语推断。

这是一个神秘的宇宙，也许正因为如此，那个高等文明才无法获取相关信息。事实上，"数学破坏"就是通过1号宇宙遗留下来的物质制成的，由于物理规律不符，在9号宇宙中，它就拥有了毁天灭地的力量。反过来，9号宇宙和10号宇宙的物质在1号宇宙也拥有同样的能力。

这个高等文明给10个宇宙都取了名字，分别是："未知宙""中子宙""海洋宙""高温宙""引力宙""硼基宙""硅基宙""寒冰宙""前宇宙"，最后一个则是我们所在的"宇宙"。

"宇宙"一词中，"宇"表示空间，"宙"代表时间，意思就是"时空"。在这10个宇宙中，空间中有着截然不同的物体和物质，但时间仍然是从1号宇宙诞生之前就存在的。换句话说，"宇"可以变化，但"宙"永远保持不变——至少在前10个宇宙中是这样的。

这10个宇宙都来源于一个奇点，它爆炸形成了1号宇宙，坍缩，爆炸，坍缩，爆炸，坍缩……产生并毁灭了一个又一个新的宇宙。

总有一天9号宇宙的故事会得到完善，我们当然也欢迎全宇宙的读者投身于这项极其伟大的事业，参与完善这10个宇宙的故事，无论通过何种方法！

番外·非三维

这个故事并没有结束！

奇点爆炸产生的10个宇宙被统称为"三维区"或"三维地区"。"地区"显然是一个更大区域的一部分，而这个更大的区域的维度不一，有些地区是零维的，有些是一维的，有些是二维的，还有些是四、五、六、七、八、九、十维的。它们都来源于三维区之外的奇点产生的爆炸，且每个"区"都有它专属的空间维度。

无论空间维度如何变化，时间永远保持不变。即便是奇点也有一维时间，只是它无限慢。没有任何一个地方有着非一维的时间。

值得一提的是，三维区中的物质总量不会保持不变，可以从其他"区"中汲取能量，再将其变为质量。

高维度物体是不能进入低维空间的，否则会被所谓的"维度势能"（Dimensional Potential Energy）压碎。维度势能和重力势能类似，具有大量这种能量的物体（高维物体）会不稳定，因此会慢慢地变成维度更低的物体，这个过程就叫作"跌落"。瑞诺斯曾经居住的那个四维空间可能是跌落了，也可能是被仙女座星系摧毁了。

根据实验发现，跌落的速度和维度几乎没有关系——意思是，五维变成四维和四维变成三维的速度几乎一样。

跌落现象经常会发生在高维度的"地区"上。这类事情发生过很多次，会造成大量人员伤亡，因此大部分文明都已经掌握或试图掌握远离低维空间的方法。

接下来，我们就来极其简略地讲述一下四维空间的故事。可能读者很诧异：作为9号宇宙银河系人类的后代，那个高等文明也应该是三维生物，是怎么得知四维空间的事件的？

答案是：道听途说。笔者一贯不赞成把真实性存疑的事件记在如此庄重的故事中，但是为了告诉读者大致发生了什么，笔者决定破例。那一片四维空间称作"四维区"，而该文明只提供了"四维区"一个平行宇宙的故事的极小一部分。我们姑且把这个宇宙称作"四维宙"，这个宇宙将在2038年彻底跌落至三维，并且并入三维区。

所有平行宇宙和"地区"都是球形[1]的，四维宙当然也不例外。公元前1945年左右，那时它还比较大，半径有900多光年。

有一颗四维的行星在那一年刚开始的时候就跌落成三维了。不过，在跌落后，从一个三维生物的视角上看，一切都是相同的。

这颗行星的跌落过程是悄无声息的。它是一颗巨行星，绚丽而五彩缤纷的光环最先坠入三维空间，宛如一双来自四维天堂的大手，缓缓伸向三维的世间；美妙的大气如同一幅婀娜多姿的油画，跌落时产

---

[1] 也可以是直线、圆形以及高维度的球体。

生极其微弱的"嗡嗡"声，既像是蜻蜓点水，又像是蜜蜂之舞；几十颗小卫星如众星拱月般围绕在它旁边，似乎是一个个的士兵要以一己之力阻挡膨胀的三维空间，但又无法力挽狂澜；最后，它只剩下一声沉闷的爆炸……

说完四维，我们来聊一聊二维。这个二维的平行宇宙"二维宙"（来自"二维区"）还在持续膨胀，吞噬着附近的三维区（换句话说，我们宇宙的一部分正在向它跌落）。与我们的一些科学家预想的不同，在二维空间也可以存在生命。它们创建了绚烂的文明，有些——如果它们是三维的话——比现在的人类发达得多。它们在你阅读这一页的时候也存在。

差一个维度，能包含的信息就差了很多。因此，这些能产生智慧的生命不仅要有非常复杂的神经元网络，而且还得非常巨大。这些生命几乎都是正方形，当然它们的"边"不是完全笔直的，但仍然很长。就拿二维宙中心的一颗星球而言，它所孕育的智慧生命的边长可以达到一公里，而且这种生物的身体外部有一层极其坚硬的外骨骼，在二维世界里可以称得上是无坚不摧。同时，这也有一定的保护作用，使它们可以直接在太空中生存。

该文明还提供了二维生物创作的一部虚构作品：《无限》。这本"书"（一本诗集中的史诗之一）中讲述了某一个二维文明试图突破维度的限制，进入三维、四维、五维……但最终失败，而一事无成。

虽然这是一场悲剧，但也从侧面反映了这些二维生物的精神，至少是它们向往的世界和生活。二维的"书"就是一张二维纸，是长而窄的矩形，作者用彩色的"墨水"把文字写在边缘，用黑色分开单词，白色分开句子，灰色分开段落。它们使用的文字是一维的，正如人类——一种三维生物——使用二维文字一样。

翻译为三维生物的语言之后，二维生物的作品似乎比原先更加耐人寻味——这也不奇怪，毕竟前者显然能传达更多的意思，也就有着很多不同的翻译方式。

换言之，一个"二维词"可以翻译成很多含义不同甚至截然相反的"三维词"，因此对于三维生物而言，同一篇故事就可以有成百上千种解读；但对于二维生物，只有一种解读是正确的，其他的都是在胡说八道。譬如，前文中提到的《无限》的标题甚至可以被翻译成"虚无""消失""存在""零"，但这些都不是它的实际含义。

"一维区"中的"一维宙"存在生命吗？

我们不得不惊叹于生物的力量，在这种简单的令人窒息的环境中也有活着的生物。它们的结构太过于简单，不可能产生智能。它们就是一根线段。你在三维空间中找到的国际单位制中有7个基本单位，对应7个物理量：米（长度）、千克（质量）、秒（时间）、安培（电流）、开尔文（温度）、摩尔（物质的量）和坎德拉（发光强度）；其中只有3个在一维空间中存在：长度、时间、物质的量[1]。

一维宙只有长度，没有宽度和高度，因此没有重量——无限细的东西没有有意义的质量。

"时间在任何地方都有，这里也仍然在流逝。"《无限》，一部二维作品，有着这句同样适用于一维世界的话。

---

[1] 物质还在那里，那些粒子当然也是，因此物质的量无论如何都是存在的。

由于一维空间中任何物体的移动范围都完全受限于周围的物体，电子几乎无法运动，更没有电流。

同样的道理，微观粒子不能移动，一切均处于绝对零度，温度在一维空间没有使用的意义。

能产生光的设备、装置，在一维宙中也只能把它的光线传播到它本身与相邻的物品，光只会在这两个物体之间不断反射。因为没有能反射一切光的物体，一切的光在一维宙最终将会被吸收，而这导致一维宙中已经没有光线了。所以发光强度这个物理量没有存在的必要性。

零维，就是一个可有可无的点。为了证明零维生命不存在，我们就要知道：根据定义，生命一定要能区分自己和外界。如果一种生命不占据空间（如零维生命），它就和周围那些同样不占据空间的物体（零维物体）没有区别，导致它不能区分自己和外界，也就不是生命。因此我们必须承认，不存在零维生命。

由于根深蒂固的物理法则，维度高于四的地区存在的生命都无法被三维仪器探测到，因此只有一、二、三、四维存在可探测的生命。

附录

9号宇宙大事年表

纪元	年份	事件
公元纪元 （?—2245）	前9852	灭神星向地狱神星发射子弹
	前7978	亚光速子弹到达地狱神星
	2045	人类全面生产人造肉和人造蔬菜
	2060	灭神星文明对地球发起战争
	2120	1379与2015相见
	2121	地球开始反攻灭神星
	2138	战争结束，地球获胜
	2139	地球共和国统一全球，毁灭地狱神星文明
	2142	巫神星对人类发起战争，人类取得胜利
	2155	地球人发现月球人
	2156	月球向地球开战，反被地球炸碎
	2157	一些月球人登上火星
	2158	第二代火星人出现
	2206	第三代火星人出现
	2216	地球人殖民内太阳系
	2230	地球人殖民外太阳系
	2245	矮行星周围的太空城建成

（续上表）

纪元	年份	事件
太阳纪元 （2246—2702）	1	太阳系联邦出现
	2	太阳系内乱开始旋即结束
	66	南门二周围出现风神星
	70	风神星被人类发现
	71	两星之间的联系建立
	152	风神星生命被摧毁
	156	上述现象被人类发现
	222	"三战"爆发，太阳系联邦灭亡
	224	"三战"停止，进入和平时期
	457	地球共和国第一次重建
公元纪元 （2703—60222）	2703	地球开始远离太阳
	2705	地球"复位"，回到原先的轨道上
	2706	世界航天局成立
	2709	"日冕号"发射，发生重大事故
	2711	火星飞船降落在地球，占领南极洲
	2740	地球人制造了一块巨岩
	2759	地球人夺回南极，火星文明灭亡
	2800	第二月球出现，成为地球的新卫星
	2870	克马尼罗出生
	2892	"时间号"发射
	2893	黄石超级火山爆发

（续上表）

纪元	年份	事件
公元纪元 （2703—60222）	4000	"时间号"发现地球进入冰河时代
	60200	第二月球被摧毁
	60200	"时间号"到达埃普莱涅特，后被驱逐
	60220	第三月球工程完工，投入使用
	60222	西里山、克马尼罗及斯卡基文逝世
地球纪元 （60227—62315）	1	地球共和国第二次重建
	2	地球上出现了大量新的建筑物
	3	地球共和国的行政区划确立
	1443	格罗比亚出生
	1453	地球共和国被"冈东孔"取代
	1460	地球共和国第三次重建
	1500	地球的发达程度超过埃普莱涅特
	1825	歌唱者出生
	2016	歌唱者第一次毁灭一个星系
	2025	斯塔尔斯成为地球共和国总统
	2026	歌唱者发现地球，用"数学破坏"将其毁灭
	2027	剩余的人类移居白星，重建文明
	2028	白星帝国建立，皇帝为尤巴斯
	2063	歌唱者又一次发现人类文明

（续上表）

纪元	年份	事件
地球纪元 （60227—62315）	2081	斯莱福鲁斯继位，成为白星的新皇帝
	2089	白星帝国灭亡，银河共和国雏形出现
银河纪元 （62316—62415）	1	银河共和国统一银河系，歌唱者遇害
	18	"数学破坏"失效，地球重新出现
	19	银河系叛乱开始，并被平定
	24	运动会间接导致的第二次叛乱出现并被镇压
	25	瑞诺斯出生
	47	仙女座星系入侵银河系，瑞诺斯当选"抗奎者"
	48	瑞诺斯发现了四维物质
	50	瑞诺斯成为"灵魂"
	55	"灵魂"的职位被撤销
	56	卡里特勒出生
	81	银河共和国开展阅兵式，星空计划启动
	90	卡里特勒当选"抗奎者"，制造微型平行宇宙
	100	9号宇宙结束

三维往事

1 Tartarus

On an afternoon in November 9852 BC, King Hilhof and Vice King Miye of the Tartarus Kingdom looked anxiously at the red dot in the palace's underground conference room, which represented a series of sub light–speed "bullets" fired by the planet Shiva, which was thousands of light–years away. Astronomers estimate that they will arrive in 7978 BC. The bullets themselves were very ordinary, made of very cheap metal, and the least almost about the size of a basketball, but their speed was very close to the speed of light, and relativistic effects gave them enormous energy.

"I cannot believe that our kingdom, which has lasted for more than 10000 years, is going to end like this. Absolutely not! That shameful civilization," said Hilhof, "intends to annihilate us and three thousand other civilizations near us in nearly two thousand years! How can we counter them?"

"Your Highness, we have now taken on the task of building a ship for generations." Miye finally got these words out of his mouth.

"You mean escaping? No, I swear on behalf of my government that we will live and die with Tartarus!"

"Your Majesty, for the safety of our people, we must go now. The ship is the only way out!"

"No, as vice king, you have no right to contradict me!"

"This has nothing to do with the relationship between the monarch and his subjects. If we stay, we absolutely cannot live!"

"This is not how our civilization should behave!"

"With all due respect, Sire. Do you care nothing for our safety?"

"Maybe, maybe not. It would be a betrayal to abandon Tartarus that gave birth to us."

"Mind you, you exist to protect this country and its people. Can you bear to see ten billion people die before you?"

"Since childhood, we aristocrats have known that integrity is more important than survival!"

"But we cannot make the decision for hundreds of millions of people of Tartarus!"

"This is our common homeland, and as vice king, you are the second-most responsible to this planet!" Hilhof was furious.

"Your Majesty, as the latest vice king, I am, of course elected by the people. Citizens also choose to build a generation of spacecraft!"

In response to Miye's retort, Hilhof was speechless and hesitated. This is because the debate is between integrity and dignity, freedom and survival.

More than 10000 years later, a poem on Earth wrote, "How can a man's body climb out of a dog's hole?" If I were to say this to the people of Tartarus, I'm afraid they would not agree; them, who struggle for freedom and happiness, have experienced countless disasters and will do anything to save the lives of most people. This "survival consciousness" drives the development of Tartarus economy, science, technology and art. Without it, Tartarus would not have achieved its brilliant achievements today. It can be said that the civilization of Tartarus is a work of art made by this "survival consciousness", a great sculptor.

But the nobles of Tartarus had received a very different education. They valued honor and money more than people's lives. All this has become a sonorous word: "No!"

"Your Majesty, how can you be so stubborn?"

"No!"

"Are you sure..."

"No!"

"Please reconsider..."

"For the last time, no!"

"Please..."

"Never! Don't talk to me anymore! Stop! Did you hear me? Never!"

Before the words were out, Hilhof's behavior activated Miye's animalistic nature. Miye lost patience with the stubborn emperor and growled, "Nonsense! Think about who you are! You are the enemy of this planet! I repeat, you are the enemy of this planet!"

He abandoned all manners and roared, "die!" like a great beast.

With a roar, he plunged a dagger he had found out of nowhere into Hilhof's chest. Hilhof groaned in pain. "Do not abandon Tartarus..." His voice was so weak that Miye knew he was dying.

Facing the dying emperor, Miet felt pity. He said to himself, "never mind. I must get rid of this enemy that threatens the lives of all the people. I'll be shot by his men if I'm found out!"

With the people outside, Miye cut off Hirchhoff's head to hide his murder.

The next day, Miye usurped the throne, declared Hilhof's death as a suicide caused by depression, and immediately ordered the construction of a generation of ships to begin.

In 7978 BC, the first "interstellar bullet" – slightly slower than light speed – hit Tartarus, and fell into the sea. It was very massive, and caused a massive explosion. Tartarus' oceans evaporated in few seconds, and parts of the land fell into the mantle. By this time, the people of this planet escaped long ago.

Three hours later, another "bullet" struck the capital of Tartarus in light speed. At that place, the buildings flattened in a very brief moment, there were cracks hundreds of kilometers long on the planet's crust, many objects went to the mantle through them, and lava flooded everything they met.

Seven hours past, the three continents of Tartarus remained with two. The oceans that were evaporated went back in the form of rain and covered Tartarus for a moment. But at this point, the third "bullet" hit the second largest city of Tartarus, and it was destroyed in few minutes. The continent it was on was ruined by the lava, and went deep into the planet. Water filled where it was. At this point, Tartarus only got one continent.

The fourth "bullet" hit this planet two hours later, it was

bigger. The land was all burnt and unlively.

Soon the fifth "bullet" came. Its mass was 10 times larger than the sum of the four bullets before. The planet were shredded into pieces.

On the other hand, Shiva was in the midst of an orgy across the country, and its longtime enemy, Tartarus, had finally been destroyed. But in fact 100 million people have escaped and survived. However, this also made Shiva the strongest civilization in the Orion arm of the galaxy. Civilizations on other planets were basically a group of primitive people in the stone age, and those stronger civilizations had been suppressed or sanctioned by Shiva in a similar way. Then, perhaps due to excessive pride, the development of Shiva began to stagnate, and they did not continue to expand until the Common Era. Shiva, the planet was called "Middle World" and was the core of this civilization. Middle World was later converted into a military base.

The long expansion lasted for tens of thousands of years. But whether the reign of Shiva would last remained an open question...

2 The Last Man

The "last" person on Earth was sitting alone in a room when suddenly there was a knock on the door...

He sighed. "Come in. The door is not locked."

The door opened, and there stood a man, who had not come in. The man in the room was so happy to had found other people that he rushed forward to give him a hug. However, his hand passed through the body of the coming person without any feelings.

He suddenly noticed something wrong with the visitor: he was naked and had no mouth, red skin, nine big, gleaming blue eyes, twenty-four strong abs, a wrinkled neck, a thick tail longer than the body, and fourteen tentacles that secreted green mucus.

Out of nowhere, it said, "Hi."

He was struck by the fact that this strange creature could understood human language. With a strange twinkle in his eyes, that was half surprise and half fear, he replied, "Hello."

There was a silence that lasted five minutes.

Finally, the creature said, "Do you know what's going on out there?"

"I do not know."

So, the creature began its brief narrative. "In 2060, the civilization of Shiva on the other end of the galaxy launches a shocking war against Earth. Shiva is very warlike, and in the war, they were overwhelming, killing all life on Earth. The survivors are all out of their sphere of influence. Its 2120 now, and for 60 years, these survivors and many of their descendants have been quietly building an army against Shiva, the nightmare of the survivors."

He was interrupted by someone in the room, "What are you?"

"I'm just a man. This image of me is not real, but a fictional projection. That's why you can't see any movement in my body. I did it because I wanted to give you a special first impression."

"I do not have a name, just a number: 1379. You can call me that. Your current number is 2015."

"There are many other non-human creatures in the fleet, even some bacteria that will fight back against Shiva in their own way. My purpose is to invite you to join the Earth's army."

"For the sake of the planet, I agree to join."

"Good. You will now be a, uh, marshal of the Earth Counterattack Force. When the counterattack is over, you will be the vice president of Earth."

"Why me?"

"You will know then." In fact, 1379 did not tell him when he should have known why. The reason is unknown.

Then the earth awakens its sleeping power.

In 2121, the war between Earth and Shiva began, and everyone began to fight. Shiva had an appearance similar to Earth, but with an atmosphere of 75% oxygen, 20% carbon dioxide and 5% noble gases. Because the people of Shiva breathed carbon dioxide, the Earth Counterattack Forces planted a lot of plants in the ground to capture the little carbon dioxide there was in Shiva's atmosphere. When they finished this work, earthlings set them on fire, burning so violently in the high concentration of oxygen that they turned the only continent on Shiva into a barren wasteland for a few years. However, according to someone's speculation, the environment would recover rapidly.

Carnivores and omnivores attacked enemies on the surface, herbivores took away the plants that Shiva depend on, and scavengers cleaned up the battlefields. Together, they made up a vast army. Aquatic animals formed the Earth's navy, responsible for attacking ships and other creatures in the seas of Shiva.

All flying birds formed an air force whose job was to disrupt the enemy. Many of the enemies were infected by viruses or bacteria released by Earth. Human beings fought in spaceships with the fleet of Shiva.

In 2138, the Earth Resistance Army had driven the surface survivors of Shiva to the poles, where they were immediately wiped out by other local animals, such as polar bears. Earth's space force worked hard to wipe out Shiva's space army. Nobody knows, Shiva still left some survivors, and they would launch another war against humanity in the future...

In this way, the Earth Resistance plundered a large amount of resources from Shiva, and humans returned to Earth altogether, left the rest of life behind forever. This was because Shiva had strong repair ability to make more suitable environment for these plants and animals.

At this point, "what will the rest of humanity eat?" was a common question asked by many earthlings. The government's answer was that artificial meat and vegetables would be fully produced by 2045, so what people eat wasn't really a problem.

3 Two Battles

May 8th, 2139 marked a milestone for civilization on Earth: astronomers had discovered another alien civilization, Tartarus. On the same day, the Earth Republic united the Earth, becoming the first nation in human history to unify the globe.

In the vastness of outer space, a huge dish-shaped spaceship was approaching the Earth. It belonged to an exoplanet nicknamed "Tartarus", which was known for extremely high temperatures on the surface. As previously mentioned, Tartarus was blown up by the Shiva civilization in 7978 BC, so they launched this ship to search for a new home in the universe. This ship had been wandering the vast expanse of space for a long time, but still had a population of only 100 million. Now they finally found the Earth.

Astronomers from Tartarus believed that Earth was a

suitable home and had plenty of resources to bring their civilization back, but all earthlings must die out.

On May 10th of this year, all mankind had been nervous, many pessimists often leaned against the wall, pale and fragile due to the excessive fear of Tartarus. That's because their spacecraft broke into Mars orbit today.

On May 17th, the spacecraft was only 400000 kilometers from Earth, a little more than the distance between Earth and the moon.

How did Tartarus want to destroy Earth and conquer Earth? By law, anyone over the age of 14 and under the age of 60 (except for technicians and security guards) must be involved in controlling the spaceship or working together to create a rock for impact on Earth. The rock is about 50 kilometers in diameter and took five weeks to complete. It was completed in 2095.

On May 20th, the spacecraft had been orbiting Earth for three days and nights. That afternoon, Hells aimed the massive rock at Earth and three days later it would launch towards Earth. In their words, "At that time, being an earthling would become a common method of suicide." This kind of confusing joke is a famous characteristic of Tartarus.

The leaders and heads of state of the various regions of the Earth Republic immediately held a major meeting and finally predicted: "After more than 200000 years of human life on the Earth, there are only three days left."

It is completely impossible to move all the earthlings to other planets in three days, and recent information that once Tartarus conquer the Earth, they will set their plans for the entire solar system, driving out all the earthlings in the solar system and robbing all available resources.

After taking away the resources of the solar system, they will return and wipe out Shiva. This may not seem to be a matter of Earth civilization, but according to the information available so far, people of Earth, Tartarus, and Shiva are all members of the so-called Galactic Race, or "Galaxians". This was one of the few intelligent races in the galaxy and there was little biodiversity.

For now, the only way to prevent Hells from invading Earth is to release antimatter weapons.

On May 21st, a hundred antimatter weapons from all over the world were gathered on a deserted island, ready to be launched by rocket.

"Three, two, one, launch!"

The rocket, *Antimatter 1*, carrying the antimatter weapons and the hope of the earthlings, was launched on May 22nd, and was still a multistage rocket. The head of *Antimatter 1* (where the weapons were located) quickly separated from the second and third stages, which had been abandoned.

This was seen very dangerous: if the rocket failed, it could accidentally set off the antimatter weapons that would destroy humanity. But now is the 22nd century, humans can control unmanned rockets with great precision.

Antimatter 1 is much faster than the *Saturn 5*, launched two centuries ago, and can reaching the Tartarus spacecraft's position in half a day, plus half a day to adjust its bearings and orbit, which can be done in a few hours.

On board the Tartarus spacecraft, a huge rock can be seen, caught between thousands of robotic arms, soon to be released. *Antimatter 1* launched a surprise attack from the side of the ship facing away from Earth, because the crew of the spaceship were mostly focused on the earth facing side of the ship, nervously waiting for the launch of the "artificial meteorite", and there was little supervision of the back side.

A hundred antimatter weapons flew in two batches behind the Tartarus ship, but because they were in space, they made no sound. A bright light appeared outside the ship. Fifty antimatter weapons had blasted through the hull and destroyed the back half of the ship. Due to air loss, many suffocated, others simply floated outside, and those within range of the blast were vaporized by the massive energy. More than 85 million deaths have been reported. Now, their civilization is at a disadvantage that is virtually impossible to reverse.

In a room located in the center of the ship, Hersokira and her daughter, less than a year old, were on the run. This single-parent family had a low standard of living, but were always active and doing what they could to survive: "Survival is better than anything," Hersokira's great-grandfather once said. This was the basic principle of every member of her family, and was the principle of the entire Tartarus civilization.

She rushed out of the room with the baby girl in her arms, and shouting in the crowd, "ahh!" The crowd froze, staring at her as she dashed through the stagnant crowd. The nearest lifeboat is only 30 meters from Hersokira. She was desperate to get there, trying to squeeze in.

Unfortunately, that lifeboat was nearly full, and there was only room for one child. She had to hand the baby over to the ship's security guards, who were responsible for maintaining order. At this time, the baby's gaze seems to say: Mom, do not abandon me...

At the moment of life and death, in the baby's eyes, Hersokira saw the hope of the civilization, that is love...

In space, the remaining 50 antimatter bombs blew a long

151

crack in the second shell, nearly tearing the ship apart, and all those who failed to escape were killed in the fire. A great number of debris flew out. The spaceship was already a brilliant blue in the heat, and finally cooled down. That rock, the product of the work of hundreds of millions of people, has been blown to pieces in this murderous space war, but it is a permanent memorial to the spirit of this civilization. This rock is also the tombstone of Tartarus civilization, which is supposed to be completely extinct. The people of Earth began to cheer because the Earth civilization had won its first space war.

Unfortunately, the engine of *Antimatter 1* was hit by a rock the size of a lunch box, and it was lost forever in space. It didn't matter because it had already done its job and wasn't carrying any antimatter weapons. According to the observation of a satellite orbiting the sun, it finally broke away from the earth and fell into the sun.

What no one knew at that time was that the nine lifeboats that had not been engulfed by the explosion formed an array that continued the dying civilization and would soon rebuild the Tartarus Kingdom on the moon.

Debris from objects inside the Hells ship formed Earth's ring, hanging like a necklace in the pale blue sky. Because the moon is within the ring range, it is often hit by debris, and the back side of the moon began to have more craters. Among the many lunar seas on the moon, many craters appear to be particularly bizarre, and are no less large than those of Tycho and Copernicus.

Despite the victory on Earth, space wars are almost endless because there are so many forces involved. Although interstellar warfare has some rules similar to the laws of war, peace is always a dream.

Tartarus had a moon nicknamed Hecate that also have intelligent civilization, and the two were on good terms and even shared the same language. A hundred centuries ago, when Tartarus was blown up, Hecate followed and built a ship. Hecate itself was then torn apart by the debris of Tartarus. The two ships were originally together, but then they got separated. After receiving the message that the Tartarus spaceship had been blown up by Earth, the Hecate people were very furious. Their spaceship flew to the third planet in the solar system at top speed.

"*Hecate*, full speed ahead!"

The Voodoo spacecraft arrived in Earth orbit on September 30th, 2142, at a distance of 350,000 kilometers, trying to hide itself with the Earth's rings. The weapon used by *Hecate* (it is also the spaceship's name) is also a rock, but only 15 kilometers across, not much bigger than the asteroid that killed the

153

dinosaurs.

In this era, there are tons of high-orbit satellites in Earth's orbit, and it is not long before *Hecate* were discovered. Earthlings also discovered that they also want to wipe out the entire Earth population with a single rock. There are only 40 million people on *Hecate*, less than half the number of the Tartarus spacecraft.

In the face of such a situation, Earth civilization has been prepared, once again, earthlings built a hundred antimatter weapons and a rocket.

Making antimatter weapons was very easy these days. The most commonly used antimatter is antihydrogen. In antimatter weapons, the antimatter needs to be turned into a solid with a very ow temperature in order to bind it to a magnetic field.

The cold is removed by a computer before annihilation, and the solid hydrogen turns into a gas. The next step is to remove the magnetic field, and the mass of gas will burst the outer shell, and since the outer shell is made of ordinary matter, annihilation will occur.

On October 18th, *Hecate* was ready to release the rock they had made. As soon as the earthlings received the news, they launched rockets. The rocket, called *Antimatter 2*, launched with a hundred antimatter weapons at high speed. *Antimatter 2* is much bigger and incorporates more technology than *Antimatter 1*.

When *Antimatter 2* reached the inside of the Earth's ring, it saw *Hecate* preparing to release the rock. It then circled around to the side of the ship facing away from Earth and prepared to attack like *Antimatter 1*.

However, a servant on the spaceship accidentally saw "*Antimatter 2*" and immediately reported it to his superiors. In a panic, the Voodoo men shot the rocket with mini nukes. Several of them hit the rocket, and sadly, they all hit its only weakness, the propeller. After it was destroyed by the nuclear flame, the internal computer believed that *Antimatter 2* had been captured by the enemy, so the rocket detonated all the antimatter bombs.

Antimatter 2 instantly turned into a flash of white light, and its explosion severely damaged the hull of *Hecate*, but only 10 million were killed, leaving 30 million.

By accident, a piece of the ship hit the spaceship's self-destruct button (designed to kill the enemy when the spaceship were captured or damaged), and it immediately went into self-destruction. There are thousands of nuclear bombs on the outside of the ship, all of which are ordered to explode at the same second.

None of the people on board *Hecate* knew what was going on, but because earthlings had satellites, they recorded the whole thing.

The nuclear bombs only hit the outer part of the ship, which seemed to be nonlethal. But everything on the inside of the ship started to heat up. Eventually, the heat caused a violent burn (there was plenty of oxygen inside), turning the ship into ash and gravel.

People crowded every escape route. When these items burn, they also burn the passageway. Hecate was known for its extremely democratic and disorder, and this is the result of anarchy.

As a result, the Earth's ring thickened by a little bit, and though it was not quite as grand and dignified and magnificent as Saturn's rings yet, but when the weather was right, you can see a beautiful and magnificent silver ribbon hanging across the sky. At night it will be matched by the moon, with stars set like blue, white, yellow and red jewels on either side of the ring. You can even see it at noon with the sun beside.

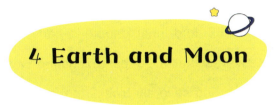

4 Earth and Moon

Speaking of the moon, it has been making chaos. The Moon civilization is the third alien civilization discovered by Earth. Lunar people are also Galaxians. The Earth's ring coincides with the moon's orbit, and some of the rocks from the ring will fall to the moon under the influence of the moon's gravity, resulting in more and more craters on the moon.

Recently, the Tartarus array landed on the moon. They formed a huge matrix that shocked the lunar people and was accepted as a member of the Moon. They are very similar so they can even interbreed.

The moon's population is about 6 billion, and its level of development is a little more than a century behind the Earth. They had mastered controllable nuclear fusion and antimatter weapons, but its technology, military and cultural level are not as developed as what earthlings expect.

Earthling and lunar humans discovered each other at about the same time. Earthlings discovered the Moon civilization in late December 2155, and lunar people in early January 2156. They also discovered that the mass extinction was caused by earthlings. Earth's ring severely blocks the moon's view of the sky, as it is mainly composed of rock and metal from the two ships, with a small amount of organic matter (possibly remnants of their bodies), which not only blocks the Moon man's view, but also reflects a lot of light.

The moon government was very angry: "why would earthlings be so cunning!" The lunar government sent a message to Earth written in Morse codes, which translated into English to read something like: "the moon have been your earth's satellite for billions of years, helping to create the tides, but now the earth is full of life and green; on the moon, however, nothing grows. You laid to rest the precious lives of 140 million aliens, who had been drifting and wandering for 100 centuries, but you brutally slaughtered them in just over a decade. If that is still fine, but you also blew up their spacecraft and smashed the remains and pieces into the moon!" When the Moon people discovered that the Earth people "love to play the emotional card", they decided to do the same and personified the Moon and Earth.

The leader of the Earth Republic responded, "they invade the Earth, we naturally would attack back, and they show no sign of surrendering or leaving, so our only choice is to kill them all. We didn't find you until after the Earth ring formed, but it was too late. On behalf of the whole planet, I am deeply sorry."

Around this time, the earthlings found a book written by lunar men, it was about the history of the whole moon, so the translation of the book's name is *Moon History*.

Earthlings found a story in the book that the lunar people had two branches before 1980, with a population of 4 billion and 2 billion, and one of them wiped out the other one with less members.

The lunar people were stunned to see that earthlings had *Moon History* in their hands: This book showed the bloody, dark side of them, and the number of deaths was three billion (one billion people died in the first branch and everybody in the second one), far more than 140 million that earthlings killed.

So, the moon went to war with the Earth. The earthlings used hydrogen bombs in this war. In this era, hydrogen bombs can even be mass–produced, thousands of miniature hydrogen bombs at a time, or dozens of normal hydrogen bombs at a time.

As we all know, hydrogen bomb is detonated by the high temperature generated by atomic bomb, and atomic bomb can be used to control explosions in the 22nd century, a very small one can turn a skyscraper into ruins. The power of atomic bomb and earthling's control of it has reached the point that people in the past are impressed, so thousands of large hydrogen bomb is completely enough. The moon's weapon, on the other hand, is a few hundred hydrogen bombs.

In case of losing the war, humans have worked together to build the most powerful antimatter weapon ever, called the "Earth Bomb". Ordinary antimatter weapons or even large hydrogen bombs are like firecrackers in front of it, which are not a level at all. On March 19th, 2156, with the exception of the "Earth Bomb," these weapons were mounted on rocket engines and were launched toward the moon.

On March 20th, hundreds of hydrogen bombs belonging to the Moon met thousands of hydrogen bombs belonging to Earth. Soon, a short war began. Since Earth's weapons are numerous and very automated, while all lunar weapons are manually operated and not very sensitive, most of the Moon's hydrogen bombs are destroyed by Earth's hydrogen bombs in a matter of minutes.

On March 21st, the "Earth bomb" was fired at the moon from the same island to let lunar civilization surrender. Unexpectedly, the moon civilization would not surrender to death, and most of them are ready to escape and another day to revenge.

So, the "Earth Bomb" passes through the Earth's ring, and the next morning, the computer inside sends instructions for it to explode. The annihilation begins just a few kilometers from the moon, over Oceanus Procellarum.

The lunar men on the far side of the moon narrowly survived the explosion, and reportedly selected 100 lucky people to build a crude craft (more than six times slower than the fastest ship on Earth) and fly off in the direction of Mars, presumably to settle there.

What people did not know was that this was performance art arranged and most of the lunar people survive. But these information were blocked by the lunar human's powerful computers. What earthlings see is: "Earth Bomb" tore out a very long crack on the surface of the moon, people fall into cracks, tens of millions of people died...

The Earthlings were not feeling bad to learn that some of the moon people had escaped, because as long as they would not return for revenge, the Earth would be safe. Even if they did return, the Earthlings would be quick to spot them, and the Lunar ships were rudimentary and prone to accidents.

Then there was an accident. According to the detection

of relevant personnel, the yield of the "earth bomb" was ten times more than the design! It was impossible to prove who was responsible for this. Had it not been for this accident, a huge impact crater would have appeared on the moon, splitting the Oceanus Procellarum, the largest lunar sea on the moon, in two. But that's not true! In fact, it was not the Oceanus Procellarum that's been split in two, it's the moon! Several huge fissures ran through the moon's northern hemisphere, causing severe gravitational anomalies, and a large portion of the Earth's ring flew over, creating wider, longer, and more deadly fissures, which eventually tore the moon apart and were affected by the debris, which quickly dispersed into the Earth's ring.

The moon disappeared, but it became the halo of the Earth. Today's Earth's rings were much more spectacular than Saturn's which together form a sphere that was only 300 kilometers across at most; and the Earth rings together to form a sphere more than 3,000 kilometers in diameter.

Tides are caused by the gravity of the moon and the sun, and now the moon has turned into the Earth's halo, although the mass is not less, but the gravity is cancelled out, so that only the sun can affect the tides.

Although the Earth's ring was much narrower than Saturn's, it was so dense that if a spacecraft were to pass through the middle, it would quickly be hit by debris and eventually be scrapped (it would have to pass above or below). In fact, the density was so high that the Earth's rings did not have any gaps.

The study of the Earth's rings led to the discovery of many secrets about the two spacecraft and the moon. There is almost no ice in Earth's rings, and even if there is, it melts, and is mostly rock and metal, unlike Saturn's rings, which are made up of rock and ice. Because the Earth's rings reflect a lot of sunlight, they appear silvery white, rather than the brownish yellow of Saturn's rings, presenting a unique beauty.

5 Mars Civilization

In a typical night of Earth, many stars inlaid in the sky, light from various buildings glowed from the ground, but their light is eclipsed by the Earth's ring. During the day, the ring will reflect the sunlight and shine brighter. When the ring blocks the sun, a small part of it will submerge in the sun's light, like a diamond on a silver bracelet. Due to the large amount of reflection, the brightness of the sun will increase greatly at this time.

But without the moon, something is missing from the night sky. Speaking of the moon, in January 2157, the lunar spacecraft was damaged as it approached Mars. The fuel tank used to power the spacecraft broke a hole. The nuclear fuel inside had a high possibility to leak and had to be parked on Phobos (Deimos was on the other side) for repairing.

The lunar spacecraft made an emergency landing on

Phobos, ready to fill holes in the fuel tank with rocks. It was also discovered that the ship had been damaged during the landing, so a lot of rocks were needed to repair it. Also, the ship was hastily assembled from several space shuttles, so it still has some cracks. Also, beneath this mask of rock and soil, Phobos has a large ice core that explains its low density, and rock is simply not enough.

After a few days, Phobos ran out of rock, exposing its ice core and making it much more reflective.

Earthlings discovered this phenomenon and confirmed that the Lunar people wanted to settle on Mars.

The lunar men's ship still has a potential danger. They took a chance and piloted their spaceship to land on Mars. But the craft couldn't be stopped, so it crashed. Out of the 100 men, only 10 survived.

For these 10 native lunar people, Mars is the hell: its thin atmosphere is nothing compared to the Moon's atmosphere which is not so much different from vacuum, and atmospheric pressure is a big deal to them; secondly, Mars has nearly twice the gravity of the Moon, making walking and any sort of moving very difficult. In addition, dust storms are common on Mars.

Under such extreme and demanding circumstances, the lunar men started building a base. First, they took the craft apart, arranged the pieces that still could be used, and filled them with Martian rock and soil, resulting in a hemispherical shell. On its inside and outside sides, walls made of Martian rock were also created. Finally, the Moon men made a hole in the wall and shell. This was a simple door with no handle or panel.

They went into the base, blocked the door with earth, then compressed all the air into a jar, and buried the jar several meters underground. The base could solve most of the problems, but they would still have to accept strong gravity.

The ship was almost destroyed and its remains were buried outside the base, along with 90 lunar men who had died in the accident. On top of them was a piece of metal that had been removed from the ship, with their names written on it. This piece of metal is their tombstone.

After the base and cemetery were built, the lunar men (now Martians) began to make all kinds of household items and furniture, such as beds and chairs. With no tools but rocks, the progress was slow. By June, most of the necessary items had been made and a large number of resources for expansion had been saved. They began to make laws and elect leaders. None of the 10 Martians have names, they only have numbers. For example, the Martian leader's number is 7, because he is the seventh oldest of the Martians. In the matter of fact, he is one of the people who escaped from the destruction of the Tartarus spaceship.

Time flies, and soon it is August 2157. One day, a Martian numbered 9 announced, "There are five males and five females among us, which makes exactly five couples. Our fertility limit is two, so we can end up with ten children. Also, the age difference between the 10 children should not be too big, otherwise they will have difficulty having children."

The view of 9 has been unanimously agreed by everyone. 9 Divide the entire Martian population into male and female, and send one representative each to play "Rock, Paper, Scissors," a game imported from Earth. The men sent 7 and the women sent 9. In the end, 7 plays "paper", and 9 plays "rock", so 7 wins.

Then 9 said, "In a moment, you'll see what I'm thinking of." She separated the two groups, took a piece of white paper out of her pocket and tore it quickly into five pieces. With a barely usable pen she had brought with her, she wrote a number in the middle of each piece of paper. These numbers represent the number of the female group. She crumpled it up into balls, and threw it away.

Next, the group of nine men were pulled to the five balls. Each man was asked to hold one but weren't allow to open it for the moment. Now everyone knew what 9 was doing: She was drawing lots in a fancy way to determine which two people would get married. "Do you see what I'm doing?" she asked.

"We see," the others replied in unison. "We swear to never go back on our word."

"Very well. Now, all men, open your balls," said 9. The group unwrapped the spitball nervously, but had no choice but to accept the result.

7 organize all the proposals made by 9 into Martian laws. Coincidentally, the spitball in his hand has "9" written on it, which means they will be a couple...

Because of the extreme conditions, five women tried to conceive on the same day, and fortunately all of them were successful once.

By the end of June 2158, ten children were born one after another, numbered 11 to 20. This period was the hardest for Martian civilization: ten newborns couldn't work, five women weren't fully recovered, and five men had to support the first two, as well as themselves, so everyone had to work extra hard.

What's more, the children's parents are from the moon, and the bones of lunar newborns are very fragile. The gravity of Mars is relatively strong, which is likely to crush them. But these hardy Martian babies have adapted to strong gravity. At the end of the year, when 11, the eldest of them, took his first steps, all the adults were delighted, especially his parents, Seven and Nine. Soon after, 11's sister, 12, also stood up and paced in the base with 11, falling over a dozen times.

It was also revealed later that 11 and 12 were the most physically fit of the second generation of Martians, but for the time being the remaining eight children were not as fit as them. 13 and 14 came up with an idea: two people land on one hand, hold each other's hand tightly with the other, put their feet on the ground, slowly release the holding hand and stand up, then release the other's hand.

Seeing this, a Martian male, number 8, suggested that to make sure there were no conflicts between the children (if there were, the Martian civilization would split into camps and eventually become extinct), they should be allowed to bond from an early age.

By this time, the remaining six children had risen in a similar fashion. Soon everyone could walk steadily and even run slowly. Much to their parents' relief, their children are better adapted to the Martian environment, where the red planet can no longer be considered a hell.

In January 2206, a new generation of Martians was also born, numbered 21 to 28. With harder bones than their parents and grandparents, they too are getting up and taking their first wobbly steps.

Two children (a boy and a girl) were born later than the other eight. They first child (29) was born at 23:52 on July 13th 2206, while her second (30) was born at 00:03 the following day. They were both children of 20.

After that, the Martians moved underground, where conditions were still harsh, and were never heard from again. In five hundred years, they might do something crazy to the earth...

6 The Solar System's Story

In 2216, earthlings divided a group of astronauts into groups to set up bases on the other three Earth-like planets in the solar system for various purposes, including obtaining resources and increasing population.

By 2230, earthlings had spread throughout the inner solar system and built six space cities around the four gas giants (two each for Jupiter and Saturn and one each for Uranus and Neptune), named after the six continents of Earth: Eurasia, Africa, North America, South America, Antarctica and Oceania.

The earthlings haven't stopped their colonization. By 2245, earthlings had established space cities around Pluto, and a few of the people inside even came to build space cities around Haumea, Makemake, and Eris. The four space cities orbiting around the dwarf planets are named after Earth's four oceans.

On January 1st, 2246, the then leader of the Earth solemnly announced: the Solar System Federation was officially established in January 1st, 2246!

The calendar used by the Solar System Federation is still the Gregorian calendar, but with 2246 as the first year. Since then, the earth people used the Solar Era. In English, the way people say a year is like "Year XXXX of XXXX era".

On February 4th, Year 1 of the Solar Era, the two space cities around Jupiter, *Eurasia* and *Africa*, fought with the two space cities around Saturn, *North America* and *South America*. Finally, *Antarctica* around Uranus, *Oceania* around Neptune, the *Arctic* around Makemake, the *Indian* around Haumea, the *Atlantic* around Eris, and the *Pacific* around Pluto were also involved.

The war is chaotic in the outer solar system, and no space city has reliable allies anymore, they only have fierce enemies.

The four planets of the inner solar system tried to stop their battle, but after the establishment of the federation, the power of the outer solar system became stronger and were completely uncontrollable. There were even several cities threatened the federal government to not intervene, or they would attack the capital of the solar system, Earth.

In November, Year 2 of the Solar Era, the war was stopped by the federation government, and the space cities got along as if nothing had happened.

It is said that a good beginning is half done. The Solar System Federation does not seem to have a good start, and serious internal contradictions appeared just after its establishment. This problem, though has not yet fully reflected, has strongly effected for the future of the Solar System Federation.

The federation grew rapidly over the next few decades in a calm, gentle and peaceful period. In September, Year 70 of the Solar Era, astronomers noticed that Alpha Centauri, which was the closest star that isn't the sun to Earth, was glowing brighter than it should be. That lasted for a while and returned to normal, but there was something missing that puzzled them.

When people pointed their telescopes at the star, what was surprising was that both Alpha Centauri B and Proxima Centauri disappeared, turning into a cloud of gas and rock! Also, A planet appeared next to the remaining Alpha Centaury A! Since it is about 4 light years from the sun, this event would have occurred in the Year 66 of the Solar Era.

Where did the planet come from? Due to the lack of observational data, solar system scientists can only speculate. It was discovered on August 1st, Year 70 of the Solar Era, and cannot be traced back any further. However, the clever humans of the solar system will connect the location where it was first discovered with its present position by a virtual line, and then extend the end of the line. This line passes through the original location of Tartarus, proving that it was once Tartarus' second moon and was later pushed away when Tartarus exploded. Eventually, it was captured by the gravity of Alpha Centauri!

Observations suggest that the planet's surface is completely covered by a 10km-thick ocean (which, in the cold of space, formed a layer of ice, now melted) with a very large liquid iron core under that. The core takes up its centre. Therefore, the planet has a very strong magnetic field, stronger than Earth, and protected this planet's atmosphere (it was once frozen, after it melt and then vaporize, it contained pure oxygen).

The ocean of this planet contain intelligent life that is as powerful as human beings in the solar system. They fired a large number of thrusters in the Year 66 of the Solar Era pushing a planet orbiting Alpha Centauri B and a planet of Proxima Centauri into the two stars at high speed, causing them to explode. The planet of Alpha Centauri B could also be the other planet of Proxima Centauri.

Their motivation was: Alpha Centauri A is a perfect parent star. It is not too big and very similar to the sun, and it is perfect for a planet as habitable and beautiful as Earth.

However, that star belonged to a system with 3 stars,

which would have messed up the orbits of the planets around it, leading to a series of disasters, so they must get rid of the other two stars. Now, there is only one star and one planet left in the system, so people call Alpha Centauri A "Alpha Centauri" and the planet "Alpha Centauri b". Alpha Centauri b is also called Aeolus, named after the Greek god of wind: this planet had fast-flowing atmosphere and frequent storms with wind speeds slightly less than the speed of sound.

In the Year 71 of the Solar Era, Aeolus had already circled Alpha Centauri in 380 days (note: this happened in Year 67 of Solar Era). This was the year that the humans of the solar system received a message of intelligent life in the oceans of Aeolus that surprised everyone with a simple word: "Hello?" The message was sent using the star as an antenna, similar to the 21st century novel *The Three-Body Problem*. Only one of the three suns in the novel remains.

In the same way, the Solar System Federation sent a very short message to the Aeolus: Yes!

In the Year 75 of the Solar Era, the intelligent beings on Aeolus received the text that the solar system sent. They sent their response in the same direction: "Best wishes to the world that replies to our message. Through this piece of information, you will have a general understanding of our world. Our planet was once a satellite of another planet, until that planet was blown up, and our planet was ejected. As you can see, we blew up two stars in this system. Traveling through the cold of interstellar space, the surface of our planet's oceans solidified, forming a layer of ice hundreds of meters thick, but the ice kept our oceans from freezing. This was similar to your Ice Age. This period spans for more than 10000 years, during which we made great breakthroughs in science and technology. However, we have hit a bottleneck, so we may need your help. And a large number of our citizens that learned your existence would like to establish relations with your planetary system."

In the Year 79 of the Solar Era, by the decision of the Solar System Federation, the Solar System agreed to establish relations with the Alpha Centauri system, which would allow both sides to develop rapidly.

From the following year, the two civilizations developed peacefully and helped each other. Intelligent life on Aeolus has made a breakthrough in the field of nanotechnology, while humans in the solar system have made significant progress in controlled nuclear fusion.

In the solar system, there have been many TV shows, movies and novels about intelligent life on Aeolus. Due to the influence of this "Aeolus culture" and the fact that they live in the sea, the crowds call the intelligent life there "sea people", or "waterman" for short.

"Sea people" are very different from humans in the solar system and other Galaxians, because they are actually fish which evolved intelligence. The brain capacity is higher than Galaxians, and they also swim very fast.

Time flies, and more than seventy years have passed. The power of both humans and the "sea people" is not what it used to be. Both systems have developed to a very high degree. In the solar system, antimatter and nuclear fusion are no longer used as weapons, and were used by the public. To self-defend, the humans surround every planet and dwarf planet with an army of 100 million soldiers and 100 thousand starships.

In the Year 152 of the Solar Era, a huge rogue planet flew by Alpha Centauri. It was a very large Jupiter-like planet. It used its strong gravity to pull Aeolus closer to its star, but because it is so fast, it wasn't captured and flew away to the empty interstellar space.

The orbit of Aeolus is lowered so much that it only takes 38 days to circle its star, a tenth of what it used to be. Such a short period of orbit means that it is very close to Alpha Centauri, so the surface temperature rises quickly, and the thick ocean above boils like a kettle of water.

The ocean was dried out, and all living things in it (including all the "sea people") were scorched, leaving only the iron core in the center of the planet. As a result, Aeolus went from a comfortable home for the "sea people" to an absolute hell.

This event was observed in the solar system in the Year 156 of the Solar Era. There are thousands of words in everyone's heart, want to express their gratitude and regret for the "sea people" civilization. After all, it was this destroyed civilization that helped the solar system and itself grow rapidly.

But, there is no turning back from the tragedy. People must recover from the temporary sadness and facing the cruel and dark reality before them. Some people even hated for the scientists and TV stations that report this information, exacerbating the conflict between the public and the scientists and making the case more serious.

In the Year 199 of the Solar Era, the federal government established a new administrative plan, which greatly improved governance and control of the different regions. In the new administrative plan, each planet/dwarf planet is a province, each space city is a city, and the continents of the Earth are different cities with full political equality with space cities. Because of the ease of governance, the Army of the Solar System Federation began to lay off staff, there is even 500 generals who were forced to resign, which later turned out to be a mistake.

After a year, all the existing space cities were renamed. For example, the two surrounding Jupiter were renamed *Jupiter I* and *Jupiter II*, and the two surrounding Saturn became *Saturn I* and *Saturn II*. The same was done for the other planets and dwarf planets. In addition, the six space cities around the Jupiter—like planets were ordered to build four new space cities, one for each planet.

Another five years have passed. The new four space cities and the previous six descend into the thick atmospheres of the planets they orbit to further explore them. The move caused huge controversy, with some fearing that the space cities would crash, just like the Galileo and Cassini probes did four and a half centuries ago. Despite repeated explanations by scientists that they has enough energy to keep it from crashing for the next few thousand years, but it was no use. The public continues to argue and that the old rift between the two is now irreparable.

The event, known as the Space City Movement, eventually evolved from a social movement into a major war in the Year 222 of the Solar Era, known as World War III, between the rebels and the government of the solar system.

According to official data, the war lasted until the Year 457 of the Solar Era, without a break. The Solar Systems Federation was destroyed in this world war lasting 236 years, and the nation developed into the interplanetary age. The solar system rebels destroyed all the space cities after the people inside were transferred to Earth. Humans from other planets have also returned to Earth. Two months later, all humans in the solar system returned to Earth and re-established the Earth Republic.

Amazingly, the federal government of the solar system has been able to resist for two centuries. Nothing natural or human factors could have caused this. Some have discovered that they possess a strange substance that can be made into bombs more powerful than antimatter weapons.

According to analysis by several expert teams, this strange material came from the inner solar system. This theory is based on the fact that the government's headquarter is on Earth, and they cannot send a probe into the outer solar system (conquered by the rebels) during the war. Since this material is in the government's hands, it must come from the inner solar system.

But where exactly does it come from?

Experts are focusing their attention from the entire inner solar system on one place: the sun. That's because Mercury, Venus, and Mars had a lot of rebels at the time because there isn't as many people belonging to the government there. In fact, people of the Earth makes up a half of the total population. The asteroid belt was in the solar system's ring of rebels, making it dangerous for the government. For Earth, the human race has never found anything more powerful than an antimatter weapon on this beautiful blue marble since its birth. So, this strange stuff can only come from the sun.

Presumably, the weapon is thought to have been made after a government probe was launched and passed through the orbits of Venus and Mercury as it headed for the sun, carrying away hundreds of tons of material from the star. This particular substance has been nicknamed "sun" in folk and scientific circles because it comes from the sun.

What is "sun"? That question can only be determined by its image, and there are only ten such images in total. From these images, the sun is a silver–white metal. Now the question is, is it an element or is it an alloy?

On April 1st, Year 458 of the Solar Era, scientists said "sun" was the element with an atomic number of 119. Chemists has been searching for element 119 since seven centuries ago, but experts from all over the world worked together for hundreds of years to find it. To celebrate this event, the Earth Republic government changed the era they use back to the Common Era. According to the Common Era, this year was 2703.

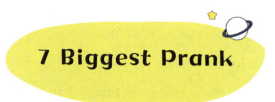

7 Biggest Prank

However, as soon as one problem was solved, two new questions arose: the sun as a yellow dwarf star was unable to produce elements as heavy as "sun", so where did "sun" come from? And why do not elements with such high atomic numbers decay?

Actually, it was a joke. "Sun" is not element 119 at all. In fact, it does not exist. The government had planned for a long time, but finally on April Fool's Day, the biggest joke in history was played on the public! The Solar Systems Federation collapsed at the beginning of the war, which lasted only three years, and the next two hundred years was entirely peaceful.

But soon, there will be a new joke to break the record, and unlike "sun", this one is devastating. On July 10th, 2703, it was discovered that the sun had suddenly begun to shrink as fast as it could be seen in the sky! In other words, the Earth is moving away from the sun!

An hour after the first sighting, Earth's orbit had reached a radius of 1.5 astronomical units, close to Mars' orbit, but because Mars is on the other side of the sun, the two planets did not collide. The sun's apparent magnitude in the sky is about −25, compared with −26 in its original orbit. While that does not sound like much, the sun has actually dimmed more than twice as then.

Another hour later, Earth is 2 AU from the sun, beyond the orbit of Mars and into the inner asteroid belt. As a result, particles from the asteroid belt and Earth's rings get mixed up.

Earthlings, on the other hand, have gone underground, because at two astronomical units from the sun, the cold has become unstoppable.

When Earth emerged from the outer layer of the asteroid belt, it had lost its beautiful ring, and the total mass of the asteroid belt increased more than twenty times in a few hours, all because rocks from the Earth's ring entered the belt.

The earth continues to move away from the sun. Another seven hours later, the Earth was 5.5 AU away from the sun, beyond the orbit of Jupiter. The apparent magnitude of the sun becomes −23.

183

Nine hours after crossing Jupiter's orbit, Earth enters Saturn's orbit, 10 AU from the Sun, which becomes a star of magnitude −21 but is still the brightest object in the sky.

For eighteen hours after passing through Saturn's orbit, people stayed underground and nothing much happened. The Earth then crosses the orbit of Uranus, a full 19 AU from the sun.

People underground were surprisingly calm, and there hadn't been any chaos. Underground people can stay warm, and the environment is not much worse than the life on the surface. Speaking of the surface, it is already snowing there: not snow made of ice crystals, but snowflakes of nitrogen and oxygen in the atmosphere, solidifying in the cold. The Earth's atmosphere was replaced by deep snow on the surface.

Twenty-two hours after passing Uranus' orbit, Earth passes Neptune's orbit with an orbital radius of 30 AU, becoming the most distant planet from the sun.

About five and a half days later (135 hours, to be exact), Earth crossed Eris' aphelion, with an orbital radius of 97.5 AU. After another five hours, the radius of Earth's orbit reached 100 AU, a hundred times more than normal. The Earth's atmosphere has completely disappeared, and the distant sun is just a star with an apparent magnitude of −16.

Today is July 18th, 2703, the day Earth becomes the furthest large object from the sun, even further than Eris, a dwarf planet in the discrete disk.

Seventy-five days passed quickly, and on October 1st, 2703, the distance between the Earth and the Sun reached 1000 AU. If a man stood on the surface of the earth, he could only see snow and stars all around him, and the sun was just an insignificant speck in the sky.

After repeated calculations, the Earth is heading in the direction of Alpha Centauri. The crowd was fearing that the Earth would collide with Aeolus, or the Earth would not reach the habitable zone, or Earth would be thrown out of the planetary system again. But none of this happened, because the Earth stopped at 1000 AU away from the sun and began to orbit it.

Then a familiar planet flew in from the direction of the sun: Mercury. Mercury is moving away from the sun four times faster than Earth, traveling two astronomical units per hour, but the exact time it started moving away from the sun is unknown. Anyway, Mercury caught up with Earth, getting bigger and bigger in the sky, until October 30th, when it became the Earth's satellite, and had slowed down by a lot.

On November 15th, 2703, due to Mercury's inertia, it broke away from Earth and flew back toward the sun. However, once Mercury had gone, Venus had followed, its atmosphere had disappeared without trace, and a layer of dry ice so thick that barely anybody could tell that the planet was Venus. Venus is moving away from the sun three times faster than Earth, but it still caught up with Earth on November 17th.

Fortunately, Venus was hit by a larger asteroid when it was 350,000 kilometers from Earth and shattered into pieces.

The fact of three planets flying away from the sun has puzzled people. And why is Mercury returning? Is that asteroid really capable of crushing Venus? Why did the Earth stop moving away from the sun? When people put their minds to these questions, it turns out that Mars was moving away from the sun on the day Venus was shattered, though only half as fast as Earth. But Mars is headed for Cassiopeia, the exact opposite direction of Centaurus.

On the morning of November 18th, Earthlings made an amazing discovery: Neptune was moving closer to the sun, eight times faster than the Earth! Just seven and a half hours later, Neptune has moved into Mercury's orbit.

The next sequence of events is a headache for Earthling, because no current theories cannot explain it at all. On November 20th, Jupiter suddenly moved directly in front of Mars from its current orbit. After Mars collided with Jupiter, Jupiter moved away from the sun at the speed of Neptune's approach to the sun and flew toward Polaris. On November 21st, Uranus approached the Sun at the same speed. After reaching Neptune's orbit, Uranus moved forward and caught up with Neptune. Due to inertia, Uranus and Neptune's debris crashed into the Sun; on November 22nd, Saturn moved away from the Sun at twice the rate of Jupiter, but also in the direction of Polaris, and then collided with Jupiter; on November 23rd, Ceres flew to Earth and went away.

In summary, the Earth becomes the only planet in the solar system. Although Earthlings have gone underground and built a large number of cities and dungeons, the surface of the earth is no longer suitable for living, and there is not enough space in these underground shelters. There is only one way for humanity to survive: push the Earth back into its original orbit.

In January 2704, humans stopped the Earth's rotation with dozens of planetary engines. Earthlings have 28th century technology, so it does not take much effort. After the Earth's rotation stopped, the sun stopped rising and setting. The planetary engine is sent to the side of the Earth facing away from the sun and then starts to run.

On April 1st, 2705, the Earth returned to the warm embrace of the sun. With the planetary engine, the Earth began to spin again, but because today is April Fool's Day, the world government deliberately pushed the planetary engine in the wrong direction, causing the Earth to spin in the opposite direction. As a result, the sun began to rise in the west and set in the east, causing people to pay more attention to the sun.

8 Antarcticians

On January 16th, 2706, the World Space Agency, or WSA for short, was established. One of its purposes was to send a spacecraft (named *Corona*) with an astronaut on board to the surface of the Sun and collect data.

And the journey was not one–way. The astronaut on *Corona* will not die in the sun's flames. Instead, he or she will use powerful engines to leave the sun and return to Earth.

Corona is scheduled to descend to the Sun's surface with a temperature of 6000 degrees Celsius, and even into the sun's inside, but that's no problem for the spacecraft, which is made of metal with a super–high melting point.

Corona was launched in May 2709 by the latest generation of antimatter powered rocket, *Star Sky 3*. *Star Sky 3* is a little different from previous rocket launches: After the second and third stages detach, its first stage simply breaks into pieces after a short flight, using inertia to propel *Corona* and the astronaut inside toward the sun. Some of the other spacecrafts do not even need a rocket. They have engines so powerful that they can be launched perpendicularly to the ground and fly on by itself. These spaceships do not have fuel, they only have containers full of energy.

Corona has powerful engines on its own, but they are turned off because it is flying toward the Sun through inertia and the sun's gravity.

The astronaut in the spaceship is descended from one of the people sent to Mars by Solar System Federation, so he, his parents, grandparents and siblings were actually born on Mars.

Just like the Martians, people on Mars base only have numbers, and this astronaut's number is 68957986. After that, he was called back to Earth and eventually selected as astronaut on board *Corona*. Right now, 68957986 is floating in the cockpit, heading toward the sun. To reach the sun quickly, he manually turned on the ship's engines and set them to full power.

20 days later, 68957986 arrived at the sun, turned off the engine, and used the spacecraft system to record data, take photos and other work to let humans understand more information about the sun. *Corona* also became the first and last

spacecraft to reach the surface of the sun.

Unfortunately, as the ship crossed the sun's surface, the hull of the ship was hit by a meteorite falling toward the sun. The whole process was filmed by the ship's monitors, but because of the meteorite's speed, 68957986 didn't have time to control the ship to avoid the collision. A large hole was broken in the hull of the ship, the heat of the sun poured out of the hole, burning everything inside the ship, including 68957986.

There was a camera on board that was connected to Corona's ground control, and it recorded the destruction of the spacecraft. Eight minutes later, fear and shock gripped the people in the ground control center as they received images and videos from the monitors.

After months of research, it turns out that small meteorites hit the sun very frequently, about once every ten seconds. Still, the fact that a meteorite hit the *Corona* exactly where it did is remarkable.

Fearing a repeat of the accident, *Corona 2*, originally scheduled for launch in 2710, was later built to be a manned spacecraft orbiting the Earth and renamed *Mediterranean*. With 10 million people living inside, *Mediterranean* was considered a major space city around the Earth.

On June 8th, 2711, the *Mediterranean* captured a spacecraft circling the sun as it approached Earth.

It was certainly not *Corona*, because on July 11th, it had approached the orbit of *Mediterranean* at great speed, and was visible to the naked eye through the windows of the space city. It was also glowing red. *Corona* could do none of these.

On the morning of July 12th, it passed the *Mediterranean*. At this point, the distance between the two is only 100 kilometers. It then flew slowly towards Earth for about 500 kilometers, presumably in free fall after shutting down its engines.

The scary things happened: it suddenly turned on its engines, flew toward the *Mediterranean*, and apparently spotted the space city. You can clearly see that they're the same size. This time, they collided directly. The attack was carried out by the solar spacecraft, which hit the *Mediterranean*'s fuel tank directly, sending it crashing to Earth, but most of the people survived.

Then, the solar spaceship plunged into the Mediterranean Sea, floated slowly back up, suspended in midair, and moved slowly eastward.

It crossed the entire Eurasian continent. It was crossing North America when it suddenly began to fly south, flew across South America, and landed in West Antarctica.

Out of the solar spaceship came an alien. He was more than

two meters tall, less than three meters tall, with long thin arms hanging down to his knees, and five very long fingers on each hand. His face was pale, and beneath his huge eyes were two tiny nostrils, followed by a large mouth with no lips or teeth, and an unusually sharp chin.

The alien is bald and has no clothes or pants. His mouth was large, but when it close, only a small gap could be seen. He had a loaded pistol in his right hand and a dagger in his left.

This alien is from Mars, not the Sun. They are the descendants of the lunar people who settled Mars. It was he who came up with the idea of building this craft after Mars left the solar system and flew back to the inner solar system. His name is pronounced "Rade'ato" and is shortened to "Rae" by Earthlings.

Rae walked straight to the nearest station, shot a glass through the window, got in, and shouted at the people inside, "freeze!"

He said it three times, first in Chinese, second in English, and third in an alien language that only he understood.

Seeing one of the men trying to escape, Ra threw the dagger from his hand and struck the man in the chest, piercing his heart. None of the others dared to move. They watched in horror as Rae pulled out the dagger and threw it to the next man.

Then, with the pistol, Rae shot everybody in the research station. All equipment that can communicate with other people was destroyed. The alien swagger back to the spaceship.

He stopped in front of the ship and shouted at it, "come out!" It was said in the alien language.

The ship's doors burst open, and tens of millions of aliens just like him poured out. Among them was an alien with a white crown on his head, clearly the leader of the aliens. Apparently, he is also a Martian, but with a different name. He is called "Xa'iwosh" by other aliens and "Xas" by Earthlings. "What's the environment like here, Rade'ato?" she asked.

"It is a nice environment here, my king," Rae said to the Sand, getting down on his knees, "but it is a little hot."

"This a good temperature is alright." said Xas.

"My king, it is winter now. When summer comes..."

"It is okay," Sand interrupted, then took what was called a "megaphone", which is a tool to make sounds louder, and shouted to all the aliens, "everybody! We are finally here on Earth, our dream home. Now, I'm going to make a significant announcement."

"First, Earth's civilization is currently weaker than ours, and we could easily take over the planet. But the rest of the earth, as Rade'ato says, is very hot. So, it is enough for us to occupy the white continent."

"Second, having conquered the continent, the earthlings must want to take it back. We must take care not to let the Earthlings take this place!"

"Third, from now on we live on the continent that the earthlings call Antarctica, and although we are still subject to Martian laws, we are no longer Martians! Today, we are Antarcticians!"

A few kilometers away at the South Pole, Xas planted the Antarctic flag designed by himself. Xas also declared the occupation of Antarctica and the establishment of the Antarctic Kingdom.

Many satellites had spotted this phenomenon, and the earthlings immediately launched a general attack on the Martians. Or, for that matter, the Antarcticains. The Antarcticians were so militarily powerful that in less than a day they were able to repel the flood of Earth's armies.

The helpless Earthlings were forced to sign the *Antarctic Independence Treaty* with the victorious Antarcticians. The treaty limited the territory of the Antarctic Kingdom to Antarctica and its surrounding islands. The territory of the Earth Republic shrunk and earthlings were not ruling Antarctica.

Since 2711, the people of the Earth Republic had held a

grudge against the people of Antarctica, who had been enjoying all the benefits of the white continent without noticing that the people of the Earth have really developed their military and technology.

In 2759, the treaty was broken, and the Earth Republic, now stronger than ever before, completely destroyed the Antarctic Kingdom. This is a wonderful thing, and it pleases all the people on Earth.

9 Recapturing Antarctica

In 2740, some earthlings suddenly remembered Tartarus. Their civilization had tried to hit the earth with a rock. That happened six centuries earlier. Although they had not succeeded, the analysis of many scientists found that this attack was extremely effective, and Tartarus had destroyed many of their rivals in this way on their way to Earth.

The Earth of the 28th century had long been capable of making such a large rock, but because the target of this impact was only Antarctica, the rock was much smaller. After the tireless efforts of tens of millions of people, a rock with a diameter of 5 kilometers was successfully created in three days to crash into Antarctica.

Fearing that the rocks would harm other earthlings in the southern hemisphere, the Earth Republic government was announcing all people to evacuate to the northern hemisphere except Antarcticians. There are nearly 80 billion people on Earth at this time, and about 30 billion in the southern Hemisphere, so the evacuation process took nearly 15 years.

The vehicles used in the evacuation were ordinary spaceships. The people of Earth meet at multiple "airports", and then the ships transported the people from each "airport" to the northern hemisphere. These spacecrafts was later given a name: Monster Passenger Ship, or MPS. Different types of MPS can carry 5000 to 10000 people at speeds of around 1000 kilometers per second. It was powered by controlled nuclear fusion technology.

People from the southern hemisphere also needs to have temporary accommodation in the northern hemisphere, so it took a while to settle them down once the evacuation process was over.

In 2755, after the evacuation, a rocket called *Star Sky 4* lifted off from the desert in the northern Hemisphere carrying the rock. The rock is headed for the southernmost continent on Earth.

The rock hitting Antarctica would generate a lot of heat, potentially causing Antarctica's ice sheet to melt, which would surely raise sea levels and flood a number of coastal cities.

It took nearly four years to let everybody leave the coast, and after all was clear, the man-made rock entered the atmosphere and crashed hard near the South Pole.

The rock moved faster than expected, melting the entire Antarctic ice sheet and raising sea levels by more than 60 meters.

Antarctica is rich in fresh water. More than half of the world's fresh water flows into the Southern Ocean. At the same time, a large number of former coastal areas were under water.

The water is diluted by Antarctica's ice sheet, causing massive damage to the ecosystem. At the same time, the increased sea water has drastically changed the Earth's climate.

Now look at Antarctica. Almost all of the Martians who settled at the South Pole died the moment the rock hit the surface, and then instinct drove the remaining survivors away from the impact, towards the sea, and into the sea in a desperate attempt to swim in an inefficient way. However, most of them died in the sea.

By the time there were only 30 or 40 survivors, including Xas, his relatives, attendants, ministers, and one or two commoners. These men sailed a speedboat to South America, the nearest continent.

There are almost no ships in the seas of the southern hemisphere due to the fact that people left the region behind.

Soon, after a satellite spotted the ship, the earthlings sent a battleship (still a crude and outdated one) and made the boat sank. All the Antarcticians on board were buried at the bottom of the sea, where their bodies were quickly eaten by the fish.

In 2760, after all was clear, the evacuees returned to the southern hemisphere, which took ten years. By 2770, the "Return" was completely over, everyone lived and worked in peace and harmony. The Earth became a calm and peaceful planet again, and its ecosystems and climate recovered at an astonishing speed.

Antarctica became an archipelago because the ice temporarily disappeared. It was also a tourist attraction. Because of its huge number of unexplored resources, Antarctica has also become an industrial base with several protected areas. In short, Antarctica became a bustling continent.

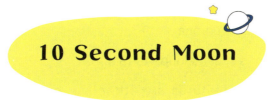

10 Second Moon

In 2800, the moon came back.

What? Isn't the moon gone?

The moon has indeed disappeared, and the moon isn't that beautiful silvery satellite of Earth. Earth's current satellite, or moon, is an ugly black and white object. That's because the satellite combines the following features:

1. The size of the moon

2. Io's volcanoes

3. Oceans of Europa, Ganymede and Callisto

4. Mimas' huge crater

5. Geysers on Enceladus

6. The canyons of Tethys, Dione and Ariel

7. Rhea's rings

8. Titan's atmosphere

9. Iapetus' colors

10. The cliffs of Titania

11. Impact craters of Umbriel and Oberon

12. Miranda's corona

13. Triton's "cantaloupe terrain"

All of these features are attractive, but they add up to something very ugly.

Because it is about the same size as the previous moon, but has only half the mass and distance from Earth, it occupies almost twice as much space in the sky. In addition, it is currently the only moon in the solar system, known to Earthlings as the Second Moon.

All life on Earth needs water. In the subsurface oceans of the second Moon, humans discovered a whole new class of creatures that would eventually destroy life on Earth.

This type of creatures were not very ancient, but they evoluted quickly. This species were about 500 thousand years. They started with a bacteria-like life. The creature, known as the primordial ball, looks like a ball with two tentacles. It had a silvery body covered with a mirror, and is 3 millimeters wide. Their tentacles are probably made of polyethylene wrapped around the nervous system, and the "ball" are made of alkanes and alkenes.

The ball can somehow send an electrical signal that causes the two tentacles to wiggle. The two tentacles of the primordial ball were very long compared to the ball, at 20 centimeters, and were used to catch food. This "food" is actually dust in the subsurface ocean, similar in composition to the body of the primordial ball.

When the primordial ball doubles in weight, it splits into two smaller balls and the process is repeated. A century later, the second Moon's subsurface sea was full of primordial balls, and the amount of dust dropped dramatically. Then, a cluster of primordial balls came together, and the ball among them merged into a larger sphere. The tentacles connected and could catch dust faster than the individual primordial balls.

Under their own weight, these larger creatures sank all the way to the bottom of the subsurface ocean. Over time, these primordial balls lost their spherical parts, leaving only tentacles, which looked a lot more like plants. The individual primordial balls became food for the "plant", hence the name "balltrap plant". Electrical signals are sent from the roots of these antennae.

Balltrap plants are actually animals, but they are rooted to the bottom of the sea and can only move with the current.

Fast forward 50 thousand years. On an unremarkable day 450 thousand years ago, the roots of a balltrap plant broke off from the ocean floor. Hundreds of millions of years later, the descendants of that balltrap plant were able to swim at will, and they looked a lot like fish on Earth. This "fish" was called "underground fish".

The underground fish fed on balltrap plants and primordial balls, both of which became extinct as their numbers increased dramatically.

With food gone, underground fish must kill each other. 30 thousand years ago, a massive natural disaster caused a genetic mutation in a handful of fish, giving them sex for the first time.

The advantage of this is that the underground fish do not have to wait until they have doubled in size before splitting off. They can go through a process similar to human reproduction. In this way, when a single underground fish is attacked, it can mate and give birth to more than 50 young underground fish, or children. Underground fish are viviparous. Also, the time from conception to giving birth is only a few seconds.

If a pair of underground fish of different sexes travel together, they can mate and give birth to young underground fish if they find themselves in danger. With their descendants as cover, two adults can escape, and most juveniles can get out of danger.

Then, some clever subterranean fish discovered: even if they were not in danger, it was necessary to have as many children as possible. In this way, the genderless underground fish will be attacked by the other ones and will be powerless to fight back.

Ten centuries later, genderless underground fish were completely extinct. The others feeding only on dust. This dust is also the food, excrement and secretions of the underground fish, and any dead underground fish will gradually turn into dust.

Because they feed on dust, they do not need to kill each other or have much physical strength, and the underground fish slowly evolved into human beings with a growing brain size.

10000 years ago, the underground fish "civilization" entered the Stone Age. These rocks came from the top of the ocean and the bottom of the sea. The first few languages of them had also emerged. Two hundred years ago, underground fish, or Second Moon men, dug into the crust above the ocean, and through this hole, they saw the stars for the first time. By this time, they were very close to the solar system.

Now, in the year 2800, the second moon has barged into the inner solar system, hurtling toward the only planet in the planetary system and becoming its satellite.

By 2185, the second Man on the Moon had exceeded the current level of technology, six centuries ahead of the Earthlings. The two technologies, which the Second Moon men excelled, were drilling and genetic engineering, far outdid those of today's earthlings.

Look at the Earth. In 2893, the Yellowstone super volcano erupted, and ash blocked out the sun, setting off a chain reaction that wiped out all but one million people on Earth. At this time, the rest of humanity chose a leader. Unfortunately, this "leader" is actually evil.

The leader called himself "Kafawantu Ronbimsin'ikan" or "Kafa" for short. Kafa created a cult and forced all Earthlings to believe. The general content was described by one of his followers as "the Earth is angry, and the evils trapped underground have been unleashed by the Earth God, and step by step they will push all life to death".

All the believers had to do was worship the "Earth God", Kafa, and save life on Earth.

The second Moon men had long set their sights on Earth, intending to claim the planet as their own. Seeing that earthlings believed in Kafa's cult and that their population was so small, the Second Moon men decided to launch an attack on Earth in 2894.

Being outnumbered, the Earthlings were quickly defeated like ants in front of Second Moon's massive army.

By 2895, polar regions, deserts, oceans, the sky, hills, basins, canyons, the underground...were taken over by the Second Moon men who destroyed almost all life on Earth.

11 Time Journey

The surviving Earthlings live in few remote corners of a cruise ship, and even so, they sometimes have to endure the Second Moon's attack into nearby seas.

One day, the army of the Second Moon finally found them. In the panic, one of them remembered that in 2892, the government had sent a spaceship called *Time* into space, which was one of the few spacecrafts that had not been destroyed by the Second Moon. They should now be circling the Earth.

The day before the Earth was completely taken over, he managed to avoid the attack of the Second Moon men and finally killed Kafa. He sent a long radio message to the ship, mainly about the current situation of the Earth people.

The second message sent to *Time* was much shorter than the first, and read as follows:

"Best wishes to the 500 crew members of your ship and hope you find your new home soon. Starting tomorrow, you will be the only people left. Goodbye."

After receiving the messages, the young captain of *Time* sensed danger. The nearest Second Moon spacecraft was only a few kilometers away. They shut down all of the lights on the ship.

He immediately decided to escape in the opposite direction of the Second Moon until there is a safe distance. They began to zigzag through time, or in other words, time travel.

So far, *Time* is the longest living human spacecraft, it can last for 100 million to 150 million years, and it can also travel at half the speed of light 50 million to 100 million years, with a top speed of three quarters of the speed of light. The ship's hibernation system can also allow people to hibernate uninterrupted for 200 million years and wake up healthy. So, there's no need for *Time* to find a new home, and their job is just explore the world.

In early 2895, the captain officially announced that they would travel to the year 3000 to see the future. Although the journey was perfectly safe, the captain was still hesitant and had a picture of his own tombstone in his mind. There was not even his name on it, only the year of his birth and death: "2870–

2895".

Traveling to the past was proved to be impossible, but traveling to the future is. They used wormhole technology to create a wormhole into a parallel universe where time flows much more slowly than in our own, making it possible to travel through 105 years in just 1.05 seconds. A second in this parallel universe is a century in our universe.

In the eyes of people in the universe, they had a long century, but the crew will actually age by just over a second so there is no problem at all.

The captain connected the ship's time machine, or the wormhole—making machine, to his laptop, using simple data cables. When the computer turned on, a window popped up. On the left is an icon of a clock, with the current time displayed below. It is accurate to the level of seconds, so it is just an ordinary digital clock. There are also two buttons in the window, "Confirm" and "Cancel", and on the right is a line of text: "the time machine is connected. please click 'confirm' to continue.

The captain maneuvers the mouse and clicks the "Confirm" button, which changes the contents of the window instantly, with the words "Please enter your destination!" at the top and a text box below.

"Wormhole entered, exit in 1.05 seconds." This appeared in the window when the captain typed in the number "3000.1.1.00.00.00" . 1.05 seconds passed quickly. The computer beeped and the window closed. In the computer's built-in calendar system, today is clearly written as January 1, 3000, as if nothing had happened; but the crew knew they had just crossed a century.

The captain closed the window, turned off the computer, and unplugged the cable. He called the crew together and said, "We have arrived in the year 3000. Go and see the Earth." With that, one of the crew members looked toward the Earth.

Earth is still a lifeless wasteland and has been used by the Second Moon men as an industrial and military base.

The captain exclaimed, "What? The Second Moon man has occupied the Earth for more than one hundred and five years!"

"Come, let's go fast forward to a thousand years later," said the Captain, resuming his calm tone. He performed the same operation as in 2895, but entered the number "4000.1.1.00.00.00" .

Ten seconds later, *Time* travelled to the year 4000. The crew was surprised to find that the Earth's blue oceans had turned white and the Ice Age had arrived.

"What about the sun?" asked the ship's co-captain.

It took a while before anyone realized the seriousness of the problem.

The sun disappeared.

"Go to hell! You have destroyed civilization and all life on Earth, and destroyed the sun! You have destroyed our beautiful seas and lands! You turned the seas of our planet into ice! You have committed unpardonable crimes! You are responsible for this!" growled the captain like a wild animal.

The captain's good mood disappeared, and his eyes, mixed with anger, shock, sadness, and fear, vaguely said: "We go to a thousand years later."

The crew imagined all the possibilities, but the reality was harsher: the Earth and the Second Moon had disappeared like the sun, leaving no shadows behind – leaving only darkness in their place.

"What's going on?" yelled the captain.

Even after the Ice Age, Earth still supports the spirits of the crew. Now the earth is gone, and in its place air and life are gone, and there is no real matter.

"In the past, no matter how far astronauts flew, there was always a spiritual thread connecting them to the Earth. Now the earth is gone, the thread is broken, we are no longer earthlings, murmured the ship's co-captain.

The pilot of the spaceship pointed his hand outside and exclaimed, "Ah! Look outside!"

"Be quiet!" the captain scolded. Then he knew what the man was referring to.

There were nothing out there.

Time is the only thing left in the vast universe. The crew felt the strain ripping at their hearts. Can anybody here be described only as lonely?

A pleasant voice from the ship's artificial intelligence said: "Data indicates that the ship's time machine malfunctioned and disconnected from the spaceship's thrusters, causing us to fail to exit the wormhole in time. The wormhole is already closed. Nearly half a minute has passed now."

Everyone was stunned. The crew were thinking of their own things, but one thought, like an electric shock, deeply planted in their minds: "No!"

At this point, the world in front of them becomes distorted, and all of them soon fall to the ground, probably because of a giant lens was floating in front of them.

It was only after nine minutes into the parallel universe that everyone returned to normal. The doctor on board finally broke the silence: "So by the time we get back, won't it have been years?"

"Yes."

"How far away are we from the Earth?" the captain asked the AI.

The AI answered: "Hundreds of millions of light years away. We must build the wormhole now!"

The captain pressed a button and the AI said, "The wormhole machine has been activated. Please do not move, or the wormhole may not be built successfully."

9 minutes and 22 seconds into the parallel universe, the wormhole was successfully created, and the ship went through at the blink of an eye. They were supposed to be in there for 10 seconds, or 1000 years in our universe, but instead, they spent 562 seconds, or 56200 years in our universe. They were now in the year 60200.

"Well?" That was the captain's first word of the year, also the first word he had spoken in thousands of years.

The AI replied: "Now we are in the year 60200, but it shouldn't matter."

The frozen Earth came into view again, and the Second Moon was still in its orbit, but the Second Moon men was gone.

The captain asked, "With the power of *Time*, can the Second Moon be destroyed? It is just too disgusting and evil."

The answer was, yes.

A few hours later, only a pile of debris remained at the original site of the Second Moon, but only a few pieces were visible at this distance. Now, the Earth is a planet without a moon.

"Let's get some energy," suggested the AI.

"All right." the captain agreed.

The ship stopped sailing for some time. "The energy is full, please confirm the next destination—huge unidentified object! I repeat, we have a large unidentified object!" the AI screamed.

12 Galactic Center Journey

"What is it?"

"The data so far suggest it is..."

The AI's words were interrupted. Everyone screamed, "An alien spaceship!"

Indeed, there was a huge alien spaceship outside the window. Unlike the streamlined human spaceship, this one was pentagonal and about ten meters thick. The alien ship was moving at a slow speed toward *Time*.

"Is there any sign of life inside?"

"Yes, absolutely," exclaimed the pilot, "isn't that life?"

Through the portholes of *Time* and the alien craft, several humanoid objects were clearly visible, along with the name of the alien craft. There were one line written in an alien language and the other in English. Both lines were beautiful and neat, but clearly they are handwritten.

Clearly, the alien ship's English name is "Zmy", so the people on *Time* called it *Z*.

The name of *Z* written in the alien language, was equally clear. It was larger, but simpler than English. No one could read it. It looked like "1 π e". "This line of writing does not have the beauty of Earth's languages," said the co-captain, "it contains something extremely simple. I think this ship belongs to a higher civilization."

The AI thought *Z* was no threat to *Time* and it turned out to be right. When the alien on board Time spotted Time, he took out a pen and wrote on the windows in english: "Hello! Can you read this line?"

In the same way, the captain of *Time* wrote: "Yes!"

The alien on board *Z* erased the first sentence and wrote:

"May you follow our ship?"

The men on *Time* replied: "Why?"

"We are going to take you to our home planet and invite you to join Planet Club."

"But how far away is your home planet?"

"It is about 25000 light years away. We can travel faster than light, so you do not have to worry."

"Z" suddenly opened a door, and at the same time, the

alien wrote: "Come in!"

Time slowly turned around and carefully drove into *Z*. When the *Time* crew came off, one men on *Z* explained, "we are flying toward the nearest wormhole."

"Which is right here!" shouted the pilot of *Z*.

"Z" at full power went into the wormhole. As the ship emerged, the crew of *Time* noticed that there were many stars around and many ships could be seen. They were like a group of peasants who had come to a big city.

"Which direction is your planet, and what is its name?" The captain of *Time* asked an alien around him.

The alien replied, "which way? I cannot see it from here, so I do not know. It is only visible from the ship's dashboard. Speaking of names, our home is called Eplanet and was named after the matter that make up the most of it, it does not exist on your planet."

The captain added, "Our planet is called Earth. Can you see your star from here?"

The alien replied, "Our home revolves around a black hole. I do not know what you call a planet like that, but we do not go around a star. By the way, our home is actually a dwarf planet."

"Thank you."

"You're welcome."

When *Z* reached Eplanet, the captain of *Time* tried to get down, but he was held back, "Please put on your protective clothing! This is a dwarf planet with no air."

"Yes, but why do not you wear them?"

"We are people just like you, but we are adapted to vacuum. So could people from another dwarf planet nearby."

The crew thought this was strange: you are human, and you think we are human, so why do you have such "superpowers" and we do not? But they didn't follow up.

They put on their protective suits and walked down the steps of the ship. Walking was easier than on Earth because gravity was way lower. The co-captain asked an alien nearby, "Do you have culture, politics and art?"

"Yes."

The captain suddenly asked the same alien, "What is the Planet Club you were talking about earlier?"

"Ha ha ha, it does not exist. We invited you here to live on our planet, and the Planet Club is just an excuse."

"You living on this planet, that is a great thing." said the captain of *Z*.

"Are there actually benefits? How can we go through our life while wearing protective clothing all day? Besides, there's too much radiation here near the galactic center. How can we possibly survive?" roared the captain of *Time*.

"You will have access to all our technology, which will benefit the people of your planet! When your planet was far from your star, it was something we did to let you know us!" said the captain of the *Z*.

"I object! I've just tested, and you're not smart enough to understand our technology, or to know that we're the ones who pushed your planet beyond the discrete disk by yourself. Plus, you're angry at us! Please get out of here," the co–captain of *Z* said, to the approval of the captain of *Z*, which left the crew of *Time* confused.

"Your behavior cannot be accepted! Do you know how much money and effort it cost us to push the Earth back into orbit?" yelled the captain of the Time.

"Then who made you have a low IQ?" the captain of *Z* pushed back.

"We curse your planet!" cried the crew of *Time*. That led the whole crew being brought to the court of Eplanet. Soon, the results came back.

With the wooden hammer in the judge's hand, the crew returned to the *Time*, but this time they were expelled.

After *Time* was forced to take off, the crew decided to return to Earth. But without wormhole technology, Time will arrive in the solar system in thousands of years, and who knows what will happen then?

So, *Time* officially changed its name to *Galaxy* and became a stray spaceship. Their current goal is still different from the one given to them by the man who killed Kafa. The new goal was: return to Earth!

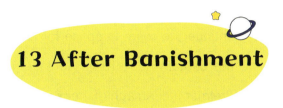 13 After Banishment

In 60201, the wormhole maker of *Galaxy* was reopened. The head of engineering discovered that it had been invaded by the inhabitants of Eplanet in a way that is extremely difficult to repair. The repairs and restarts alone took eight years. During that, the rest of the crew did not waste their time, they were guiding *Galaxy* through the collection of scientific data.

These data will not be buried in the dustbin of history; they will be useful in the future.

In 60210, after thousands of test runs, the wormhole maker restarted after a decade!

In less than half a minute, the crew was back to Earth. It was still covered with ice. It is freezing, and the only heat on the surface is probably volcanoes.

The earth had become frozen, with only microbes like

bacteria roaming above and below the ice. The conditions were so bad that *Galaxy* left without looking. Leaving behind a planet that had once hosted all kinds of life.

The Galaxy continued to roam in space for another decade. Over the years, the captain had often had a dream about an angry old lady in a helmet staring at him, her bright eyes shooting flames through the helmet's mask. The meaning was clear: You left me alone, twice!

One day in 60220, the captain understood. That person represented the "Earth". The captain ran out of his room with a gun with only one bullet in it.

Do not underestimate it, this bullet is a mini atomic bomb. When the captain pulls the trigger, the ship's crew will be buried in space, and the last humans will be extinct.

The captain put his gun to the pilot's forehead and shouted, "argh!" With that, he gently placed his index finger on the trigger.

The pilt felt an indescribable fear. He involuntarily raised his hands, and everyone else did the same.

There are nothing except for a pistol that was about to kill 500 people and silence.

One second passed.

Two seconds passed.

Three seconds passed.

On the one hand, the captain's mind is occupied by infinite hatred, "Earth" and the captain's dialogue kept appearing in his mind. On the other hand, he thought he would be executed by the world, so the captain delayed pulling the trigger.

With a smile, the captain said in a voice only he could hear, "there is no one else. Now I am the leader of the race, I can…"

The voice of the mysterious woman in the captain's head went, "Go ahead and kill everyone!"

"No! I cannot exterminate the human race, " the captain said, teeth grinding, "I cannot kill my crew who have been with me for tens of thousands of years!"

He did not put down his gun. He threw the gun out, and it flew into the captain's room and into the drawer where it had always been.

That night, the voice of the Earth appeared again in the captain's dream, but with a young man beside her. The man was tall and handsome, with a loud voice, but his face was gray, with no expression on it, only dark spots. He was near the earth all the time. The two people said at the same time, "hello! You…" That was interrupted by the captain's sleep words:

"The moon! You're still there! You weren't bombed by our

ancestors!"

The captain dreamed that he rushed forward excitedly, but was pushed away by the moon.

"Listen, boy," snarled the man called Moon, "we are your elders. Show some respect!"

The moon recovered his normal voice and spoke again: "Although I have been blown to pieces, the civilization I nurtured still lives on! Everything you've heard before is wrong: there were indeed lunar men on Mars. They were volunteers, used to cover up the fact that none of the Lunar men were killed. Most of the Moon men, that is, all but the hundred, escaped."

The moon's words were again interrupted by the captain: "Oh."

"The remaining Lunar men used their stock of ships (traveling at half the speed of light) to land on a planet in the center of the Milky Way called Plumbia by its natives."

"This planet, like the moon, has no atmosphere, but the surface soil is rich in lead. Of course, the metal is not toxic to lunar people. We quickly adapted to its environment and integrated into the planet.

The indigenous peoples and other nearby civilizations were much more technologically advanced than we are. Because we had broken the laws of Plumbia, we were transported by the natives to other planets, tortured, and freed nearly fifty years later, exiled into space. Then we realized that many civilizations in the galaxy were far more developed than we were. Now, I sincerely invite you to join us."

At last he added, "I can do this because we have learned how to control and divert dreams. The rest of the crew was having the same dream. If you want to join us, press one; Otherwise press zero."

The next morning, the crew shared the dream with each other. But no one knows the last sentence's meaning yet.

Suddenly, out of thin air, a square keyboard appeared. It had one and zero and another key below it saying "confirm". The keyboard has an area of 4 square meters and each side is 2 meters long.

"I think we should help them for the following reasons: first, they are also an oppressed race and should be rescued; second, we should be on our guard against planets like Plumbia, and do our best to please them, for obvious reasons; third, once we've united with the Lunar men, we will have the opportunity, the confidence, and the weapons to take revenge on Eplanet, who exiled us; fourth, There are more races at the heart of the galaxy, and contact with them will help us understand other planets. So, I think we should press '1'," the co-captain said.

The captain agreed with his co-captain, pressed "1" decisively and then clicked "confirm"; the keyboard turned into a window. That said, "Please send your coordinates." Below the line is a text box and a fluorescent keyboard. When the captain entered his coordinates, a ship arrived, and it was later revealed that this real-time communication and high-speed ship was only possible through a wormhole.

The craft is spherical but has a crater in the surface, much like the Death Star from Star Wars. The name of the craft was clearly visible: "Luna". It was called Luna by the crew. Those who disagreed to pressing "1" were told off by the captain for calling the ship "the Moon of Death".

Below that is a line in an alien language, much like Chinese. The captain read, "The left side of the first word is '人', the right side is '一'. The top of the second word is '从', and the bottom part is '龙'. The third word is '从' and the fourth word is '皿'. It seems to correspond to the letters 'Luna'."

Luna fired an arcing, unknown substance through the crater and sucked *Galaxy* into it.

The captain of *Luna* came over and said, "hello! In fact, our real intention is to invite you to join us in building a new planet, because we, just like you, have become wanderers like Gypsies, and we need to build a planet. However, we only have raw materials, not enough technology; You only have technology, not enough materials. Of course, I am talking about the corresponding fields. Our comprehensive level of science and technology is much higher than yours. That's why you were invited here. As for this ship, it was built before our exile, as a precaution against danger."

"Lying to us. Here we go again..." the crew grumbled.

The captain of the *Galaxy* was the first to calm down: "It is not lying. But cannot we just live on your ship?"

One of the Lunar men shook his head slowly and said, "No, no. Such a relatively small ecosystem is also vulnerable to the harshest thing in the universe: time. Huge bodies like the Earth and moon can experience strong winds and waves without being damaged; And our ships, even if they sail in small drains, will eventually capsize."

A look of surprise gradually appeared on the captain's face. The sailor immediately guessed what he was thinking. He laughed and said, "although I come from the moon, where there are no ships, waves, or little drains, I do know what they are." Other *Luna* crew members agreed.

"But what is this artificial planet even for?"

The moon crewman replied, "there are two options: one, become a generational ship that roams the universe; two, continue to orbit the Earth."

"In short, it is either a headless fly aimless in space or a new satellite of Earth." Seeing that the crew of the Galaxy did not understand the meaning of the man, the co-captain of *Galaxy* blurted it out.

"Can you get all the data from the ship? We're going to start building the planet," the moon crewman added.

"How long would that take?"

"I do not know, maybe about a year."

"So soon!"

"Well, yes. Before we were exiled, we got a lot of technology from Plumbia. Also, you are Earthlings, less than a thousand of you, and there are nearly 10 billion lunar men here. You are obviously unable to adapt to our lives, so you can transfer your consciousness and minds into the bodies of lunar men."

"What about the original consciousness of the body?"

"Those bodies belong to the ones who does not care their own lives. In our society, such consciousness is extremely rare and immoral," this tone was strange to come out of his mouth,

"you should have no objection to the fact that we have replaced the owners of these bodies with your noble consciousness. Of course, they're all healthy. You do not have to worry about that."

"Through you, I know a little more about the moon's culture! I totally agree with that."

Two days later, the minds of the 500 crew members were transferred to the bodies of Lunar men, whose original bodies were being studied by scientists.

Then, an artificial planet has been built, taking the second option proposed by the Moon crew. It looks and acts almost exactly like the original moon and was called the Third Moon, where 10 billion lunar people will settle and establish the Lunar Republic.

14 Third Moon

All the data from *Galaxy* was stored in one of the tallest buildings on the Third Moon. It was called the Lunar Database. It stored all the information known to the Lunar people, and it also deduced new knowledge from the known information. All the people with relevant documents can go in to inquire about the information. The Lunar Database was an e−book, a library, and a computer. Of course, the Lunar Database was always heavily guarded, and illegal access was not easy.

As for the *Galaxy* itself, it was preserved in the Third Moon First Museum, where anyone could come and see it.

It was only a month after the Third Moon was built that the captain learned the name of the lunar crewman: Sikakiwin.

During a conversation, the captain (who was no longer the captain and now serves as the Vice President of the Lunar

Republic, changing his name to "Kermaniro") asked Sikakiwen (another vice president of the Lunar Republic), "Sikakiwen, what did you do?"

"What do you mean by 'do', Kermaniro?"

"Career, of course."

"I used to be a helium-3 miner. On the moon, this job is also known as 'miner'. Later, I became a soldier, and a astronaut, hibernating for a long time, then at last, I went to this ship to serve as a co-captain."

"You were the co-captain!" said Kermaniro, surprised.

"Yes."

A week passed and the two men again had a private conversation. "Why does not the Lunar Republic have a flag?" Kermaniro asked first.

"A flag? Are you kidding? What is a flag?"

"No kidding. A flag is a piece of material on Earth used to symbolize a country, or in other words, rectangles that represent a country."

Sikakiwen hesitated, "Can you show me some flags?"

"How can I remember so many flags? I'm going to check out the Lunar Database."

From the Lunar Database, Kermaniro found several flags from the 21st and 22nd centuries.

Sikakiwen finished, shook his head and said, "It is too complicated. You've lived on the moon for a long time. Did you know that the moon people worship white? I'm sure you know. Adopting these colorful flags as the national flag…just does not fit. We could make a proposal to the president, or design a flag. By the way, your flags has a very clever meanings."

"Yes, I cannot agree more."

At the end of 60221, the president of the Lunar Republic and the former captain of Luna, Ceelesan, planted a solemn and pure white flag on the South Pole of the Third Moon under the gaze of ten billion lunar men.

Since there is no wind on the moon, the flag is not hung the same way it is on Earth, or else it will fall down. The flagpole is T-shaped, about 2 meters high, and at the very top is a 1-meter-long stick from which the flag hang.

The lunar flag, like most flags in Earth's history, is rectangular, with the most common ratio of 3:2. Kermainiro thought: does flying the white flag means to surrender?

Thought of this, he smiled. Ceelesan snapped, "Why are you laughing?"

"On Earth, the white flag means surrender."

The good news for Kermaniro was that Ceelesan heard the word "surrender" as "peace" and Kermaniro received no punishment.

Unfortunately, Ceelesan died in 60222. Kermaniro and Sikakiwen discussed and decided to store their minds, or souls, in one body and be the president. Eventually, for reasons everyone knows but no one dares to say, they decide to put the two minds in Sikakiwen's body.

When their minds were united, they changed their name to Cysas, which means "new president" in a Third Moon dialect. According to the laws and regulations of the Third Moon, both people were considered "dead" even though their consciousness was still there.

Ironically, the captain (Kermaniro), who thought he was going to die while time traveling, miraculously lived tens of thousands of years. 57352 years to be exact.

The day Cysas took office was later designated as the Lunar National Day, which is April 2nd. In 60223, Cysas started the Third Lunar Era, or "Lunar Era" for short.

On April 2nd, Year 2 of the Lunar Era, the Lunar Republic had its president election. By all accounts, Cesar is very popular, with an approval rating of 81% at the first year of the Lunar Era, which is pretty high on the Third Moon.

In addition, Cysas was recognized as one of the most wise, powerful, kind, intelligent, and fair presidents in lunar history, every bit as good as Ceelesan. People thought he will be a popular figure to be followed by all presidents after him. But in a bizarre twist of fate, Cysas failed to serve for another term.

A week later, with a heavy heart, Cycas exclaimed in public (as part of the Lunar Republic's presidential handover ceremony), "I give the title of President of the Lunar Republic to Hurninau."

Hurninau is the new lunar president, whose name means "Son of God" in one of the moon's ancient languages.

Over the course of his presidency, Hurninau, who calls himself the "Moon King", has transformed a prosperous republic into an immaculately corrupt kingdom.

On his eleventh day as president, Hurninau announced that he would rename his country the Lunar Empire.

Since Hurninau's succession, Cysas has not been seen in public, living in a tiny house on the outskirts of Tycho Crater on the Third Moon. On the day the Lunar Empire was founded, he suddenly came to Hurninau's house and shouted, "go away! You do not deserve to be president of the third Moon!"

Hurninau mistakenly believed that a normal was Shouting outside and sent his own guards to arrest him. The guards, however, were dumbfounded at the sight of the man they were about to arrest, and immediately bowed in horror before

Cysas, not even daring to approach him. The leading guard said,

"Forgive us, my Lord." With that said, he led all the guards into Hurninau's house and escorted him out.

Cysas gave the lead guard a stern look. He pulled out a knife and put it around Hurninau's neck, to the cheers of the crowd.

A pleading look flashed into Hurninau's eyes.

Suddenly, the crowd fell silent. Cysas, they thought, was a benevolent president who had never allowed any executions (on the Third Moon, executions cannot be done without the president's approval). But he also hates people like Hurninau. The crowd fixed their eyes on the three people.

Cysas thought that some people had developed sympathy and pity for Hurninau, and if Cirnino was not executed as soon as possible, there would be no chance to do so because the crowd would oppose him. He said, "Without further ado, are you willing to kill him?"

Hurninau's hope came back, but his despair also developed a little more. The two emotions made him shake his head violently.

Then Cysas remembered all of his crime. It was clear that his soul was struggling. There was no reaction from the crowd; they are also hesitating, waiting for the president's next instructions.

After reading the crowd's intentions, Cysas said quietly,

"If you are silent, I will execute him; if you present your opinion, then I will decide."

The crowd remained silent, whether they wanted the execution or were hesitating. This is Cysas's genius: even if some people are still deliberating and silent, he can still justify the execution of Hurninau.

Cysas smiled and added sternly, "On the count of three, if you do not speak..."

He looked back at Hurninau, "Then you're going to die!"

He shouted, "Three! Two and a half! Two! one and a half! One! A half! Zero!"

Cysas was not in a hurry, pointing a finger at Hurninau. "You only have seconds left to live. What else can you say?"

"I have nothing more to say." Hurninau said slowly.

The silent crowd suddenly shouted, "Kill him!" Apparently, what they were looking forward to finally happened.

15 To Earth

The next day, Cysas announced his succession and made a public speech. In the middle of the speech, he recited a poem and said, "In this poem lies my great goal. Of course, it is not deeply hidden."

As he recited the poem, his tone was very composed, and his voice was low and slow, quite different from the impassioned speech:

"Funny people, living in a crowded place.

Everyone knows, there's an empty one.

That has these wonders: wind, fire and lightning.

But no, nobody knows it is the blue star in the sky.

The ignorant, that star is in front of you.

Where is it? The crowded place goes around."

In the audience, someone asked, "Find a blue star?"

"Not quite."

"Living in space?"

"No."

The correct answer came from a five-year-old (maybe a six-year-old) who said, "go to Earth?"

"That's right! Tell me how do you know, child."

Speaking to the president under the attention of so many people, the child was not nervous at all. She said calmly, "there are already 10 billion people on the moon. For a moon with a diameter of only more than 3000 kilometers, it is obvious that it is crowded; the earth is empty now, and there is no one living there; on earth there is wind, fire, and lightning; the earth is a blue planet, which is the blue star in the poem; the earth is the nearest celestial body to us; finally, the Earth is the planet which our moon orbits."

"So that's it. It seems that you are not only smart, but clever! Also, I noticed how confident you were when you spoke. Good!" Cysas praised. Returning to his usual tone, he concluded:

"The third Moon simply wasn't big enough, because we didn't have enough material to construct it. Therefore, we need to migrate to the Earth which is larger. Although our population growth has been slow, but we still have a lot of people, the (third) moon cannot support our life. In order to adapt to Earth, we need to 'become' Earthlings!"

He hesitated and continued, "In fact, the spaceship *Galaxy* from Earth has all the physical information about a normal Earthman and the body of the same person. This man was a member of the ship's crew when he is alive. We can take this information and his body and 'make' an Earthling. Then, we'll clone this person 10 billion times. Scientists have shown that when cloning an Earthling, the individual's memory is not preserved, and we will have to transplant the consciousness of each Lunar man into the body of these clones."

A day later, the "manufactured" Earthman has appeared, and Cysas' speech continues, but the content is less important.

Two days later, his speech had stopped. Using a technique that has never been revealed, they cloned 11 billion people in four minutes (the extra billion were spares) and then transplanted the consciousness of all the Moon men into their bodies.

The police of the Third Moon took advantage of this opportunity to arrest a large number of thieves, bandits, and wanted criminals. The police forbade their consciousness to be transplanted. They either came to Earth and died because they didn't adapt, or were executed by the government on the third Moon and had no way to live. A common way in lunar history of weeding out baddies was banning them from an event in which the whole nation participates.

Now, the moon people are all Earthlings.

Since there is no sun, the surface of the Earth is frozen and unimaginably cold. So, the third Lunar government converted nuclear fusion engines of *Luna*, which provided kinetic energy, into an artificial sun, which provided heat. The nuclear fuel on *Luna* made up more than 90% of the spacecraft's mass, and because it was hydrogen and highly compressed, there was plenty of it. The Third Moon man made a star called the Second Sun, and it was a real star.

The Second Sun has almost the same diameter, temperature, and distance as the sun, so it can provide enough heat. Later, it was also called the "sun" and, aka "Child of the Sun God" by some non-mainstream religious groups.

At this point, I have to mention the religious culture of the moon. The moon had a religion before AD 1389, with factions large and small, collectively known as Heliosism. The moon's rotation period is very long, so the days and nights are very long. During the long night, these then uncivilized lunar people lived very hard and invented the so-called Sun God. In 1389, someone finally suggested that the night must be followed by the day, and gave a systematic way of surviving the long night. Overnight, most of the moon people stopped believing Heliosism.

As the nuclear fusion of the Second Sun began, the Earth's ice began to slowly melt. To speed up Earth's thaw and turn into a habitable planet, a suitably sized rock was taken from the Third Moon and hurled at Earth, using the resulting heat to melt some of the coldest ice sheets.

Because the rock was small enough, the surface temperature of the Earth was still suitable for Earthlings, and certainly for these Moon people with Earthlings' bodies.

By this time, the busy people had cloned all the harmless creatures on Earth, which was not a problem for such anadvanced civilization. It only took one year.

In Year 4 of Lunar Era, the 10 billion Earthlings and creatures who were about to return to Earth set out from the third Moon. All the plants are cultivated, or planted, in one space, with separate compartments for animals and huge cockpits packed tightly with humans. At Luna's speed, the journey would take only thirty minutes, so the men would have to endure only half an hour of crowding.

Inside, Luna was equipped with a number of airplanes that took all the plants and animals to their original habitats before landing. In the end, the only living things on the ship were some bacteria and Earthlings.

The Luna slowly touched down on the beaches of East

Asia. This beach was once part of a bustling city of more than 20 million people in the 21st century AD, and although it has been ruled by the Earth Republic and the Solar System Federation, and its name has changed many times, the city's bright lights and tall buildings have not changed at all during those times.

The Second Moon men had destroyed all life on Earth, and these tall buildings had long since collapsed. Now their ruins had been taken away by the planes of the spaceship. Traveling much faster than the Earth's escape velocity, these planes carried the traces of Earth civilization into space.

The ship landed and the humans went home. The hatch of Luna opened, the gangway buzzed down, and Cysas got off first.

An hour later, all the Earthlings were off the ship, and with everyone watching closely and carefully, Cysas walked into the sea. These people had never seen Earth's oceans so close, so they followed him.

When they reached knee-deep water, Cysas and his men fell on their knees, raised their heads to the sky and screamed, "ah!"

He was a man with two minds, and the emotions that filled his brain at this time made him suddenly lost all grace.

He stood up and pounded his chest like a gorilla. He said, "I'm back!" The crazy crowd followed him.

That night, the new Earthlings were very excited. After that, the crew began to dismantle the ship and build a building. During that time, 10 billion people on Earth lived inside the spaceship. They are a crazy race, and this is a crazy plan, mainly because this building could support 10 billion people living inside.

But it does not matter, the moon was originally a place where alien lunatics and psychopaths were exiled.

Each room has a bunk bed, and food is delivered by waiters (more than 100 million of them). Earthlings will live in this building for a year.

In the Year 5 of the Lunar Era, Cysas declared the Terran Era, changed the country's name to Earth Republic, and succeeded the president. At the same time, more and more buildings, mostly houses, are being built around the world with the help of robots.

In the Year 2 of the Terran Era, buildings such as shopping centers and office buildings began to appear one after another. The original building has been razed to the ground, and all its components have been recycled.

A digital version of the lunar database is also there, stored in a building next to the Earth Republic's presidential palace. Items from all lunar museums, galleries and exhibitions are also now in the building in digital form, the new Lunar Database.

As for the Earth Republic's presidential palace, its located on the Earth's capital, the great city in East Asia.

Next, the last big thing before the government was to decide the administrative division. It took a year to complete, and the Earth was divided into 21 regions: North America, Rockies, Great Lakes, Central America, Andes, South America, Northwest Europe, Southern Europe, Eastern Europe, North Africa, West Africa, Central South Africa, East Africa, North Asia, West Asia, Central Asia, South Asia, East Asia, Southeast Asia, Oceania, and Antarctica.

The Earth Republic was very much the same as the one founded in the 22nd century. They even had the same flag. The people have no complaints, the economy was growing steadily, and all corruption problems were solved.

But the good days would eventually pass and the great wheel of time continued to roll forward, unstoppable. No one or thing could stop it. In the Year 1453 of the Terran Era, the Republic was declared dead, just like how the Byzantine Empire had fallen in AD 1453. The Republic became a land of corrupt officials, robberies and separatist forces.

The Earth Republic of the Year 1452 of the Terran Era was still a "healthy" nation, but after the year passed, the Earth plunged into endless darkness, as if a sorcerer's magic to maintain youth had suddenly failed and the long history of it, about one thousand and five hundred years, had suddenly been revealed.

The name of the Earth Republic had been changed to "Cantoncong Empire", and the land area was only 200000 square kilometers. True to its name, it has become an empire headed by Calori, a fierce, cruel and vicious emperor. Calori had ordered officers to imprison captured soldiers and abuse them.

The Earth was divided into hundreds of various powers, and wars were fought over and over. The World War IV finally began.

In the Great War, the Cantoncong Empire won every battle , and unified the world in less than a year, except for Antarctica.

The Earth needed a god who can unify the world, but not as brutal as Calori. This man was the eldest son of the last president of the Earth Republic, and his name was Globia.

Globia was born in the Year 1443 of the Terran Era. Ten years after he was born, the republic collapsed and he was secretly sent to Antarctica, the most peaceful place on Earth. His father, the last president of the Earth Republic, and his mother were murdered.

In Antarctica, Globia was accompanied only by a bodyguard who also served as a teacher. There was also a police dog.

Many citizens fled from Cantoncong to Antarctica. In order to live a peaceful life, they: did not fear the cold; made Globia the president; came to Grobia's banner.

So Calori sent the army to invade Antarctica. These armies are not really under the command of him. In fact, if he were dead or missing, the Empire would cease to exist. Globia discovered this and sent ten assassins to kill Calori but none of them succeeded. Fortunately, the tenth assassin escaped and stole a huge amount of information to bring to Grobia.

When Calori attacked Antarctica, Grobia sent out hundreds of thousands of wanted posters: "Whoever brings Calori's head to me will be rewarded!"

As the saying goes, a great reward makes a brave man. As soon as these wanted posters were posted, the queen of the Empire came to reveal them. She did this because she had been forced to marry Crowley, and she did not like it.

That night, she pulled the knife from under his pillow, and a minute later came to the harbor with his head in her hands.

She took a boat to Antarctica, met Globia, and laid the bloody head of Calori down at Globia's feet. As she was about to sail away, Globia placed two bags of gold on her ship.

In the year 1460 of the Terran Era, Globia re−established the Earth Republic. This time, it grew faster and faster, catching up with Eplanet in the Year 1500 of the Terran Era.

In the Year 2025 of the Terran Era, a man named Stars

became president and announced the colonization of nearby planets. Not only that, Stars was a crazy careerist, he was trying to take down the entire galaxy and make this country rule the milky way.

What he didn't know was that there was an alien civilization in the universe hiding in an unknown place and had once wiped out all life in a planetary system, but no one outside knew about it.

16 Hidden Dangers

This civilization is Shiva. They left only a handful of survivors after their planet lost the war with Earth. Thus, they became an interstellar civilization, its name is officially changed to "the Hidden". there are individuals of the Hidden throughout the galaxy.

The Hidden are down to 10 million members, most of them were living on ships. 1% of the population consists of their leaders, called "master". With the exception of the masters, almost all of them were called sweepers, or usually cleaners, who attacked and exterminated civilizations weaker than themselves.

Cleaning was a humble occupation in hider culture, but one that was very successful in battle could become a master. Of course, the cleaners were also divided into different levels.

In the year 2026 of the Terran Era, a cleaner named Singer discovered Earth while wandering. It was entirely accidental, and he was not concentrating as he did so. He was singing a song.

Compared to the masters who have an average age of 600, the singer is still very young. He was born in 1825, and was 200 years old. He didn't have any outstanding achievements then, so Singer is the lowest and most common type of cleaner.

Ten years ago, in the year 2016 of the Terran Era, Singer discovered a group of inferior civilizations at the galactic center. There is no connection between them. Singer used antimatter weapons to turn every planet in their planetary system into a barren field. Together, these civilizations are far less powerful than the Earth Republic, much like the Earth of the Middle Ages. He sang the same song while discovering these planets and the Earth:

"How wide is the world!

It has beautiful spots in spacetime.

We hide in the dark universe.

Waiting for the next prey.

Let all things bow down at my feet.

It is my pleasure to conquer and rule.

I'm moving forward unscrupulously!"

This time, however, the discovery of the Earth Republic led

Singer sensed an opportunity for promotion. "A belated 200th birthday present," the Singer called it. Although the Earth Republic was at a lower level of development than the Hidden (estimated to be only one-third of it), it was one of the strongest civilizations Singer had ever seen. Once Singer wiped out this civilization, then⋯

Not daring to think any further, the singer hurried to the nearest master (beyond 100 AU) and applied for a weapon called mathematical destruction.

The elder questioned, "do you know the civilization, singer? We are a cautious civilization. Cautious!"

The singer questioned, "why cannot I use mathematical destruction? You mentioned our civilization. Do not you know the phrase 'act first, think later'?"

"Oh, why do not you see? This weapon has never been used or even tested. It is not safe. I am looking out for your safety. Do you have any idea how much a 'mathematical destruction' can cost? The answer is one million, enough to buy 500 million bottles of water. Do you know how many of these weapons there are today, Singer? Why take the risk?"

"How many?" Singer really does not know that.

The master held up a finger, "one."

"Excuse me, master. The civilization I just discovered

calls itself mankind, and they are so powerful. If they have a technological explosion, they will find us. Besides, our planet was occupied by them before," replied Singer.

The elder shoved the weapon at the end of Singer's forelimb and interrupted very impatiently, "Yes, yes, take it."

The singer arrived at the shuttle, pressed a button on the wall, and the machine controlling the shuttle throws "mathematical destruction" at the capital of the Earth Republic, Earth. The singer was only 20 AU away from Earth, not far from the orbit of Uranus.

In ten days, it was expected to turn Earth into a very scary world. In that world, zero equals any number, and math and science will collapse.

Mathematical destruction was a weapon based on mathematical laws, which was said to be the terminator of mathematics and technology, because when zero equals one, if you multiply both sides of the equation by any number, then zero can equal any number, and therefore any number is equal.

When all numbers are equal, all living things die, and nothing can live in this world, for obvious reasons. In ten days, humans must escape from the world where the only number is zero.

17 Micro Universe Room

Time flies. Nine days had passed. Humans had heard of "mathematical destruction", and they tore the space, created a crack that led to a region independent of this universe.

This space was like a micro parallel universe but not a parallel universe exactly, due to its independence, people could escape the attack of "mathematical destruction". It was a cube, one kilometer on each side. It had resources to let one person live for two years, and its time passed at the same rate as the universe, hence was named micro universe room, or MUR. If there were two people, they can only live for a year, which is enough time to find new planets.

As unfair as it is, only two citizens will survive.

The entrance to MUR is a door two meters high and one meter wide, with no door panel and only a glowing border to show it is position, which is like a rectangular icon taken from the computer, a symbol of simplicity. The door, which was once a kilometer in the air, has now been pulled to the ground. The two people that is lucky enough came to the door, one of them was the Earth Republic President – Stars, and the other was just a woman with no name. Soon they were jumping through the door, hand in hand.

When they entered MUR, a soldier at the door pressed a button, and the glowing border suddenly went out (it is actually flying to space in light speed). The people were furious because they had lost their last chance of survival. There is a difference between the door and a wormhole, and that button controls its position.

A woman tried to get through the door where it should have been, and a man threw stones and sticks at it, but nothing happened as if the door had never existed.

Another woman shouted at the soldier, "Open the door! Open the door!"

The soldier held the switch that opened the door to the universe, and under the pressure of the crowd, he pressed the switch and opened the door, that is, moving it to earth again.

The crowd went forward, and the soldier stopped them with one hand. Under the gaze of tens of thousands of eyes, he saw the two people on the opposite side.

The soldier threw in gate's switch, and the nameless person caught it. The soldier shouted, "Click! Click it! Yes!"

She and the crowd outside were stunned when Stars grabbed the switch and pressed the button on it.

Among the crowd, a tall, fat, big, fast-eyed young man pushed his way through the crowd as the door closed and came to the door.

He's racing against time, he's racing against the universe, he's racing against survival, he's racing against the gate...

Sadly, he came last in these races. The door flew up in the air again, and he could only pull back the hand he had almost put in.

He was very angry and began to hit the soldier who threw the switch into MUR. Five minutes later there was only a dead body and a lot of blood where the soldier had been standing.

After entering MUR and leaving the rest of the people behind, the two calmed down immediately. It is not enough to rebuild a civilization with just two people. "It requires turning us into robots." said the woman.

Stars laughed, "Correct! You guessed it! Look, I have got a robot ready. That door can be moved at our will, and we can use it to find habitable planets – for robots. After that, you can put somebody's consciousness into the robot, and then let the robot through the door. Of course, robots won't be able to reproduce, but robots can make humans out of the database."

"So how do we get there?"

"There is also a door in MUR, just behind us."

"So how do we control the gate to move to a habitable planet?"

"The switch can control the movement of the door according to our instructions and move to a habitable planet, as long as the temperature and other parameters of the target planet are right."

Time flies, and the computer finds a suitable planet a year later (2027 in our universe). It was not only habitable for robots, but also for humans, only colder and bigger than Earth with an average temperature of exactly zero Celsius. The planet orbits a star much like the sun, but with a much larger orbital period.

There is only one robot, so whose consciousness should we put in the robot?

"Of course, it is me." Stars' answer was this.

"Mind you, there are only two people left," the anonymous sneered, "In this case, are you still president?"

"Of course, it is!"

"You are so self-centered. I am a civilian, you are the

255

president, and the 'equality' that you politicians broadcast so hard still does not disappear?"

Stars was speechless. He noticed that the woman who was questioning him was pulling a cold glittering dagger from her waist. He shouted, "Stop! Hey, stop it! Everything can be done by communicating properly. We shall put consciousness into it at the same time, just as Sikakiwen and Kermaniro did more than 2,000 years ago."

"Good." Although the anonymous agreed, she was still very rude in her words.

Ten days later, the consciousness of the two was put into the robot called Xenon, named after the planet's xenon-rich atmosphere. The pair painted the name on Xenon's back with purple paint.

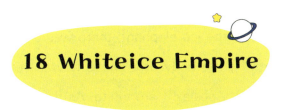

18 Whiteice Empire

The planet was almost transparent, with some whiteness from the ice sheet, so Xenon called it Whiteice.

Further detection revealed that Whiteice was actually less similar to Earth than previously thought. The oceans, deserts, and mountains that the Earth has were not found in it. Whiteice only has endless ice sheets. The term "ice sheet" was also inaccurate, because the planet was entirely made up of ice, and underneath the ice···was still ice. In the planet's inside, water molecules were compressed so the water is still ice, but in a different form. Whiteice was much less dense than ordinary terrestrial planets, but very large, so the surface gravity was about the same as Earth's.

On the surface of Whiteice, there was a creature that looks like a mammoth, but was taller, heavier, slower and more docile, called an "icelephant" which did not need to ingest food or excretion, but only needed to eat the ice under its feet to replenish water.

In addition to the ice elephant, there was a creature called the "snakefly", the body of a snakefly was very similar to the cobra, but its "scales" are white. As the name suggests, snakefly could fly. Interestingly, flying snakes fed on ice elephants. Of course, it was a large group of flying snakes against ice elephant.

Xenon not only held the consciousness of the two, but also held all the information in the original lunar database, so it pulled all the information of a male and a female Earthman from it, creating a pair of Earthmen.

Then it repeated the process, creating 50 million pairs of Earth people, 100 million in all. Its thought at this time was simply, "human civilization can survive!"

After Xenon left all of its stored information to the 100 million people, it self-destructed, believing that its presence would interfere with the re-emerging human civilization.

The new humans fed on the icelephant, which provided a lot of nutrients and energy, and its tusks could also be used as tools. This creature was extremely productive and abundant, and did not become extinct because of the arrival of humans.

In the Year 2028 of the Terran Era, mankind elected an emperor, whose name was "Yaubas". Yaubas was the first leader in the history of Whiteice.

In this year, Yaubas founded the Whiteice Empire. In the Year 2031 of the Terran Era, Yaubas released Xenon's remaining data and ordered the technology to be redeveloped. In the Year 2052 of the Terran era, the Whiteice Empire was restored to its former level of technology.

If you drew a ball with a radius of 20 light-years around the white star, then every planet in the ball was part of the empire.

In the Year 2063 of the Terran Era, Singer, at the age of 237 (by this time he had become a master), rediscovered humans, and upon further investigation, he discovered that they were descendants of the Earthmen he had extermination 37 years earlier. He calculated thousands of calculations, never thought that the earth people made MUR and survived. In thirty-seven years, the population of the Hidden Civilization had multiplied fifteen times to 150 million, and the population of the Empire was about the same.

Human civilization and the Hidden civilization may begin to kill each other.

Singer was very angry, he knew he couldn't use the mathematical destruction this time, the only one had been used by himself. Although he had been valued as a master, he is really only a noble cleaner. Either cleaning, or working for the government.

To calm himself down, Singer began to sing again. This time, he sang the song:

Universe is closed to me forever. Time eclipsed, space narrowed.

After singing, Singer chose silence, and did not report the news to his superiors. He thought, "Human beings are also a great civilization, they can survive and pass my test, just let them live."

The Whiteice Empire was still expanding, and human civilization had gained great prestige in the universe. In Year 2081 of Terran Era, Yaubas died and his son Srefrus became emperor after a royal dispute. The pace of expansion was certainly not stopped by this battle for the throne. In his words, "the unification of the galaxy is within reach, and the destruction of the Hidden is at hand."

However, as a large country with a large population and territory, monarchy was not feasible. In Year 2087 of Terran Era, a rebel group, calling itself the "Second Force" emerged among the people of the White Star Empire. It can be said that the constitutional monarchy adopted in this country is the cradle of the "second force".

The Second Force was a secret society or underground party that was never seen in public, so the government knows little about them. The members of the Second Force all agree on: if you want to rule the galaxy, you must overthrow the emperor!

Moreover, the name "Whiteice Empire" was full of anthropocentrism, which demonstrated the disrespect to other species and even other civilizations!

For Srefrus, emperor of Whiteice Empire, such an underground party could not affect his rule, so he did not care. This eventually led to the growth of the Second Force. In fact, he was not a wicked king, nor did he do anything particularly bad.

The officers soon discovered that the Second Force wanted and always wanted to overthrow the Empire, but they were afraid to tell this to the public, because Srefrus had executed someone who had previously said so. In Year 2089 of Terran Era, when the Second Force invaded the capital of the Whiteice Empire, Slevorus woke up, but it was too late. He let out a deep sigh, "Alas! The tide has turned, I should have listened to them..."

In the end, the leader of the Second force, Milky, was elected president by the masses who were relieved by the demise of the Empire.

However, some believe that the actions of the Second Force are transgressive and should be condemned rather than celebrated by the masses. Most of them were rich and powerful people, and their power and money came from the emperor, so they supported the old government. Of course, these people were very few in number and were soon completely overwhelmed as remnants of the empire.

19 Galactic Republic

As his name "Milky" reflected, he inherited the ambition of Stars. His great ambition was to unify the Milky Way and establish a galactic republic!

In the same year, this wish was carried out, and the Galactic Republic established by Milky unified the galaxy within a year, known as the "Galactic War".

The Whiteice Empire had been replaced by the Galactic Republic. At this time, humans had a ship called *Orion Arm*, which opened the entire network of wormholes in the Orion Arm, and each planet had a wormhole port near it. The Galactic Republic had the conditions to create a wormhole 50000 light-years across, so it immediately came to the opposite side of Orion arm, in the direction of Sagittarius.

Regions 30000 light-years away (or further) from the

galactic Center were difficult to harbor life, but the reason was unknown. Because there was less life here, it was also very easy to occupy. Three months later, the Galactic Republic became a ring, with the galactic center inside.

The galactic center was the region where most advanced civilizations were located. That sounded very strange, because the cosmic rays were so strong here that it was already difficult to emerge life, and it was even harder to give birth to civilization.

More than 90% of these organisms were not carbon-based, and therefore they had extremely strong bodies, some of which could even not breathe air.

Most of these life-bearing planets had a so-called "element field" that could isolate the surface from cosmic rays and gave these creatures a high intelligence.

Eplanet, for example, was a planet orbiting a black hole that was smaller than Earth, or even Mars, but also hosted intelligent life.

Most of these planets were friendly, and the rival planets were united at wartimes, so it was not easy to fight them. In fact, it was a very difficult task, even a giant political entity, the Galactic Republic, took nine months.

For example, one planet had a weapon called a "planet lighter" that could burn the surface of any Earth-like planet to ashes; several other planets had large reserves of poison gas; another planet used an artificial element field to destroy no fewer than five planets belonging to the Galactic Republic; the Hidden, who destroyed the Earth, were hiding in this area; the craziest part was that some planets employ armies that did not even have real intelligence...

None of this had stopped the Galactic Republic. The planets were eventually conquered and most of their citizens surrendered...

The Galactic Republic set its capital at Eplanet (in the galactic center).

The epoch used by humans had changed many times. However, on January 1, Year 2090 of the Terran Era, as if he did not feel chaotic enough, he changed it to "Galactic Era". The Terran Era that lasted 2089 years is over.

Changing the era was actually a very troublesome thing, for example, many computers had to make some adjustments, and the printing house had to print a new calendar, which brought a lot of difficulties. Like the Moon people, today's humans also admired white, because white was the color of the Milky Way. In the first year of the Galactic Era, this color was designated as the "symbolic color". The old era was still used in some areas, and the Year 1 of the Galactic Era is the Year 2090 of the Terran Era, but it is no longer used as a year after the Terran Era was abolished by the Galactic Republic few months later.

There was a lot of fun happening in the Galactic Republic. The term of the President of the Galactic Republic was ten years, and Milky was re-elected once. In the Year 17 of the Galactic Era, a person who lived in the Centaur Arm came to the galactic center and made suggestions to Milky. The guards at the presidential palace let him in and immediately saw the president. When he noticed a group of serious looking people around him, he ran out again. After he got out, he thought to himself, "I came all this way, just to run around the presidential palace?" So, he came running back.

He looked directly at the serious-looking president, hesitated to speak, and lingered for a few minutes before making that bland suggestion, which made people laugh. The story was later turned into a fable called "Running Around." In moral classes at Galactic Republic's schools, teachers often tell this story and tell the students, "This tells us that we must be determined to do things."

Some students, however, interpreted the matter differently. Some people think that this fable expresses "do not be nervous when speaking" and "wasting includes wasting time, which is equally shameful" ...

In the Year 18 of the Galactic Era, the "mathematical

destruction" failed and Earth reappeared. If Singer knew that, he would be very upset...

But the singer could never know, because he died in the Year 1 of the Galactic Era, at the age of 265, because of murder. This rarely happened, but when he was promoted to elder, others were jealous, and a group of people who opposed and envied him prepared carefully for many years. One day, while Singer was on a spacewalk to repair the shuttle, the murderer pierced his spacesuit mask with a micronuclear bomb, shattering his brain and killing him instantly.

The Galactic Republic of course did not know this, and entered a brief period of peace and prosperity. Just as astronomers in the 20th and 21st centuries searched for extraterrestrial life, astronomers in the Galactic Republic began searching for life beyond the Milky Way. Since galaxies outside the Milky Way are called "extragalactic galaxies", life outside the Milky Way is called "extragalactic life".

With galactic human capabilities, it was theoretically possible to travel to the nearest large galaxy, Andromeda, because humans had long been able to travel faster than light by creating wormholes. However, this would take a long time. Therefore, the relevant institutions of the Galactic Republic had not been approved, which was equivalent to creating a half–natural and half–artificial barrier for human beings in the Milky Way.

As for other galaxies, they were either thought to be devoid of life, or so far away that no one can go, so nobody had ever explored extragalactic life.

In the Year 19 of the Galactic Era, Milky retired and returned to his home, Whiteice, to work as a hunter. The Galactic Republic elected a new president, but he turned out to be an ineffectual one. His policies made the government so unpopular that rebellion broke out.

At a critical moment, the incumbent president was ousted by the masses, who were sworn to defend their country, and a new one was hastily elected. The new president rescinded all the policies enacted by his predecessor, stepped up the training of the army, and the rebels signed a peace treaty with the government, which temporarily restored calm.

One wave followed another. Another rebellion ensued. The second rebellion began in the Year 24 of the Galactic Era. That year, the government held an intergalactic games, like the Olympics (but called "Milkypics") at the center of the galaxy, and traffic problems made spectators miserable. What followed was a chain reaction in which a traffic jam led to a mutiny.

Fortunately, the rebellion was put down by the government forces in time. The age of peace continued again, and the great wheel of time continued to roll on.

20 Andromeda Galaxy

One year after the rebellion was put down (the Year 25 of the Galactic Era), a person, named Renos, was born. In the Year 47 of the Galactic Era, invaders from another galaxy attacked the Milky Way. Renos was a university student at the time. When the attack came, he and all the other students were asleep, because it was night.

The war between Andromeda and the Milky Way began.

In the war, Renos would be the hero who saved the galaxy...

Two months later, after lunch, he founded himself sitting next to a classmate named Misa, though Renos did not remember her name at the time.

She immediately noticed the look of Renos, and for the first time, saw a wisdom, strength, and vicissitudes very unsuitable for his age in Renos. They looked at each other and suddenly remembered who the other was.

When he was five years old, his parents divorced and gave him a large sum of money for tuition and living expenses. He lived alone in the house that his parents left for two years, when, in his words, "I lived with five things. Learning, fun, money, food and loneliness."

When Renos was in year two, Misa's family moved into his neighborhood, right next door. After the family lived here, Misa was encouraged by his parents to get to know the neighbors around him and met Renos. The two attended the same school but did not communicate at school due to their age difference.

When Renos was in middle school, the family moved to another building, though Misa tried to persuade them. Since the two did not go to the same school, they lost touch.

After making many friends in secondary, Renos gradually forgot Misa, only vaguely remembering a lost neighbor; Misa, for her part, remembers her neighbor as a child who could not speak with a tone – not even a sentence with a question mark or an exclamation mark. Today was the first time he knew that his childhood playmate was in his own school.

The two looked at each other for a long time without speaking. Renos already deeply felt the message expressed by the other person's eyes, "I know you! I must have seen you somewhere!"

After the Andromeda Galaxy (which was like the Milky Way, they both has been unified by a nation) attacked the galaxy, the Galactic Republic government was recruiting two people who can fight off Andromeda.

The two men were called "thinkers".

After a while, Misa broke the silence and said to Renos, "All these years, I never forgot you... From what I've known about you⋯Let me rephrase that, when I saw you today, my first impression was that you would be a suitable thinker."

Renos stared ahead, then suddenly turned and smiled, "Of course I haven't completely forgotten you. There will always be a place for you in my heart. You think I'm a good thinker. Yes. Ha ha ha..."

Misa asked in horror, "Renos? What's the matter with you?"

"It is all right." Renos could see that Misa had understood what that meant. Renos put the meaning of this sentence into perspective:

"I said yes because I will be graduating and will have nothing else to do. I will run for the job."

On October 15th of that year, Renos and countless others filed applications to become thinkers. Through a series of serendipity, he was chosen.

The other thinker went to work as soon as he was selected, but his plans seemed to reflect only the naivest illusions. His absurd plan was to build two wormholes on the way from the Galactic Center to the Andromeda Galaxy, passing the center of the Local Group, and then build a network of wormholes in the Andromeda Galaxy. At this point, it's time to send the fleet to them.

He gave his opinion after requesting permission to speak. Renos stood up and retorted, "sir, your wormhole project is perfectly feasible in theory, and we already has the technology and financial resources necessary to carry it out. However, you are not taking the reality into account. The Galactic Republic already knows that Andromeda has a strong military, much stronger than ours. There are about as many soldiers and soldiers left in Andromeda as there are in all the armies in the galaxy."

He paused and took a sip of water, "Because of the problem of resources, the fleet we send can only be thirty percent of the entire army of the Galactic system, and it cannot attack Andromeda at all. Besides, the people of Andromeda are smart and have more advanced weapons than we do. With only 70% of the galaxy's army left, it could easily be wiped out by the Andromeda's expedition, even just in numbers. In doing so, you would give the galaxy to invaders, and that is something that no one here wants to see..."

"Shut up, Renos! You don't even have a plan, and you are going to argue with me? Who do you think you are?" The other thinker suddenly stood up and shouted.

"Please watch your language." Renos said together with the president.

Seeing that someone wanted to speak, Renos raised a hand to stop them and continued, "I am not finished. The other thinker, your plan is an outcome that no one here wants to see. No plan is better than an ending that will lead to the conquest of the galaxy by invaders. We know that a good plan takes time."

Renos turned to the thinker, "you have shown only three things in your plan: ignorance, rudeness, and impossibility," he said, turning back to the group. "you are all peaceful, and we do not want to talk to Andromeda on the battlefield. And I actually have a plan in place."

"Can it be made public?" The president asked.

"Mister President, no. Once it becomes public, there may be some people who take the plan out of context and it will end badly."

It could be clearly seen that the president was using silence as a weapon to threaten Renos to speak. Renos relented, "But if that is what you want, I will say it."

The president nodded.

"With the help of one of my best friends, I discovered a flaw in the Andromeda Army: there are one 'leader' ship out of every 10000 ships, and once its computer is destroyed, the 9999 ships it leads will explode out of control, at least lose their attack power, and only serve as obstacles. If you ask why do some people take it out of context, because it is the kind of things that is common in our movies, but now, it is real," Renos told all about his plan.

"Using normal fighting method, attacking these 'leader' ships can achieve a phase that leads to victory. According to our research, ships that lose attack will self-destruct, and then you just have to clean up the battlefield."

"So, what do we use to attack these 'leader' ships?" asked another thinker.

"Sir, I was counting on you to invent a super weapon to help me. But after what you just said, I was disappointed."

The hearing was not held in secret, but was broadcasted on television. The audience was very excited.

That night, Renos returned to the apartment where he had just rented and fell asleep. He woke up at 10 o'clock the next day, ate a quick breakfast, ran to his phone, and texted the president, "We can attack the 'leader' ships with antimatter weapons!"

A year later, during the sixth hearing of the thinker program, the Galactic Republic's Defense Minister pointed a bitter face at Renos and said, "Dear Mr. President, his plan is indeed possible, or viable, but after our enemy discovered that we knew their weakness, they adopted a different tactic, which was to protect the 'leader' ship with ordinary ships, and our army suffered from heavy losses."

Renos broke in, "That is right. I have a solution for your problem. In a experiment, my team triggered a special mechanism to obtain a technology that had previously existed only in science fiction: four-dimensional matter." He added, "everybody knows that we can already travel through a wormhole, that is, folding the three dimensions and entering four dimensions. That allows our travelling takes much shorter time than usual interstellar traveling ways."

Some members of the crowd looked puzzled. Renos explained, "Note that Galaxy, or Time, also made a significant leap across space into a region where time is slow. That is what happened when it traveled through time using a wormhole, so technically they did use the wormhole to leap over large spaces. But, they eventually returned to Earth, where it was originally located. In addition, their purpose is not to travel through space."

He went back to the point and said, "We had not found four-dimensional matter before. This matter is far more complex than we can imagine. For example, a four-dimensional atom might be a four-dimensional sphere, but its electron cloud is crossed, twisted, and complex. Anyway, it's not something I can explain in three dimensions. I can use it to attack Andromeda, but I can't disclose the method, or their subatomic bugs, or listeners (that is how we called it), might learn about it and find a way to counter it."

The discovery of four-dimensional matter had made Renos a fortune, and the Milky Way, on the other hand, was holding Andromeda hostage: if the Galactic Republic did not do as it was demanded, there would be no good end. The one who could hold Andromeda hostage was Renos, known as the "Spirit of the thinkers", or "Soul" for short. He eats and lives in a small room, and if the enemy does something unacceptable, Renos can remotely destroy the interior of the Andromeda galaxy.

In the Year 50 of the Galactic Era, Renos officially became a soul. He thought the profession would stay with him forever, but he was wrong.

On the first day, he was a little out of place, because seeing four-dimensional matter was an extremely strange experience. The next day, it was all right. People built a bedroom inside this place. In the extra time after production, others could read books, or look at computers.

When the Andromeda Galaxy learned of the existence of four-dimensional matter, they felt helpless. After much deliberation, it decided to test the soul.

Andromeda's attack on a planet was discovered by the Galactic Republic Army, who immediately reported it to Renos, who did not hesitate to kill the supreme commander of the Andromeda Army in a unique way: adjusting the position of four-dimensional matter, moving it to Andromeda in four dimensions, and making it hundreds of kilometers in three dimensions. Under the gravitational influence of four dimensional matter, the ship carrying the supreme commander of the Andromeda Galaxy Army explodes. Instead of annihilating the Andromeda galaxy, Renos used this incident as an excuse to force Andromeda to circle the republic's baton.

Renos asked the Andromeda galaxy to provide the Galaxy with material and knowledge for free, and they must do so. This made the name Renos synonymous with evil in the Andromeda galaxy, while in the Milky Way, he was seen as a world-saving hero and even a righteous angel sent by God.

By the Year 55 of the Galactic Era, the technological level of the Milky Way had far surpassed that of Andromeda, which no longer had the knowledge or materials to offer the former, and therefore had no need for the Milky Way to exist. Renos used his personal fortune to purchase several ships equipped with the hibernation system and personally presented them to Andromeda with the message, "Thank you for your help, you can leave the Local Group."

The reader may ask, why not kill them all? The answer is: this is not necessary, and will be a waste of resources.

Under the duress of the soul, the people of Andromeda literally left the Local Group, never to be seen publicly again.

With them gone, the soul was no longer necessary, Renos left the four dimensional space where he had lived for five years, surrendering its use to the government, but stating that he had the right to continue studying it.

Renos had thought he would spend the rest of his life in that space, hidden from the sun, but he had no idea that it would take him only five years to fight off the enemy.

After stepping out of the four–dimensional space and taking his personal belongings with him, he was surrounded by reporters and the crowd, who asked all kinds of questions. After listening, Renos wrote down the important questions and his answers and gave them to the secretary for him to answer, and then took the spaceship back to his hometown: Earth. In fact, Renos was born on Whiteice, but because he is an Earthling, he has deeper feelings for the Earth. He quit living in the apartment where he once lived and bought a medium—sized villa on Earth.

21 Universal Epilogue

Renos lost contact with Misa during the time being a thinker and a soul, but were now back to normal. During these years, Misa became a famous military scientist, and it was she who first discovered the existence of "leader" ships and told Renos about it. Later, Misa moved into Renos' house, and their relationship began to warm up. They married the same year.

On March 5th, Year 56 of the Galactic Era, Misa, who was pregnant, was awakened in her sleep by an idea: why is there a four–dimensional space in a three–dimensional universe? Was the universe originally three or four dimensional?

The tired Misa did not think much and fell asleep.

On March 20th, Misa gave birth to her baby with Renos in the hospital.

The child's name is Qalitra, which in the language of his

birthplace means "you are a human being, a very important human being".

The only thing that filled the hearts of Misa and Renos was happiness, a happiness that could not be described.

Time flies. Qalitra went to primary school, secondary school and university...

Before graduation, he seemed to be just a person who studied well; was healthy; had many talents and friends. In addition to these characteristics, Qalitra was not very different from his classmates.

Once, he got chance to go to space. In order to save money, he chose Alpha Centauri, the closest place to the Earth, as his destination. Aeolus the planet has been destroyed in the Galactic War, so it is still a naked star without planets.

His ship flew dozens of astronomical units from the sun and burrowed into the wormhole. By the time the spaceship came out, it was very close to the star, and the border between safety and danger was thousands of kilometers ahead.

Qalitra asked the pilot, "How much further can we go?"

The pilot replied patiently, "About two thousand kilometers. After that, the ship will deform and sometimes break apart and melt."

"Then drive to the limit. As far as I know, these civil

spaceships have shuttles inside them, which are made of materials that are more resistant to high temperatures, but because of the high cost of this material, there is only one for each ship." Qalitra said so.

"Well, yes. Specifically, it is composed of ultra-high melting point alloy, and there are some strong nanomaterials that help keeping them together. The shuttle is in front of the cockpit and uses neutron material." The pilot then led Qalitra to the shuttle.

Upon his return, Qalitra went to work and was soon well on his way to becoming an astronomer. In the Year 81 of the Galactic Era, the Galactic Republic held a grand military parade, which took three days and three nights. In addition, the government has launched a program called the Star Program. The project is named after the *Star Sky 3* rocket that launched *Corona*. Selling some stars to the public is like selling private islands. Due to the number, one star only costs about as much as an old Earth recreational vehicle. As long as it is legal, the government has no right to interfere with anything for private stars.

Qalitra wanted to buy a star for the purpose of studying , but he thought it would be expensive to buy rare blue or red giants, and there was nothing special about common red dwarfs. He chose the middle star: a yellow dwarf.

He had come to a space city in the galactic center to buy the yellow dwarf, and the star assigned to him was in Orion Arm. The salesman told him that the star was called RA1093 and handed him a bag containing proof of ownership and extremely precise coordinates. What the salesman didn't know was that the star was the sun.

The sun was later artificially created by the lunar people, not naturally formed billions of years ago, but in Qalitra 's view, there was essentially no difference between the two.

He had read Earth history as a teenager, knew that the sun had been extinguished by the Second Moon men, and that this sun was artificial, and knew that there was only one planet left around the sun, Earth. But it didn't matter to him, because to him, planets were just dust that could give birth to life.

In the Year 87 of the Galactic Era, he resigned as an astronomer to devote his research to cosmology. He discovered how and when the universe really would end, and while he was not deterred by the fact that it was dark, it did make him fear that the universe would end in 14 or 15 years, possibly sooner.

In the year 90 of the Galactic Era, a catastrophe occurred, and a wormhole appeared in the center of the sun. Unfortunately, there was also a black hole at the other end of the wormhole, and this black hole used the powerful hand of gravity to cause the sun to collapse from the center and move into the black hole at the other end of the wormhole.

The sun being sucked into a black hole is already a catastrophe. But then the wormhole closed. The sun was cut directly into two parts: the part that entered and the part that did not enter the wormhole. The core of the Sun was sucked into the black hole, that is, at the other end of the wormhole. Meanwhile, the rest of the sun collapsed violently after losing the core, taking up the space where the Sun's core used to be.

It would have been lucky, because the sun was still there. However, after these parts collapsed, they exploded under too much pressure, creating a gorgeous and terrifying planetary nebula that, had no White Dwarf (the remains of a star's core) at its center! This nebula is the Solar Nebula, and it had a brilliant red color.

From all corners of Earth, ships are heading out into space, and everyone wants to escape the solar nebula, a place of death and fear that everyone wants to avoid.

According to the rules of the Star Program, if a purchased star is artificially destroyed, the owner of the star can request a new star. After that week, the salesman gave Qalitra proof of ownership of Alpha Centauri.

Qalitra owned a ship, and he took his parents with him when the disaster happened, and now the whole family lives in the Space City of Alpha Centauri. The space city is a bunch of ships (triangular, rectangular or hexagonal) that connects and inlays, each with a door in the middle.

Later, they were told that Andromeda's enemies had never left, and the black hole and wormhole were made by them. Andromeda then attacked the Milky Way again. The fourth dimension has suddenly disappeared for some reason, and no one has yet found a way to fight against, or at least counter, the Andromeda galaxy.

In folklore, Andromeda's enemies are referred to as "andrebandits", and various fictional works continue to pour out to express hatred for them. The Galactic Republic has reinstated the position of thinker.

Although the Galactic Republic did not prefer haematism, Qalitra became the only thinker. Oddly enough, at the time he came up with his plan, regional forces were using extremely strong element fields to directly disintegrate the Andromeda life into atomic particles, and no one has yet been able to explain how. His original plan was also to use the element field, but instead of attacking Andromeda, he would attack the black hole at the center of the Milky Way. Under the influence of the element field, the black hole will emit a large amount of energy, and the unprepared enemy will be destroyed.

Qalitra lost his chance to shine, and he was so upset that he never appeared in public again. It turned out to be a stupid decision – the people no longer respected him, public opinions kept attacking him. He endured hundreds of times more pain than ordinary people and suffered from severe depression. So, he created a miniature parallel universe. In the parallel universe, he wrote a few words in pencil:

It is too late. The man who wrote these words, Qalitra, had just discovered an earth–shattering fact that had been my lifelong research. There were eight universes before this one, and next, its about to be destroyed. After traveling into this miniature parallel universe, I saw a [illegible] piece of that recorded the [illegible] of the universe.

The universe will collapse, and all life, all celestial bodies, all memory, will be compressed there. The universe can store information, and its memory is infinite. It's all been read by me and saved here with a quantum computer. You can come and replicate this universe in a new one.

Run for your life!

The last sentence were also engraved in rock.

Later, out of despair, he spent the rest of his life in his own miniature parallel universe.

At the end of the Year 100, Galactic Era, Qalitra returned to the Earth in the big universe, looked up at the Milky Way in the sky, and gently said, "Your end is coming. Goodbye..." With that, he jumped into the abyss in front of him.

Public opinion had been attacking him, and many people were excited by the news of his's suicide. Later generations said of his life, "conditions gave him many opportunities, but he never caught them." Little did they know, as Qalitra had predicted, the end of the world was coming...

On December 31st, Year 100 of the Galactic Era, the New Year Eve is coming just like always. After the second of 23:59:59 passed, a moment before the beginning of the Year 101 of the Galactic Era, the universe restarted. Everything suddenly collapsed into a singularity, and at this moment, time stopped flowing for the first time. In several billion years, it had never stopped. For many years there would be no living beings who could be called "human." The Galactic Era was over, and it was exactly 100 years long.

The universe collapsed into a singularity.

In that instant, the whole universe was rebooted in a big bang, it was like somebody pressing "power on". The structure of the new universe was basically the same as the one before it: a three–dimensional darkness plotted with stars and planets, stars forming galaxies, and galaxies forming clusters of galaxies.

Some civilizations had built structures such as micro universe room, and according to incomplete statistics, there were at least 10 million of them. They ranged in size from the size of a ship to the size of a galaxy.

They took a lot of matter out of the universe, so what happened in the new universe is not quite the same as what happened in the previous universe, and even the laws of physics were slightly different. Someone may have a few molecules missing in their brain that cause them to think or say different things; a planet may no longer exist in the new universe; a galaxy may have merged with another galaxy at different times...

What I want to say here is that the concept of "parallel universes", or its synonyms, are mentioned several times in this book. The universe is finite, and when you, without warning of course, reach the edge, you shall be blocked by a mysterious force. You can only cross this boundary by the door that once lead Stars and the nameless person to the Micro Universe Room. Unlike some of the science fiction in our universe, parallel universe means: the universes before or outside our universe.

And these words don't belong here, they belong in the last

universe. That universe is the ninth universe of all time, a more crazy and exciting universe, with beautiful spots and streaks throughout its history. By comparison, this universe, Universe 10, is rather dull and boring. It can be said that all the text above is an interpretation of the history of Universe 9.

The content of the book is completely true and reliable, and every character has existed, but their ideas and dialogue are based on speculation by the author, and the author has omitted a lot of details. The physical laws of the two universes are also slightly different, so some of the slightly absurd scenarios actually make sense for Universe 9.

The author is not from Universe 9, but got information from that universe. These information comes from an advanced civilization that lives in a parallel universe who call themselves the descendants of the galactic humans Universe 9. That is why the book centers on humans.

The author wrote down their words, and the book was produced. It is worth mentioning that this civilization refers to Universe 9 as the "pre-universe" .I believe that they also accept the fact that their own universe is destroyed because "the new replaces the old" is the basic law of the world.

However, there is no practical point in writing out ideas, conversations and details. The advanced civilization that handed the information to this writer proved that the universe is a computer – that the universe has the ability to store the state of every elementary particle.

Hopefully, humans will reach that new level of development and be able to look at the data in this computer – that is, know the history of the universe; I also hope that readers can get some inspiration from this "cosmic romance".

In short, a new universe is coming, a new world is coming.

22 Before Us

Although our universe is only a small village in the vast world, I still have to admit that the story of Universe 9 is relatively interesting. However, Universe 8 is complete weird. This universe existed tens of billions of years ago, the average temperature was much higher than the current universe (that was close to absolute zero), about minus 10 degrees Celsius. Because most of its mass was water, and water froze in such temperature, so there were icicles extending for hundreds of light years or more, forming a huge system. Yes, just one – all these icicles were connected.

These icicles even harbored life, history, culture, language, technology, and war. Looking at the sky from these icicles was like looking at a giant spider web from a tree branch, except that these icicles were almost transparent, and you can see more complex structures behind them...

There were no wormholes or time travel in this universe, nor was it theoretically possible. But in this universe, where the speed of light approached infinity, everything was seen as it is now. For reasons unknown, Universe 8 lasted only 5.7 billion years before collapsing to form the much more complex Universe 9.

As for Universe 7, it had been around for 16.3 billion years and was very hot, around 100000 degrees Celsius. This universe was rich in hydrogen and helium just like ours, and interstellar dust formed many nebulae, most of which gave birth to stars. The interior of a star was much hotter than the outside, and when the conditions for nuclear fusion were reached, heavier elements were continuously produced.

There was no carbon-based life in this universe because beryllium-8, produced by the collision of two helium-4 atoms, was stable in this universe. In our universe, beryllium-8 is unstable, so the collision of three helium-4 atoms to produce carbon-12 is relatively common. The result was that in Universe 7, hydrogen, helium, beryllium, nitrogen, and oxygen were the most common elements, and life depended on silicon, which is much less abundant. The silicon-based organisms of Universe 7 used water or hydrogen fluoride as a solvent, beryllium's hardness gave them a hard shell, and their bodies were various compounds made of silicon. In addition, in Universe 7, the nucleus of silicon–28 was extremely stable, even more stable than iron in our universe, so once it fused into silicon, nuclear fusion stopped, and there were no heavier elements – the periodic table in Universe 7 only had 3 periods and 14 elements.

Due to the limitations of silicon itself, life in this universe did not develop civilization and was eventually submerged in the long river of history. Based on a specimen made by a living creature left over from that era, later civilizations created a replica. Both had been lost. The only evidence we have was a three–dimensional model based on a replica of them, which showed that this creature, called "rock brain", was a small rocky object with extremely slow physical activity. They did not live as individuals, and in some places you can see a large number of them, but no one ever saw a single living individual of it. They used hydrogen fluoride to corrode the soil underground, digging underground channels to deliver nutrients to each individual; It would also add a "ramp" near each channel to transport information.

Universe 6 was only 3.6 billion years old before it collapsed, which was exactly twice the average lifetime of stars in that universe. That universe contained a lot of boron, and life was boron–based life. Because boron lacks electrons, it can form very complex structures, and life in this universe is much more advanced. Perhaps for this reason, boron–based life developed quickly, dominating the universe within tens of thousands of years. Of course, we have to admit that Universe 6 is small, only one–third the size of our universe.

Finally, a crazy person tried to smash the basic structure of space–time, and the result can be imagined: a place of space–time fell deeply into it, forming an extremely massive black hole, and the surrounding space–time was constantly swallowed up and became part of the black hole. After thousands of years, the whole of Universe 6 sunk in, and the universe became a singularity. The end of Universe 6 can be said to be man–made, but Universe 5 is different.

After Universe 5 exploded, it expanded very slowly because it contained many dark matter. At its largest, it was only 52 light–years across. Next, the gravitational pull took control of its fate. It heated up rapidly, and everything was eventually squeezed together by two demonic hands until it became a singularity and officially declares collapse. The universe was only 1.8 billion years old.

In Universe 4, the evolution of life has been a mystery. It was later found that they were almost immortal and could transform, so there was no need to evolve. The basis of their life was hydrogen chloride, and breathing was the most important life process, which completely supported their lives. First, the "trachea" was used to absorb the external hydrogen and chlorine gas, the "lungs" further pushed the gas to achieve breathing, and then lit up them, making it into hydrogen chloride that flowed into the "heart". After the gas was pushed out, the "arteries" controlled the flow of gas to every part of the body, and the "veins" let the flue gases back to the "heart" and got pushed out.

Universe 3 had been around for much longer, even more than 100 billion years. It was also mainly composed of water, but because its temperature reached 25 degrees Celsius, so the water it contains was liquid. So there was a spherical ocean over 60 billion light years deep, its water filling the entire universe, and the celestial body was composed of impurities, their size could be compared with planets today, that moved chaoticallu. These impurities were mainly insoluble salts, barium sulfate took up the most. There is a high probability that no life exists here, and the speed of light is currently the slowest, only 841 meters per second.

Universe 2 is similar in appearance to our Universe 10, but has existed for 68.4 billion years, and none of the elements have stable isotopes. In other words, every element is radioactive, the longest half-life belong to hydrogen which finally decays into neutrons (in Universe 2, free neutrons are also stable). In this universe, neutron is the ultimate destination of all elements. The neutrons used to make shuttles that can go into stars came from this universe, also known as "neutronite".

The story of Universe 1 is completely unknown, but it is certain that it existed for hundreds of billions of years. Beyond that, I know nothing about it, and can only infer them from the fragmentary words left by that higher civilization.

This is a mysterious universe, and because of this, the advanced civilization has no access to obtain information about it. In fact, the "mathematical destruction" is made from the material left over from Universe 1, and because of not conform to the laws of physics, it has the power to destroy heaven and earth in Universe 9. Similarly, the matter of Universes 9 and 10 will have the same ability in Universes 1.

This advanced civilization has given 10 universes names. They are: "unknown universe", "neutron universe", "ocean universe", "hot universe", "gravity universe", "boron universe", "silicon universe", "ice universe", "pre universe", and the last one is where we are – "universe". They provided an acronym for the universes before us: Under the notebook, the oar, or the hat? Gosh, I bet it is sitting inside a park!

All ten of these universes came from a singularity that exploded to form Universe 1, collapsing, exploding, collapsing, exploding, collapsing... Creating and destroying new universes.

One day the story of Universe 9 will be perfected, and we certainly welcome readers from all over the universe to join us—to write the story of these ten universes, using any ways possible!

Addendum: Not Three Dimensional

This story is not over!

The ten universes we had mentioned were created by the same singularity, and were collectively referred to as "three-dimensional region", or TDR. The region is obviously part of a larger piece of space, and this larger space has different dimensions, some regions are zero-dimensional, some are one-dimensional, and some are two-dimensional; others are four, five, six, seven, eight, nine, ten dimensional and so on. They all come from explosions generated by a corresponding singularity, and each "region" has its own spatial dimension. In other words, this singularity generated this "region" with a dimension of x, that singularity generated that "region" with a dimension of y.

No matter how the spatial dimension changes, time always remains the same. Even for the singularity, it is still one-dimensional time, as well as infinitely slow. Nowhere has time that is not one dimensional.

It is worth mentioning that the total amount of matter in the three-dimensional region does not remain constant, and energy can be drawn from other "regions" and turned into mass.

High dimensional objects cannot enter low dimensional space, otherwise they will be crushed by so-called "Dimensional Potential Energy". Dimensional potential energy is similar to gravitational potential energy. Objects with large amounts of this energy (high dimensional objects) become unstable and therefore slowly become objects with lower dimensions. This processis called "falling". The four-dimensional space that Renos once inhabited may have fallen, or may have been destroyed by the Andromeda Galaxy.

According to experiments, the speed of falling has little to do with dimensions. By that I mean, the time it takes to make five dimensions become four and the time it takes to make four dimensions become three, are almost the same.

Falling often occur in high-dimensional regions. This kind of thing has happened so many times, with so many casualties and victims, that most civilizations have learned or tried to get away from low dimensional space.

Now, let's tell the story of the fourth dimension very briefly. Readers may be surprised: as the descendants of the human beings in the Milky Way of Universe 9, that advanced civilization should also be three–dimensional organisms, how did they know the events of the four–dimensional space?

The answer is hearsay. I have always frowned upon the inclusion of questionable events in such solemn stories, but in order to give the reader a general idea of what happened, I have decided to make an exception. That four–dimensional space is called the four–dimensional region, and this civilization provides only a tiny part of the story of a parallel universe in the four–dimensional region. Let's call this universe the "four–dimensional universe". This universe will completely fall to three dimensions in 2038 and merge into three–dimensional zone.

All universes and regions are spherical, and the four–dimensional universe is certainly no exception. Around 1945 BC, there was a four–dimensional planet that fell into three dimensions at the beginning of the year. However, in the fall, from the perspective of a three–dimensional creature, everything is the same.

The planet's fall was silent. It was a giant planet, gorgeous and colorful rings first fell into three-dimensional space, like a pair of big hands from the 4D heaven slowly reaching out to the 3D world; the wonderful atmosphere was like a graceful oil painting, which produced an extremely weak "buzz" sound when it fell; dozens of small satellites were dancing around it, like the stars around the Moon, they were like soldiers trying to block the expansion of three-dimensional space with his own force; in the end, it was just a dull explosion...

Having four dimensions said, let's talk about two dimensions from the "two dimensional region". This two-dimensional parallel universe is still expanding, swallowing up nearby three-dimensional regions (in other words, parts of our universe are falling). Opposite to what some of our scientists think, life can exist in two dimensions. They created splendid civilizations, some — if they were three-dimensional — are far more developed than today's humans, and they are existing just now, when you are reading this page.

With one dimension going out, space contain a lot less information. Not only do these intelligent beings have very complex networks of neurons, they must be huge. These lives are almost all square, even their "sides" are not perfectly straight. Take a planet in the center of the two-dimensional universe, its life can reach a side length of one kilometer, and the outside of the body of this creature has an extremely hard exoskeleton, which can be indestructible in the two–dimensional universe. At the same time, this also has a certain protective effect, so that they can directly survive in space.

The civilization also offers a fictional work created by two–dimensional creatures: *Infinity*. This "book" (an epic that is in an anthology) tells the story of two–dimensional civilization trying to break through the limitations of dimensions, into three, four, five... But they ultimately failed, and accomplished nothing.

Although this is a big tragedy, it also reflects the spirit of these two–dimensional creatures, at least the world and life they aspire to. A two–dimensional book is a two–dimensional sheet of paper, a long, narrow rectangle that the author writes on the edges with colored "ink". Black separating words, white separating sentences, and grey separating paragraphs. The text they use is one–dimensional, just like humans, a three–dimensional creature, using two–dimensional text.

Translated into the language of three–dimensional creatures, the works of two–dimensional creatures seem to be more intriguing than they were originally – which is not surprising, given that the former obviously conveys more meaning, and so can be translated in many different ways.

In other words, one "two-dimensional word" can be translated into many "three-dimensional words" with different or even opposite meanings, so that for three-dimensional creatures, the same story can be interpreted in hundreds of ways. But when it comes to two-dimensional organisms, only one interpretation is correct, and all the others are nonsense. For example, the title of *Infinity* mentioned above can even be translated as Nothingness, Disappearance, Existence, and Zero, but these are not its actual meanings.

Is there life in the "one-dimensional universe" of the "one-dimensional region"?

We have to appreciate the power of life, that there are living things in this environment – a simple, hopeless, unlively, static line segment. Their structure is too simple to produce intelligence.

There are seven basic units in the international system of units that you find in three dimensions, corresponding to seven physical quantities: the meter (length), the kilogram (mass), the second (time), the ampere (current), the kelvin (temperature), the mole (amount of matter), and the candela (luminous intensity). Only three of them exist in one dimension: length, time, and quantity of matter. I will tell you why now.

The one-dimensional universe only has length, no width or

height, and therefore no weight – infinitely thin things have no mass that is meaningful.

"Time is everywhere, and it is still passing here." *Infinity*, as a two-dimensional book, have this sentence that also apply to one-dimensional world.

Since the range of movement of any object in one-dimensional space is completely limited to the surrounding objects, electrons can hardly move, and that leads to no current.

In the same way, microscopic particles cannot move, everything is at absolute zero, and temperature has no use in one-dimensional space.

In the one-dimensional universe, a device that can produce light can only spread its light to itself and its neighboring objects, and the light will only reflect continuously between the two. Because there is no object that can reflect all light, all light in the one-dimensional universe will eventually be absorbed, and as a result, there is no light in the one-dimensional universe. Therefore, there is no need for the physical quantity of luminous intensity to exist.

Zero dimensions is a point that is dispensable. To prove that zero-dimensional life does not exist, we should know the life must distinguish itself from other not living things. If a life does not occupy space, it is not different from other objects around it that do not occupy space too, and you cannot distinguish the to. That makes it a thing that is not living. This makes a paradox: life is not living. To avoid this, we must declare that zero-dimensional life does not exist.

Because of the entrenched laws of physics, life in dimensions higher than four cannot be detected by three-dimensional things, so detectable life only exists in one, two, three, and four dimensions.